MW01154413

Tim

Julian

Dave

4d6

by

ROBERT BEVAN

I HOPE YOU ENJOY MY GENITAL HARPIES.

All content edited by Joan Reginaldo.
Layout design by Christopher Dowell.

ISBN: 1537338390
ISBN-13: 978-1537338392

SPECIAL THANKS TO:

First, I'd like to thank Joan Reginaldo for her invaluable criticism. It's tough to find a good beta-reader. I went through a few before I met Joan. I can't stress enough how important it is to find someone who understands your vision and is able to help you achieve it. There's so much more involved than pointing out misplaced commas (though she did a lot of that, too).

Next, I'd like to thank my beautiful wife, No Young Sook, for her constant support, and for getting up to get the kids ready for school every morning because I left early to go to the office to write some books.

Next in line to be thanked is my brother-in-law, No Hyun Jun. Every cover of mine you see is the end product of a communication struggle, his English being about on par with my Korean. But the guy can work some Photoshop magic. And he also helps out with the kids quite a bit. Thanks, Hyun Jun.

Finally, I'd like to thank all of you wonderful people who like my Facebook page (www.facebook.com/robertbevanbooks).

TABLE OF CONTENTS

Djinngle Bells
ROBERT BEVAN

DJINNGLE BELLS

(Original Publication Date: December 10, 2015)

Tim fell backwards a short distance, his ass crushing something cold and wet where his upturned bucket had just been. Everything around him was cold and wet. And dark. Why was it so dark? He couldn't see shit.

"What the f-f-f-fuck?" The sudden change in temperature was taking over his sudden blindness as a priority. "Where the f-f-f-fuck am I? Julian! Dave! Cooper!"

He felt around. Soft, cold, crunchy. Snow. He was stuck in a small cavity of fresh snow. Did he get caught in an avalanche? How much had he had to drink?

No. No no no. That couldn't be it. He was at the Whore's Head Inn, and it was still late summer. He knew he was there because that's why he'd been in a sitting position. Where the hell did his bucket go? Where the hell did all this snow come from? Shit! How much oxygen did he have?

Tim concentrated on what way was up. His feet were on solid ground, so up was the opposite way. He clawed frantically at the snow, widening the cavity above him and packing the snow more tightly near his waist. If he packed it tight enough, it would support his weight, and he could keep climbing.

"F-f-f-fuck it's c-c-c-cold!"

His fingers were starting to numb, and he had to take a piss. Two birds, one stone. He unlaced his pants and pulled out his little halfling dick. The pee was good and warm on his hands, but not so good for the structural integrity of the step he was trying to make, as he found out when his foot went right through it.

"Goddamn it!"

"Tim?" Julian's voice was faint above the snow, but it was definitely him.

"Julian!" cried Tim. "I'm down here!"

"Where?" Julian was getting closer. "I can't see you!"

Tim needed a signal. He felt around to see what he had on him. He still had his crossbow. Perfect. He loaded a bolt, cocked it back, aimed up, and pulled the trigger.

A gurgling whinny answered his signal.

"Shit."

The darkness broke as the head of a white, wide-eyed horse crashed into Tim's snow cavity, spraying blood out of its neck. Tim covered his eyes. When he looked again, the horse had disappeared. His bolt lay in a patch of orange snow. He dipped it a few times in some clean snow, then packed it away. Waste not, want not.

Julian, who had obviously been riding the magically summoned horse that Tim just accidentally murdered, stood up and shook the snow off of his serape and quarterstaff. The snow was only up to right below his chest. "Was that really necessary?"

"S-s-s-sorry," said Tim. "I p-p-p-panicked. W-w-w-where the ffffuck are we?"

"I don't know," said Julian. He averted his eyes as he reached down to help Tim up. "Why are your pants down?"

"I had to — Oomf!" Tim's hand slipped free of Julian's, sending him face first into the blood and piss stained snow.

"Dude!" said Julian. "Is this pee on your hand?"

Tim spat out some soiled snow. "And now in my mouth, thank you very much."

"Julian!" called Dave. His voice was clear. His head was obviously above the snow.

Julian nodded. "Hey, Dave."

"Don't Hey, Dave me! What's with all the snow?"

"How should I know?" said Julian. "I guess it's just one of those game things."

"No," said Tim, lacing up his pants. "There's nothing in the game that makes a group of people spontaneously teleport from a pub to a fucking tundra for no reason."

"You think we were teleported?"

"What else could it be? I've been pretty fucking drunk in my life, but I've never woken up in Antarctica."

"Shit!" said Julian, as if only now realizing something was amiss.

"What?" asked Dave.

"Cooper." Julian turned frantically, looking in every direction."Has anyone seen Cooper?"

"I've been down here in this hole," said Tim. "I haven't seen shit."

"Cooper's bigger than any of us," said Dave. "If anyone's not going to have a problem with a couple of feet of snow, it's him."

Julian pulled on his long elf ears. "He was passed out on the floor. What if he didn't wake up, and he's buried in snow? He could suffocate." He pulled the left side of his serape back and looked under it. "Ravenus. I need you to scout the area."

"It's so cold, sir," said the bird. "And I really am quite drunk. Couldn't you send the big fellow, just this once?"

"Cooper's missing. I need you to go look for him."

"Righty-ho." Ravenus feigned enthusiasm for his task through a stifled yawn. "Pip.Pip. Here we go."

Julian launched Ravenus into the air. Ravenus got in about three good flaps before he plummeted into the snow.

"Ravenus!" cried Julian. "Are you okay?"

"I am now, sir," said Ravenus. "My, but that's invigorating."

Tim could barely see Ravenus's dark form through the falling snow as he passed overhead. It was coming down hard, and Tim's hole was starting to fill back up. Every trace of urine and horse blood had been whitened away with a blanket of pristine snow.

"Hey!" Tim called up to Julian. "You mind getting me out of this hole now?"

"Did you wash your hands?"

Tim grabbed a handful of fresh snow, rubbed his numb hands together, and flung it down at his sides. "There. Are you satisfied now, mom?"

Julian forced his way through the snow into Tim's hole. "I don't know what you're so keen to get out of there for. There's nothing to see." He picked up Tim and put him on top of the snow.

Tim looked around. Julian was right. Nothing but snow as far as he could see in any direction, which admittedly wasn't very far. Still, it was nice to have some freedom of movement.

Between his high Dexterity score, his small size, and his proportionally large halfling feet, Tim found he was able to traverse the surface of the snow without sinking. He took careful steps to the edge of the trench Dave had carved.

Dave's head barely broke the surface. He must have had ten pounds of snow in his beard alone.

"Jesus, Dave," said Tim. "You must be freezing."

Dave shrugged. "Dwarves are built for this sort of thing."

Tim traced Dave's trench to the end, then the trench that Julian's horse had carved before Tim accidentally shot it, then looked at his own hole. He forced himself to remember where everyone had been at the Whore's Head Inn.

"Guys," said Tim. "I think our starting positions here are relative to where we were at the Whore's Head when we got teleported. If Cooper is here..." He turned around and faced an empty snowscape. "He should be a few yards in —"

"I've found him, sir!" cried Ravenus, flapping in from the direction Tim was facing.

"Good job, Ravenus!" said Julian. "Cooper! We're over here!"

"That won't do you any good, sir. I believe he's still asleep."

"Then how did you see him? Why isn't he covered in snow?"

Ravenus raised his wings in a shrug. "That is an excellent question, sir."

Tim's prediction on where to find Cooper was confirmed by the direction Ravenus had flown in from. He didn't wait for directions.

Moments later, Tim was standing at the edge of a crater in the snow. Cooper lay sound asleep in the middle of it, with only a light dusting of snow on his body.

"That's strange," said Tim. "How do you suppose he —"

PRRRFFFBBBBTBTBTBTBTHBBBBTTT

Cooper's loincloth fluttered as a long, noisy fart instantly melted what little snow had accumulated on him since his previous fart.

"Oh my god," said Tim as the noxious gas invaded his eyes, nose, and mouth. "What the fuck did you eat last —"

The fart-weakened snow gave way beneath Tim's feet, sending him crashing to the bottom of the crater.

"Tim?" Julian called out.

"AAAAUUUUGGGHHHH!" Tim replied. Cooper's fart was apparently denser than air, as it was much more concentrated inside the snow crater. Tim scooped up a big ball of snow, packed it hard, and threw it at Cooper's face.

"Dude," said Cooper without opening his eyes. "Knock it off. I'm trying to sleep."

"Fuck you!" said Tim, and hurled another snowball at Cooper's face.

Cooper yawned, stretched, and finally stood up. He walked to the edge of the crater and pulled up his loincloth. A steaming jet of dark yellow piss sliced through the snow like a ten-foot-long light-saber. "It's kinda chilly in here."

Tim hurled a third snowball at the back of Cooper's head. "Dude! You need to wake up!"

Cooper turned around, cutting down the top foot of snow around half the circumference of the crater, except for the part that Tim blocked with his face."Oh, shit. Sorry about that."

Tim scooped up some white snow and scrubbed his face. "Is it too much to ask to go through a single day without being covered in piss?"

Cooper squinted, looking to his left and right and scratching his balls. "Something's different."He farted again, and the section of crater wall behind him melted into a pool at his feet.

"Cooper!" said Julian, trudging through the snow. "Thank goodness you're all right! I was worried you might have — Oh my God! What's that smell?" He'd broken through to the fart crater.

"Help me!" said Tim.

Cooper picked up Tim. "You guys need to grow the fuck up." He tossed Tim out of the crater.

Tim spread out his arms and legs, maximizing the surface area with which he'd hit the snow so as to minimize how far he'd sink. It worked. He barely left an imprint as he belly-flopped onto the cold white surface.

Julian did a dolphin jump over the side of his trench, diving into a patch of snow that wasn't connected to the pipeline of concentrated fart.

"Oh man!" cried Dave, the top of his helmet visible above Julian's former trench. "What is that — It's like bacon and cheese, only terrible!"

Ravenus flew into view and perched atop Julian's quarterstaff just as he was standing up in his new trench. "Where's the danger, master?"

"It's okay, Ravenus," said Julian.

"I sensed you were being violently choked. Show me who assaulted you, and they shall feel the fury of beak and talon!"

"It was Cooper's ass."

Ravenus looked at Cooper, then back down at Julian. "Forgive me, sir. My loyalty has boundaries."

"Don't worry. We're not in any danger." Julian hugged himself. "I mean, aside from being inexplicably lost in a snowy wasteland without food, shelter, or adequate clothing."

"I spotted a cave not far from here, sir."

"Sweet!" said Tim. "Let's get moving. Lead the way already!"

Ravenus looked blankly at Tim, then down at Julian. "Is he talking to me, sir?"

"Oh, for fuck's sake," said Tim. Julian had made the mistake of

choosing Elven as the language his familiar could speak, and so the bird couldn't understand anything anyone said unless they were speaking in a British accent. Tim cleared his throat. "Tally-ho, good chap! Start flapping ye collywobbles and show us to the goddamn cave...mate."

"Right," said Ravenus. "This way, gents." He launched himself from Julian's quarterstaff and flew into the snow-filled sky.

Cooper effortlessly plowed through the snow after Ravenus.

"Horse," said Julian. The horse that appeared beside him was brown this time, and did not look at all happy about suddenly materializing in a snowstorm. Julian mounted the horse and guided it around the circumference of Cooper's fart-hole.

Tim looked back. Dave's head was buried in the side of his trench. Tim threw a snowball at him.

"What?" said Dave.

"Ravenus found a cave. Let's move."

Dave pulled his head out of the snow. His face was red and his beard was white, kind of the opposite of normal. He looked across the crater at Cooper. "I don't think I can make it."

"Don't be such a baby," said Tim. "Just keep your head held high. The fart-air will sink as it flows into your trench."

Cooper farted, melting the sides of his new trench immediately behind him.

Tim shook his head. "That is, if Cooper doesn't keep filling it up. Can't you plug that up with something?"

"Sure," said Cooper. "Come on over here."

Dave scooped up two handfuls of snow, pressed them against his face, and took a long deep inhalation. He didn't exhale as he waddled into Cooper's fart cloud.

It only took a few minutes before a piece of the horizon grew darker, then the cave entrance sharpened into view. This place seemed like a barren wasteland, but with only twenty feet of visibility in any direction, they could be in the middle of a thriving metropolis for all Tim knew.

The mouth of the cave had the appearance of natural rock,

but was a little too symmetrical. Tim suspected nature had had a little help. The same went for the stairs that led down inside. No one step was the same height or width as another, but they were too flat and functional to be completely nature's handiwork.

"Should we go in?" asked Julian once he, Tim, and Cooper were all under the lip of the cave. The cautious tone of his voice suggested he didn't think they should.

"Fuck yes," said Tim. It was nice to be out of the snow, but his clothes were soaked, and he was freezing. He and Julian looked up at Cooper for an opinion to tip the scale.

Cooper shut his eyes, grimaced, and stopped breathing.

Tim frowned. "Coop? You okay?"

Cooper exhaled as a jet of greenish-brown liquid shit squirted out from the bottom of his loincloth and pooled behind him like a large, circular welcome mat for Dave, who was just catching up.

Dave fell backwards in horror, then rolled out of the way as a shit-tendril flowed down an uneven section of rock toward him."Jesus, Cooper!"

Cooper wiped some sweat off his brow. He was breathing hard. "Oh, man. Sorry if I've been short with you guys. That's been trying to get out of me since I woke up. Fucking chili."

"What do you think, Dave?" asked Julian.

"I think there's only so much you can blame on a low Charisma score."

"I meant about the cave. Do you think we should go in?"

Dave stepped carefully around the huge shit puddle. "I don't see how we have much choice. It's either go down the stairs, wander back out into the snow, or stand here and watch Cooper shit himself until we all freeze to death."

"But what if somebody lives here?" asked Julian.

Tim shivered. "Then they can tell us where the fuck here is, and how to get the fuck out of here."

"I just don't like the idea of barging into someone's home."

Tim made a show of examining the mouth of the cave. "Well, I don't see a fucking bell."

Julian peered down the stairs. "Hello?" The tremor in his voice was amplified by echoes bouncing off the cave walls.

After thirty seconds with no response, Tim looked at Julian. "Satisfied?"

"Not remotely."

"I can't take this smell anymore," said Dave. "I'm going down."

The steps hadn't been designed for dwarves or halflings. Even a tall human probably would have found them uncomfortably steep, but Tim and Dave had to descend each one like they were climbing down from a wall. Tim hoped there was something worthwhile down there, because climbing back up was going to be a bitch.

Tim knew Julian and Cooper were following by the sound of hooves clopping against rock.

"Do you really need to bring the horse?" asked Tim.

"I'm not going to leave him outside. It's cold out there."

"Why don't you just dispel it?"

"We might need him."

"How do you even get a horse to go down stairs?" asked Dave. "I read somewhere that they won't do it."

"It's a magical horse," said Julian. "It will go wherever I want it to go."

Shortly after the curvature of the staircase blocked Tim's view of the outside, it became too dark him to see. This didn't affect his rate of descent, as he was operating mostly by touch anyway, and he was following Dave, whose dwarven eyes could see in the dark, but was always slow.

The darkness didn't last long. There was light coming from deeper within the cave, faintly illuminating the rough rocky walls of the staircase.

"Do you see that?" Dave whispered.

"Of course I do," said Tim. "It's all I fucking see."

Dave scrambled down the last couple of steps. "Oh. My. God." His face was illuminated by bright white light. "You guys aren't going to believe this."

When Tim reached the bottom of the stairs, he saw something which, however briefly, brought warmth to his cold drunk heart. "It's a goddamn Christmas tree."

The centerpiece of the subterranean room was a fifteen-foot-tall conical tree in a bathtub-sized brown clay pot. It was decorated with red ball ornaments and white lights, like the 'classy' trees they have in department stores.

"Whoa!" said Julian and Cooper upon reaching the bottom of the stairs.

"Are you quite all right, sir?" asked Ravenus. "I'm sensing feelings of bedazzlement and wonder which I can't account for."

"Ravenus," Julian whispered, not taking his eyes off the tree. "Do you know what this is?"

"It's a tree, sir."

"It's more than a tree, silly bird. This is a Christmas tree."

"I'm afraid I'm unfamiliar with that particular species."

Julian laughed. "This is a custom from our world. That means that whoever lives here must be —"

"Welcome, gentlemen," said a fat dwarf with green overalls and a bushy white beard who had just stepped out from behind the tree to make his presence known. Tim picked up a hint of malice in his voice.

"Are you from Earth?" asked Julian excitedly.

"From where?" said the dwarf. He looked flustered. "Do you honestly not know who I am?"

Cooper's eyes widened. "Santa?"

"What? No!" The dwarf's fat little fists shook with rage. He thought for a moment. "Here. See if this jogs your memory." He lay down on the floor and writhed as if in agony. "Oh! No! It's everywhere! It's all over me! It's in my eyes and in my beard!"

Tim, Cooper, Dave, Julian, and even Ravenus glanced at each other uncomfortably until the dwarf looked up at them expectantly.

"Dave's mom?" asked Cooper.

Dave punched Cooper in the arm.

The dwarf frowned and stood up. "My name is Gabruk."

Tim shrugged. "That name doesn't ring any bells. I think you might be mistaking us for someone else."

"Oh, it's no mistake!" said Gabruk. "How's this for ringing a bell?" He reached into the front pocket of his overalls, pulled out a small brass bell, and rang it vigorously.

Tim looked at his friends, who could only offer shrugs. He turned back to Gabruk. "Good, I guess?"

"Seize them!" said Gabruk, his eyes focused on something behind them.

Tim turned around to find a giant green-skinned man, solid from the waist up, but merely a cloud of vapor where his genitals and legs should be, smiling down at him.

"Whoa!" said Julian, waving his hand through the giant's gaseous crotch.

"Please stop doing that."

Julian jerked his hand away and stepped back. "Sorry."

The floating upper-half of a green man folded his hands and bowed his head graciously as if to say all was forgiven.

"Are you some kind of air elemental?" asked Julian.

"I am djinn."

Cooper pursed his lips and scratched the back of his head. "Like that Korean dude from LOST?"

"I gave you a command, Bazuul," said Gabruk. "Seize them this instant!"

The djinn bowed his head. "If that is your wish."

"Wait! No! Stop!" Gabruk waved his hands in a panic. "That wasn't a wish. It was a command. I am your master!"

"I am beholden to you for three wishes," said Bazuul. "Nothing more. When you make the third, our bond is dissolved."

"Hang on," said Tim, glaring at Gabruk. "Did you wish us here?"

"Not exactly. I wished to confront you alone. The djinn distorted my wish, cheating me out of my third wish."

"I will not have my honor besmirched in my own home," said

Bazuul. "You wanted to confront your enemies alone. This is the most isolated place in the world."

"Wait," said Tim. "How are we your enemies? Who the fuck are you? And what's with the Christmas tree?" He looked at the tree. Julian's horse was eating one of the ornaments.

"I'll tell you who I am," said Gabruk. "Two moons ago, I was but —"

Cooper raised his head and slapped his thighs. "I've got it! It all makes so much sense now."

Tim was willing to listen to any explanation he could get. "What have you got?"

Cooper looked around excitedly as everyone, including Gabruk, Bazuul, and even Julian's horse, stared expectantly at him. "Jin was the smoke monster."

Julian shook his head. "What?"

"Think about it," said Cooper. "Did you ever see those two on the island together?"

"Spoilers, man!" said Dave. "I've only seen through season two."

"Well whose fault is that? The show's, like, ten fucking years old."

"Hey! Hey!" said Tim. "Will you guys shut the fuck up about LOST? We're in a situation here." He turned to Gabruk. "Please continue."

"Two moons ago." Rage burned in Gabruk's narrowed eyes as he recounted his tale. "I was but a humble cobbler, but I had the love of a beautiful woman from a noble family. We were to be wed in secret that very night. We were nervous, as you might imagine, and decided to step into a little tavern and settle our nerves over a bottle of stonepiss."

Tim nodded. "I'm with you so far."

"On my way from the bar to our table, I slipped in a puddle of urine." Gabruk glared up at Cooper, who appeared to still be thinking about LOST. "And you! When I tried to stand up, you broke wind in my face!"

Julian stepped forward. It was Diplomacy time. "I'd like to apologize for our friend. He has a low Charisma score, and —"

"The time for apologies is past!" shouted Gabruk. "The four of you laughed as I writhed on the floor, soaked in urine and the rancid vapor of a half-orc's bowels!Tell me, do you remember me now?"

Tim shrugged. "I don't know, man. That could have been any number of nights. It sounds like we were pretty wasted."

"Felicia, the love of my life, broke off our engagement! She said I smelled like her father and she couldn't go through with it."

"Oh, man," said Tim. "That's rough... and weird."

"I would have my bride and my vengeance!" said Gabruk. "I traveled the land far and wide, seeking someone who could grant me both. Eventually, I found and captured Bazuul." He nodded up at the djinn.

Tim looked up at Bazuul. "How did an NPC cobbler manage to capture a djinn?"

Patches of pink faded into Bazuul's green cheeks. "I was drunk."

Gabruk turned and walked further into the cavern. "Would you like to meet my bride-to-be?"

Tim followed, wanting to get a better idea of his surroundings. Beyond the still-unexplained Christmas tree, the cavern was shaped like the top two thirds of a perfect sphere, carved out of solid rock. The base was lined with bookshelves, a polished wooden bar, a fireplace, and a long curving sofa, on which sat a short fat dwarven woman with a closely cropped black beard. She wore a yellow and green kimono that looked like it had been made out of someone's grandmother's curtains, and showed off her hairy cleavage.

"Felicia," said Gabruk. "Bid good day to our guests."

Felicia stood and bowed. "Friends of Gabruk the Magnificent are friends of mine."

Gabruk stood by his special lady. "These are not friends, my dearest. These are the ones who would break our bonds of love."

"Gabruk the Magnificent?" said Tim.

Gabruk looked at the floor. "The wish for her affection was very potent."

"You used up a wish on that?" asked Cooper.

Julian elbowed him. "Don't be rude!"

"What?" said Cooper."She looks like Dom DeLuise in drag."

Felicia turned to Gabruk. "Our bonds of love can never be broken." She grabbed his arm and crotch. "Take me now, my love. I thirst for your seed!" She shoved her own face into his and slathered him in slurpy kisses.

Tim averted his gaze, which landed on Julian, who was cringing.

Cooper looked down at his crotch. "I'll never have an erection again."

"This is wrong," said Dave.

"So, so wrong," said Cooper.

"That's not what I meant. This is no better than slipping a roofie into her drink. It's unethical." He took a step toward Gabruk, but Bazuul floated into his path.

"I can allow no interference," said the djinn, "nor harm to come to my master while I am under his command."

"Ha!" said Gabruk, prying his face away from Felicia's. "That's right!" He rubbed his hands together. "Now there's the matter of my third wish. I have a bit of a dilemma, you see."

"How's that?" Tim asked distractedly. He was still trying to get the mental image of two bearded dwarves sucking face out of his head. Was that racist? Or homophobic?Both? No. It was the slurping and sucking noises that had gotten to him.

"I now have to choose between wishing myself and Felicia back home and my original plan to have you all vomit up your own internal organs until you died an agonizing death."

Julian frowned. "That seems... What's the word? ...disproportionate to our —"

"Come on, man," said Tim. "So we laughed at you for slipping in piss and getting farted on. That's objectively funny."

Gabruk stomped on the floor. "You ruined my life!"

Julian put his palm out at Tim. "Please. Let me talk." He turned to Gabruk. "Think about what you just said. Take a look at your life."Diplomacy check."You've got everything you ever wanted right there beside you. You've got the love of a... beautiful woman."Bluff check."And you earned it. Look at the feats of greatness you've achieved in the name of love. Who are we, if not the catalyst which inspired you to achieve those feats?"

Gabruk looked at the floor, as if considering Julian's words. Tim gestured for Julian to keep talking.

"Your first wish was born of love. Don't let hate poison the well. You have one wish left. You could do or have or be anything you want. Do you really want to waste that kind of power on us?"

Gabruk looked at Julian, then at Felicia. "I... I need to think."

Tim was hoping Julian would steer his speech into a suggestion that he'd use his last wish to send them all home, but not murdering them wasn't a bad compromise. Still, if Tim was going to wind up vomiting up his internal organs, that wasn't something he wanted to do while sober.

"This is a nice place you've got here, Bazuul."

The djinn flashed a wide grin. "Thank you, halfling. I built this place ages ago. Here I can rest my body and spirit."

Tim pushed his limits of subtlety. "That's a really nice bar."

Bazuul's eyes widened suddenly, like a light bulb just went on in his head. "Say! Are you folks thirsty?"

"Fuck yes!" said Cooper.

Tim nodded eagerly. "What have you got back there."

"Wait 'till you see it!" said Bazuul, suddenly rising up from behind the bar with a silver pitcher in one hand, and a tray full of glasses in the other. "You're not going to believe it."

Tim licked his lips. "What is that?"

Bazuul set the tray down and pointed at the pitcher. It rose from the bar and poured bubbly golden liquid goodness into six tall glasses. "An invention of my own devising.The Decanter of

Endless Beer."

"Brilliant," said Dave, his eyes welling up with tears. "Absolutely fucking brilliant."

Tim watched in awe as the foam rose over the rims of the glasses. "If I had three wishes, I'd use them all on this."

"I'd throw in a nut," said Cooper.

Everyone in the room, including Felicia and Gabruk, stood transfixed by the flowing beer. Even Ravenus perched, mesmerized, on the edge of the bar.

Bazuul passed full glasses to Tim, Dave, Cooper, Julian, and Felicia. "And one for the bartender."

Gabruk cleared his throat.

"Oh, I'm sorry!" said Bazuul. "Did I forget someone? Here you go, little guy." He snapped his fingers and a small glass bowl appeared in front of Ravenus. The pitcher floated over and poured beer into the bowl.

Ravenus bobbed his head. "Much obliged, sir."

Gabruk's fists started trembling at his sides again. "Of all the... Bazuul, I would like a drink as well."

Bazuul smiled at him. "Is that right? Tell me, master. Just how badly would you like that drink? Your wish is my command."

Gabruk shook his fist at the djinn. "I could wish you into oblivion!"

"Don't bother, friend," said Bazuul. "I'm about to get there on my own."

Gabruk's anger was short-lived. He turned to Felicia. "My dear, would you mind giving me your beer?"

Felicia handed over her glass. "Anything for you, my dearest love."

Gabruk grinned, raised the glass to Bazuul, and began to pour the contents into his mouth.

Bazuul snapped his fingers, and Gabruk spat out a mouthful of what appeared to be salt. He hacked and coughed and spat out more of the white granules.

Tim licked the tip of his finger, and touched the bar where

some of the granules had landed, then tasted it. Definitely salt. It was almost too cruel.

"WATER!"Gabruk rasped.

"I'm afraid I don't have any water on hand, master," said Bazuul. "But if you wish, I'm sure I can conjure some up."

"Brraaaaauuuuuggghhh!" said Gabruk, flinging down the glass of salt as hard as he could.

The glass didn't hit the floor. It floated up and over the bar, right into Bazuul's hand.

"Be careful, master. This is glass."

Gabruk stomped around in a little circle, his face turning beet red as he tried to spit more salt out of his dry mouth. Suddenly, he stopped and looked past the Christmas tree. "Snow!"

He ran past the tree. Julian's magical horse whinnied as Gabruk shoved his way past it.

The beer was delightful. Light and refreshing, it was the kind of beer Tim could drink all afternoon, getting steadily buzzed, but without getting drunk enough to start texting ex-girlfriends. It was the perfect beer, and this big green fucker had an infinite supply.

"I've gotta know," said Tim about halfway into his third glass. "What's with the Christmas tree?"

Bazuul furrowed his brow and looked at the tree, then back at Tim. "Do you mean the pukka pukka tree?"

"What the pukka pukka are you talking about? I mean that big-ass tree right there, with the lights and red ornaments."

"Those are pukka pukka nuts."

"Get outta town. Are you fucking with me?"

"See for yourself." Bazuul pointed his palm at the tree. One of the ornaments flew from the tree into his waiting hand.He gave it a gentle squeeze until it cracked. He lay the two halves on the bar, revealing a thick, light-brown layer under the shell, glistening with liquid of the same color.

"Well I'll be a motherfucker," said Tim. "Is that edible?"

"It's delicious!" said Bazuul. "Here, try some." A silver spoon popped into existence on the bar in front of Tim.

Tim scraped some of the nut meat out with the spoon and put it in his mouth. The djinn had not steered him wrong. It was like a mix between chocolate and coconut.

"That's fantastic!" said Tim. "Can I have some more beer?"

"Of course," said Bazuul. When his back was turned, Tim slipped the spoon into his vest's inner pocket.

Bazuul held the pitcher over Tim's glass, but didn't pour. When Tim looked up, the djinn was frowning down at him.

"Sorry," said Tim. He reached into his pocket, but the spoon wasn't there. Panicked, he looked up. Bazuul was holding the spoon. He tapped Tim lightly on the forehead with it and poured the beer.

"That explains the ornaments," said Julian. "But what about the lights?"

"I wouldn't recommend eating those," said Bazuul. "They are enchanted stones."

Julian nodded. "I understand that much. But why did you decorate the tree with them?"

"That they are decorative comes secondary to them being necessary for the life of the tree. I live in a cave, if you haven't noticed. The pukka pukka tree is tropical, and requires much light."

Now that Tim thought about it, the answer seemed so obvious as to make the question sound stupid.

"I must say," said Bazuul. He had forgone the use of his glass, and was now drinking straight out of the Decanter of Endless Beer. "I built this place as a means to get away from everyone, but it's nice to have some company." He slammed the decanter on the bar. "I like you guys!"

"I like you, too," said Julian. He raised his glass. "Salut!"

Tim and Cooper clicked their glasses against Julian's "Salut!"

Dave wasn't so enthused. He ignored them and grumpily sipped his beer.

Bazuul smiled at their strange custom. "Salut!" he shouted, and smashed the decanter into their glasses, destroying them utterly. "Sorry about that."

He raised his hand over the bar, pointing down toward the mess. His fingers twisted around each other, which looked extremely painful for a split-second, until his hand turned into a miniature whirlwind at the end of his arm. He lowered it onto the bar, sweeping up all of the beer, broken glass, and the salt he hadn't bothered cleaning up before. He lowered his swirling hand under the bar. When he raised it again, it was a normal hand, holding a tray with three new glasses.

Tim, Julian, and Cooper applauded while Bazuul filled their new glasses.

While Tim sucked the foam off the top of his fresh glass, Bazuul waved one hand over the other, producing four more silver spoons spread out like a fan. "Can I offer you good people a taste of the pukka puk—"

"Whaaaa!" cried Gabruk from what must have been close to the top of the cavern stairs. "Oh! Ooh! Ah! Eee! Ugh! Oh! Ow! Ugh! Ooooh!" Each exclamation was nearer than the last. The final one sounded like it was just beyond the pukka pukka tree. "Oh, my head. I'm okay." His breathing was labored. "I'm okay. I just need a moment to —"

NEIGH!

THUNK!

"Oomph!"

SMACK!

Thud.

Silence.

Julian's face turned pale. "Oh no." He, Cooper, and Tim hurried around the tree with Dave waddling behind.

"Fuck," said Tim. The scene didn't leave a whole lot to the imagination. Gabruk sat on the floor against the wall, his head slumped forward. His chest was caved in with a hole about the size of a hoof, and there was a splatter of blood on the wall, smearing down from where the back of the dwarf's head hit the wall down to where he now sat.

Julian pulled on his ears. "Everybody knows you're not supposed to stand behind a horse. They spook easily!"

Tim glared at him. "Just get the goddamn horse out of —" The horse disappeared. "What happened? Did I do that?"

Julian shook his head. "The spell duration timed out."

"Thanks, horse," said Tim. "Perfect timing, asshole. Dave! Where the hell are —"

"I'm right here!" Dave put his palm on the top of Gabruk's head. "I heal thee. I heal thee!" He shook his head. "Sorry, guys. He's gone."

Felicia started screaming from back near the bar. Her voice was fast and excited, and clearly very upset, but she was too far away for Tim to be able to make out what she was saying.

Julian shivered in spite of the sweat beading on his brow. "What are we going to tell Felicia?" he whispered. "I just killed her fiancé!"

"It's not all your fault," said Dave.

"That's right," said Cooper. "Dave fucked up his healing spell too."

Dave glared up at Cooper. "I was talking about you, asshole. Look at his boot."

Cooper looked down at Julian's boots. "Um... Sweet boots, Julian. What are those? Deer leather?"

"Not Julian's!" said Dave. "Look at Gabruk's boot. Recognize anything?" Everyone looked at Gabruk's boots. The bottom of his left boot was smeared with greenish-brown shit. "He slipped in your shit-puddle. That's what sent him bouncing down the stairs."

Felicia's screaming subsided as suddenly as it had started.

Tim patted down Gabruk's pockets. "Man, he'd be pissed to know that's what did him in."

"What are you doing?" asked Julian.

"I'm looting his corpse."

"Doesn't that seem... I don't know... kind of —"

"This is Caverns and Creatures. That's just what you do when someone dies." He pulled a small brass bell out of the front pocket of the dead dwarf's overalls. "Three wishes, and he doesn't have a goddamn cent on him." He pocketed the bell.

"May I have his eyes, then?" asked Ravenus, perched on a branch of the pukka pukka tree.

"No!" snapped Julian.

They walked back around the tree as solemnly as if they were walking toward their own executions.

Felicia was passed out on the floor.

Bazuul grinned at them from behind the bar. "Why so glum, chums?"

Julian stepped forward. "I'm sorry. Gabruk—"

"—took a nasty tumble down the stairs," said Dave. "I patched him up. He'll be okay, but he's going to take a little nap for a while."

"Super!" said Bazuul. "Who's up for another round?"

"We are!" said Dave, more enthusiastically than he'd ever said anything as long as Tim had known him.

"Dude," said Tim out of the corner of his mouth. "Now may not be the best time —"

"I have an idea," said Dave, less convincingly, out of the corner of his mouth.

Bazuul didn't seem to pick up on their secret conversation. He lined up their glasses and spilled beer into them, as well as all over the bar.

"Hey!" said Dave, once the beers had been poured. "You know what I'd like to see right now?"

"Your mom's hairy balls?" suggested Cooper.

Bazuul sprayed the whole bar with beer from his nose and mouth.

Dave sucked in his pride and continued. "I'd like to see Bazuul and Cooper arm-wrestle. Wouldn't that be fun?"

"Yeah," said Tim.

"Woo-hoo," said Julian.

Bazuul flexed his huge arms. "What do you say, half-orc?"

"Uh... sure." Cooper put his elbow on the bar and held open his hand.

As soon as Bazuul locked hands with Cooper, Dave grabbed Julian's arm, pulled him down, and started feverishly whispering in his ear.

When Dave had said what he had to say, Julian straightened up. "I don't think that's going to work. I mean, he's drunk, but he's not that drunk."

"He might be!"

"Excuse me, Mr. Bazuul?" said Julian.

Bazuul and Cooper were surprisingly evenly matched, their joined hands trembling above the bar.

"Yes?" said Bazuul. His voice was strained.

"What happened to Felicia?"

"She... had... some kind of... panic attack." The tendons in Bazuul's neck were taut as he spoke. "'Where am I? Who are you? Why am I wearing this?'Crazy drunk talk. She's kind of a lightweight for a dwarf. I cast a Sleep spell on her."

Dave pulled Julian down to his level again. "He doesn't even understand why Felicia snapped out of her trance. He is that drunk!"

"I'm... really... angry!" said Cooper. His body hulked out in Barbarian Rage, and the tide of arm-battle started to swing his way.

"That's cheating!" said Bazuul.

"No, it isn't!"

"Then neither is this!" Bazuul's arm morphed into a gigantic black tentacle, with which he threw Cooper into the pukka pukka tree, knocking the whole thing over and revealing the dead dwarf.

"Ow!" cried Cooper, struggling in the branches. "Fuck, that hurt!"

Dave looked up at Julian. "Hurry up!"

"Ventriloquism," Julian whispered. He cleared his throat and cupped his hand around the side of his mouth. When he spoke next, in a pretty terrible Gabruk impersonation, his voice came from Gabruk's dead body. "Oh, Bazuul! I'm ready to make my third wish!"

Bazuul floated over the bar and toward Gabruk's body. "Very well, master. State your wish. Try to make it an easy one. I've had a lot to drink."

"I wish to be alive!"

Bazuul rubbed his chin. "Hmph. I think that's a first for me. There's something weird about that, but I can't quite put my finger on... Ah, whatever. A wish is a wish." He snapped his fingers. "Your wish is granted!"

Gabruk's sternum crunched back into shape and the hoof dent disappeared as he raised his head and sucked in a deep, wheezy breath of air. As he exhaled, his head slumped forward again, but his chest was moving. He was alive, but unconscious.

Bazuul shrugged. "He wished to be alive, not awake." He began to rummage through Gabruk's pockets while Dave and Julian returned to their drinks. Coming up empty, he searched more frantically.

Tim didn't know why a djinn, who could conjure up anything he wanted with the snap of his fingers, was so hell-bent on squeezing every last copper piece out of a dwarf's clothes, but he admired his thoroughness. When Bazuul magicked Gabruk's clothes off and started shaking them vigorously, leaving the unconscious dwarf naked on the floor, Tim decided enough was enough.

"Don't bother, man,"he said, taking the bell out of his pocket. "I cleaned him out earlier. He didn't have anything on him but this stupid bell." He gave it a little jingle.

Bazuul turned around and looked at Tim like he was made of spiders. "No!"

"What's wrong?" said Tim. "What'd I do?"

The djinn narrowed his eyes, then smiled. "Nothing. I was thinking of something else. It's the drink. Let's carry on then, shall we?"

Tim shrugged. "Sounds good to me."

"I'll admit when I'm wrong," Julian said to Dave. "That was a good idea you had. Cheers." He raised his glass.

"Hmph," said Dave, abandoning his fake enthusiasm. He listlessly clinked his glass against Julian's. "Cheers."

"What's wrong with you, man? I was paying you a compliment."

"I know. I'm sorry." Dave gulped back the last of his beer. "I'm a dwarf. This stuff might as well be water. I wish we were drinking stonepiss."

Bazuul grinned in a way that made the hairs on the back of Tim's neck stand up. "Your wish is granted. You were drinking stonepiss." He snapped his fingers.

Tim's stomach began to churn. "What? What's going on?" Thoughts raced around inside his booze-addled brain. The bell binds the djinn? I rang the bell. Why did Dave get a wish? Holy shit! All that beer I drank is turning into hard liquor inside me. He knew he didn't have much time to present an argument, and that Bazuul wasn't likely to care, but he had to try. "Subjunctive!" he cried. "SUBJUNCTIVE! SUB-BLAAUUUUURRRRGGGGHHH" Vomit spewed out of him like his mouth was a busted fire hydrant.

Julian was next, followed by Cooper. The three of them hosed down everything in sight with puke you could fuel a jet with.

"Hey guys," said Dave. "Maybe you should take it easy on the *hiccup* sauce."

Tim wanted to tell him to go fuck himself, but it came out as "BLAAUUUURRRRGGGGHHH". Julian and Cooper offered similar retorts.

When Tim's guts had given all they had to give, a wave of darkness washed over him, from which he feared he may never return.

*

Tim returned, but immediately wished he hadn't. He woke up with a headache he wouldn't wish on Hitler. Every heartbeat pounded inside his head like one of those big-ass marching band drums. And then there was the sucking and slurping, like two dire slugs fucking inside his ear canal.

"What the fuck is that noise?" said Tim, opening his eyes. Two hairy beasts were wrestling on the sofa, one with red hair and the other with black. No, that wasn't quite right. It was Dave and Felicia, and they were naked.

"Oh my god." Tim turned away and tried to throw up. He was past empty. He heaved and heaved, but not even a tendril of spit escaped his lips. "Dave!" he groaned. "What the fuck did you do?"

"How about some privacy, huh?" said Dave, and resumed his walrus mating ritual.

How long had Tim been out? He looked around for something to anchor his mind. Cooper and Julian were still passed out on the floor. Julian's foot was close enough to grab without moving, so Tim gave it a wiggle.

"Julian? Julian, are you okay?"

"Please don't do that, sir," said Ravenus from up on top of the bar. "My master doesn't feel well." He staggered to the edge of the bar. "Rise and shine, sir. We must get you hydrat—" He fell off the bar like a bag of rocks.

"Nnnngggg," said Julian, then resumed sleeping. He was alive. That was good enough.

Now to check on Cooper. Tim couldn't risk looking at Cooper without getting Dave and Felicia in this field of vision, so he — Dave and Felicia. How did...? He didn't! He did.

"Dave, you selfish son of a bitch!"

Dave stopped slurping. "What?"

"You used another wish, didn't you? On that fucking she-bear!"

"Hey, man. Watch your mouth. I'm a dwarf now. I don't subscribe to the same ideals of beauty as you do."

"Don't get on your fucking soapbox with me. What about that

sermon you gave Gabruk? You just mind-roofied his girl right after he did."

"Uh-uh," said Dave. "This is different. She loves me, and I love her."

"Are you even listening to yourself? She doesn't love you. She's just in another wish trance, and you're drunk as fuck."

"I'm telling you, man. I didn't use a wish!"

"Bullshit," said Tim, pulling the bell out of his pocket. "I'll settle this right now.Bazuul!" He rang the bell.

"Unnnnngggghhhh," said Cooper. "My head! Knock that shit off."

"Hello, master," said Bazuul, who appeared above Tim. His tone was different somehow, more businesslike. "And how are we feeling this morning?"

"Like shit," said Tim. "Hey, listen. Dave claims he didn't use a wish to get in Felicia's pants over there, and I claim he's a fucking liar. Can you tell us who's right?"

"Of course I can," said Bazuul. He raised his eyebrows. "Do you wish to know the answer?"

"Why the fuck would I have asked the question if I didn't want to — Hang on a minute. Are you trying to trick me into blowing our last wish?"

Bazuul raised his palms innocently. "No trickery intended. I was simply stating the terms of the bargain. You may have the truth, but it will cost you a wish."

Tim sat up. "It's just a question, dude. When did you turn into a huge dick? I thought we were cool."

"I thought so, too," said Bazuul. "Right up until you decided to enslave me."

"Listen, dude. I didn't know about the bell! Oh, and that reminds me. Why does Dave get to make wishes when I'm the one who jingled the bell?"

Bazuul folded his arms. "You all had your parts to play in the ruse, and so you may split the three wishes among yourselves however you see fit."

"What ruse?"

"It was very clever, I'll grant you that. The half-orc defecates all over the top of the stairs, providing a nice frozen, slippery surface. The sorcerer's horse is conveniently left at the bottom of the stairs. The dwarf gets me good and drunk."

"You offered us the beer!"

"And the sneaky rogue swipes the bell away. Tell me, Tim. How long have you been planning this?"

"Are you fucking kidding me? The four of us couldn't plan a goddamn barbecue without winding up on eight different terrorist watch lists. Do you realize how much planning what you're proposing would take? Do we look like criminal masterminds to you?"

"Your bumbling idiots act is all part of the ruse. It is very convincing."

"It's no act, friend. We are the genuine article. Think about this. If we're so smart, why would we blow our first wish nearly killing ourselves with alcohol poisoning?"

"Even geniuses make the occasional mistake. I merely took advantage of your friend's slip of the tongue."

"Speaking of slippin' the tongue," said Tim. "How about our second wish? You think the four of us all cooked up this master plan so that Dave could fuck Paul Prudhomme on your sofa?"

"I'm warning you, Tim!" said Dave. "One more crack about Felicia, and I'll come over there and kick your ass!"

"Yeah, just put some clothes on first."

"Sir!" said Ravenus, hopping on Julian's chest. "You'd better wake up, sir. I don't understand exactly what's going on, but there could be trouble afoot."

"Jesus," said Cooper. "Could somebody shut that fucking bird up? I'm trying to sleep."

"Felicia!" cried Gabruk, having finally woken up. He either didn't realize he was still naked, or he didn't care. He had enough body hair so that it almost didn't matter. The tip of his dick was barely visible, peeking out from the thick salt-and-pepper crotch forest of pubes. "What have they done to you, my love?"

Tim sighed. "Fuck."

"I'll never love you, Gabruk!" said Felicia. "Not after what you've done to me!"

"Whatever they told you, my dear, it's a damned lie!"

"Is it?" asked Dave. "Explain how she got here, then, if not for you wishing her here and dressing her up like your own personal whore!"

"At least when she was my whore, she was dressed!"

Tim and Bazuul exchanged a glance and a grimace.

Dave's helmet flew across the room and hit Gabruk in the chest. Tim wasn't sure whether it was Dave or Felicia who threw it, but it pushed the confrontation from run-of-the-mill drunk, naked, fat people fighting to full on Jerry Springer.

"I'll kill you!" shouted Gabruk, nakedly waddle-running between Tim andBazuul. He tackled and straddled Dave's nakedness, and they tried to strangle each other while Felicia nakedly pulled Gabruk's hair.

"Didn't you say you aren't allowed to let harm come to those who command you?" Tim asked Bazuul.

Bazuul shrugged. "I removed all of your weapons when you arrived. I don't foresee any serious harm coming to Dave. Are you honestly telling me you don't want to watch this?"

"Not at all," said Tim. "In fact, do you know what might make it even better?"

Bazuul looked at Tim inquisitively.

"Throw a Grease spell on the floor."

"Hmm..."Bazuul nodded slowly. "I think I like where this is going." He snapped his fingers.

Felicia's feet slipped out from under her, and all of her weight came down on Gabruk, who found himself sandwiched between his rival and his former lover.

"Get off of me!" Dave croaked as he toppled the sandwich, sending Felicia across the floor on her belly like a fat hairy penguin on a Slip 'N Slide.

Bazuul looked down at Tim. "Would you like to... um... grab a beer maybe?"

Tim smiled. "You bet your green smoky ass I would."

Ravenus pecked frantically on Julian's chest. "Please wake up, sir! I have no idea what's going on, and I'm terribly frightened."

"For fuck's sake!" groaned Cooper. "I wish someone..."

Tim's heart skipped a beat. "Cooper, no!"

"...would tell that fucking bird..."

"Shut up! Shut up!" There was no choice. It was act now or risk being stuck here forever. "I wish we..."

"...to shut..."

"...were all back..."

"...the fuck..."

"...at the Whore's..."

It was a photo finish as to whether Cooper said "up" first or Tim said "Head". Tim looked at Ravenus, who was now flapping and hopping more frantically than ever, now that no sound was coming out of his mouth.

"Oh no!" Tim looked around at what might be the only home he would know for the rest of his life, and the people he'd have to spend it with. Dave and Gabruk were on their knees in a glistening grapple stalemate. Felicia was sobbing nakedly on the floor. With Ravenus silenced, Cooper rolled over and farted himself back to sleep. Julian was still out cold.

"I'm sorry," said Bazuul. "I'm going to miss you, Tim."

Tim looked up at the teary-eyed djinn. "What do you mean?"

"Your friend spoke the truth. Felicia was drunk, and sought some measure of vengeance on Gabruk. Or maybe she just wanted to make him jealous. No wish was involved."

"Then that means..." Tim saw Bazuul's hand raised, fingers about to snap. He lunged onto the bar and hugged the Decanter of Endless Beer.

The next thing he knew, he was back in the Whore's Head Inn, his arms wrapped around a splintery wooden table leg instead of a silver pitcher of infinite beer. Ah well, he'd tried.

"Jesus, Dave!" cried Tony the Elf. "Get off me! Why are you naked... and slimy?"

Tim stood up and confirmed that Julian and Cooper had both arrived as well. They were still sound asleep on the floor, as if nothing had happened. Maybe nothing had. Maybe it had all been a bad dream.

Tim sighed, slipped his hands into his pockets, and nearly had a heart attack when he felt something long and metallic in one of them.

The bell! Bazuul forgot to take it. Tim had a second chance. He could do it all over again, making real wishes this time. He could wish himself and all of his friends back to Earth, back in their real bodies.

He nervously pulled the item out of his pocket, and discovered it wasn't a bell at all. It was the silver spoon Bazuul had provided him with to taste the pukka pukka nut.

Tim smiled at the spoon. "Well played, friend. Well played."

The End

GENITAL HARPIES
ROBERT BEVAN

GENITAL HARPIES

(Original Publication Date: February 26, 2016)

Julian laid down his cards. "Three deuces." He carefully kept his expression neutral to avoid indicating that he already knew he'd won.

Raggart, the leader of their bugbear captors, grinned at him from across the crude three-legged table. His yellow fangs pointed every which way, like a pack of blind people trying to give directions. He calmly laid his cards flat on the table next to the small pile of copper and silver coins which had accumulated over the past few rounds. "It seems your luck has run out, elf. I have a pair of nines."

Ideally, poker a game in which all players should be familiar with the rules. That was especially true when money was involved. That was even more especially true when one's opponent was only keeping one and one's friends alive for the entertainment they could provide. It was Julian's high Charisma score, and the ranks he had in the Diplomacy skill, which had made the difference between being brutally murdered and enjoying a friendly card game. These same character attributes had also served him well in patiently and delicately explaining how "all reds" did not constitute a flush. He didn't know how much further Diplomacy could carry him.

Julian swallowed hard. "I'm afraid three twos beat two nines."

The fur on Raggart's forearms bristled out as his grin changed to a sneer. "How can that be? Three twos only adds up to six. Two nines add up to..." He frowned, counting on his black-clawed fingers until they were all used up. "... more than six!"

"That doesn't matter," said Julian. "A pair of anything isn't as... Three of a kind is harder to..." He was choking. He needed to hand this off to someone with a higher intelligence score. "Tim, you want to field this one?"

Tim looked at Julian like he'd just asked him to disarm a bomb with a pair of hammers. "Fuck no!"

They were unarmed and outnumbered. The only thing keeping them alive was this game. He might be only prolonging the inevitable, but it was better than giving up now and dying.

Julian looked at Cooper, who was three knuckles deep into his left nostril. Not exactly a think tank. Dave was terrible under pressure, and apparently a shitty poker player as well. Tim was just this side of sober, he and Ravenus (and, of course, the bugbears) being the only ones who could stomach the snot-like booze the female bugbears had been serving them. It was up to Julian to come up with a plan, but he needed Tim to help buy some time. He looked pleadingly at Tim.

Tim rolled his eyes. "Fine." He looked at Raggart, who was impatiently drumming his claws on the table. "The values of the numbers on the faces of the cards only come into play when two or more players have equal numbers of matching cards."

Julian understood why Tim had been reluctant to explain. Julian could barely wrap his head around that explanation. He didn't know what the bugbears would make of it. Tim needed a nudge. "For example..."

Tim flipped over the remainder of the deck. The top two cards were a king and a queen. "Okay, this works. Let's say two of you have a hand where nothing matches, but one of you has a king, and the other has a queen. Who wins?"

"The player with the king," said Horrig, a fatter bugbear with a long scar running down his left cheek seated between Dave and Cooper.

Tim nodded. "That's right. Because a king is higher than a queen."

"He likes to think so," said Grella, who Julian had come to assume was Raggart's wife, or whatever the equivalent was in this tribe. She looked at Julian's empty bowl. "Oh dear, you must be starved. Do you want some more stew?"

Julian looked down at the crude wooden bowl. Whatever that stew was, it smelled like diseased rat boiled in raw sewage. Of course, Ravenus had lapped it up like it was made of cotton candy and heroin. Julian was just thankful to be able to get the bowl away from him.

"Thank you, ma'am. I couldn't eat another bite."

Ravenus flapped his wings excitedly. "I could!"

Julian replied in a British accent, hoping none of the bugbears were familiar with the Elven tongue. "Eat Tim's." He passed his empty bowl up to Grella and switched back to the common tongue. "It was delicious."

"Thank you," said Grella. "That stew has been in my family for five generations."

"The recipe, you mean?"

Grella snorted through her ursine snout. "Heavens no. There's no recipe to speak of. We just throw whatever we catch into the cauldron. Aside from that, it's just a matter of keeping the fire going."

The fact that Julian and his friends were included in "whatever we catch" was clearly not lost on Tim. He was as white as a sheet. Julian nodded for him to continue his card lesson.

Tim rifled through the deck until he found another queen. "What happens when the king faces off against two queens?"

"Good times, eh Chief?" said Flargarf, seated between Raggart and Julian. He was the only bugbear Julian had gotten a glimpse of during the ambush, easily recognizable by his red right eye. Where the 'whites' of the other bugbears' eyes were a milky yellow, Flargarf's right eye was blood red, like maybe a blood vessel had burst in there. Julian hoped it wasn't a bad case of pinkeye.

The rest of the bugbears laughed and gulped back their dog-snot drinks, but Raggart merely grinned in appreciation for his

friend's lewd remark. He was clearly more interested in the rules of the game. "Whether it be in bed or in battle, surely the king wins."

"Wrong," said Tim, less diplomatically than Julian was comfortable with.

"How dare he call himself a man, much less a king, when he can't best two —" Raggart's eyes darted toward the back of the cave where his wife was tending the bubbling cauldron. He leaned in and lowered his voice. "— women?"

"The statistic improbability of obtaining a higher number of matching cards is more important than the rank of any individual card." Tim's explanation was once again lost on the bugbears. "Let's continue with the example and see if you get the hang of it." He spread the cards around on the table until he found a second king, which he placed next to the first king, opposite the two queens. "There. Now we have two kings. Who wins?"

Horrig scratched his furry chin. "The one who isn't stabbing himself in the head?"

"What? No. That's not even —"

Flargarf pounded his fist on the table. "Trick question! It's the one with the larger army."

Tim buried his face in his hands, then let out an exasperated sigh. "Come on, guys. I'm trying to make this as simple as I can."

Flargarf stood up and wobbled for a moment. He steadied himself against the table and leaned over Tim, making clear their vast difference in size. "Take that tone with me again, halfling, and tonight I'll be picking halfling meat out of my teeth with halfling bones."

Julian was close enough to smell that horrible drink, thick on the bugbear's breath.

Tim held his cup with both trembling hands and stared wide-eyed at the Flargarf's jagged and crooked teeth.

"Sit down, Flargarf," said Raggart. "I believe I understand now." He looked at Tim. "In theory, seven ones would defeat one eight."

"Correct!" Julian blurted out when he saw Cooper start to speak. To placate Cooper, he added, "In theory."

Raggart spoke to his two comrades in their native tongue, which sounded like a bear speaking German while being stabbed. When he was finished, the other bugbears grumbled and nodded.

He shoved the pile of copper and silver coins toward Julian. "Very well, elf. You win again."

Julian shoved the pile back to the middle of the table. "Winning is easy when your opponent doesn't understand the game."

Raggart grinned and shoved the coins back toward Julian. "Losing is easy when you're planning to eat your opponents after the game is done."

Flargarf and Horrig chuckled. Cooper let out a long, rumbling fart, the smell of which was masked by the overpowering stench of bugbear stew. Tim and Dave looked expectantly at Julian.

Julian kept his cool. He had no doubt of the bugbears' intentions, though he hadn't expected them to lay them on the line quite so soon.

See and raise.

"Now that we're on a level playing field, what do you say we make it interesting?"

Raggart narrowed his eyes. "What did you have in mind?"

"One more round," said Julian. "You and me. If I win, we walk out of this cave alive. If you win, you all can eat us."

Raggart nodded. "You have yourself a deal, elf." His companions, predictably, chuckled softly to themselves.

"I'm afraid I'm going to require some sort of assurance that you're going to honor your end of the deal."

"Is my word not good enough for you?" Raggart challenged Julian. "Have you the audacity to come into my home and call me a liar to my face?"

"Dude," Cooper said to Julian. "That is kind of rude."

Julian couldn't believe he had to defend himself to Cooper. "We didn't ask to come into his home. They beat us unconscious and dragged us here in sacks." Diplomacy wasn't always about sugar coating. Sometimes it involved telling it like it is. He turned to Raggart. "If you would murder us, it's probably safe to assume you would lie to us as well."

Raggart frowned. "What kind of assurances would you like?"

"Give me a minute," said Julian. "I haven't thought that far ahead." What kind of assurances would be acceptable by both parties? Any guarantee regarding their safety was also dependent on their word that, upon losing, they would voluntarily allow themselves to be boiled to death in a cauldron. Julian couldn't see the bugbears accepting those terms.

"Swear to Zabir," said Dave.

The bugbears' eyes widened. Dave had apparently struck a nerve, but Julian had no idea why. He was about to ask, when Cooper beat him to it.

"Who the fuck is Zabir?"

"Bugbears are goblinoid creatures," said Dave. "Zabir is the deity of the goblins."

Cooper scratched his ass thoughtfully. "I thought that was David Bowie."

Dave ignored Cooper. "They may lie to us, but they wouldn't dare break an oath they made to Zabir."

"You ask too much, dwarf," said Raggart. "These terms are unacceptable."

Screw that. Dave was rarely useful for anything more than a healing spell, but he had just rocked the shit with this one.

"If you intend to honor your part of the agreement," said Julian, "then you should have no problem with Dave's terms. Maybe you're just afraid of being outmatched." He glanced down at Raggart's empty glass, then back up at Raggart.

Raggart, Horrig, and Flargarf were the only three bugbears in the cave who hadn't already drunk themselves into comas, but they weren't far off. Julian's group, with the exception of Tim, was stone-cold sober. If it came to a fight, a bugbear victory was no longer a foregone conclusion.

Julian was impressed with himself. If Raggart had picked up

on his innuendo, he would understand that Julian was presenting him with a gift. He was making the cowardly-but-smart option (letting them go to avoid bloodshed) seem like the brave option (not being afraid to accept Julian's challenge). He wasn't this devious in the real world. This was the result of having put all of those ranks into his Diplomacy skill.

Raggart placed a large, red-hilted dagger on the table and raised his right hand.

Flargarf grumbled something in their native language. He raised his voice, looking back at the cauldron, and then at Raggart.

"I am afraid of nothing," said Raggart. He sliced his open right palm with his dagger. "I swear by the mighty Zabir, I will be true to my word."

Julian looked back at Dave, who nodded. "Good enough for me. Dave, could you give him a quick heal so he doesn't bleed all over my cards?"

"Sure." Dave reached over and touched Raggart's fingertip. "I heal thee."

Raggart sighed with the exhilaration that came from magical healing and wiped the blood from his palm on Horrig, who had by now fallen asleep.

He stared coldly at Julian. "Deal the cards, elf."

Julian's handmade cards were too big for his slender elf hands to shuffle the conventional way, so he shuffled like a six-year-old, smearing the pile of cards all over the surface of the table, then shoving them all back together again.

He dealt the cards until he and Raggart each had five. His crude shuffling saw Raggart right out of the gate with three kings, a far better starting position than his own hand of complete crap. The Arcane Marks that Julian had put on the back of all the cards identified each card with electric blue light that only he could see, but they weren't going to help him this time. They were fucked.

"I'll take two cards," said Raggart, much to Julian's complete lack of surprise.

When Julian looked across the table, he was shocked to see that the cards Raggart had discarded were two of his three kings. Was it possible that he was this stupid? No. He was intentionally throwing the game. Julian's innuendo had successfully made Raggart reassess the situation he was in, and the likely outcome.

Julian slid the six off the top of the deck, along with the Jack underneath it, giving Raggart a nice hand of sweet fuck all.

There was just one problem. Raggart's decision to sabotage his own hand left him with a king high, which still beat the crappy hand Julian had dealt himself.

The Five of Clubs sitting on the top of the deck wasn't going to help him, but he really only had one choice. Discard everything and hope for a pair of something or an Ace.

He slid the Five toward him, then stifled a sigh of relief at the Ace underneath it. The next three cards were crap, but he had what he needed. He gulped as he looked at the front of his cards, then gasped in fake horror.

"Cooper, Dave, Tim, Ravenus," Julian said as solemnly as he could. "I'm sorry. I've failed you."

"Fuck," said Cooper and Dave. Tim snored. Fear of being boiled to death was clearly not enough to keep him from slipping into a booze-induced coma.

"I must say, sir," said Ravenus. "I admire your calm in the face of impending doom."

"Shut up, Ravenus," Julian snapped. "I'm not calm. I'm very nervous and scared."

"But you don't seem nervous to me, sir. Quite the contrary, you seem —"

"Shut up, Ravenus!"

"Very well, sir."

Cooper and Dave were buying Julian's act, as were the bugbears, if Farlgarf's hungry grin was any indication. It would take more than a gulp and a gasp to override Julian's Empathic Link with Ravenus, though, which was now letting him know that Ravenus' feelings were hurt.

Suck it up, buddy. We're almost out of here.

"The game isn't finished until the cards are turned over," said Raggart. He flipped his hand over, and Julian feigned amazement.

"Sorry, fellas," said Julian, flipping over his cards. "Looks like it's just not your day."

The bugbears' reactions were the exact opposite of what Julian had anticipated. Flargarf's grin widened as he lifted a crude club with spiked with nails.

Raggart looked alarmed rather than relieved. He drew his dagger and slapped Horrig in the back of the head. "Wake up!"

"What the fuck, dude?" Cooper asked Flargarf.

Dave backed away from the table, his forearms raised to shield his face. "Did you forget the oath you made to Zabir?"

"The terms of the deal were clear," said Flargarf. "If you lose, then we get to eat you."

"But I didn't lose," said Julian. "I won."

Raggart frowned and lowered his dagger. The panic on his face was replaced with confusion. "You did?"

"Liar!" said Flargarf. "Look at the cards. Neither hand has any cards that match. And the chief's king beats your nine."

"But it doesn't beat my Ace."

"I'm about to beat your ass."

"Not ass. Ace!"

"Stand down, Flargarf," said Raggart. "Tell me, elf. What is this 'Ace' you speak of?"

Julian slid the Ace of Diamonds away from the rest of his hand. "This is an Ace."

"Is that not a one?" said Raggart. Clearly, he still wanted to avoid violence, but had to make a show of strength in front of Flargarf.

"In some games, an Ace counts as a one, but in most games, including this one, it's the highest card in the deck."

"I see."

"Have you gone mad, Chief?" cried Flargarf. "This elf has won

every match simply by conjuring up a new rule on the spot. Now he claims a one, the lowliest peasant in the kingdom, is mightier than a King. If you believe that, then I say the dumbest bugbear in the tribe is wiser than a Chief."

"It's an Ace," said Julian. "Not a one. And the numbered cards aren't really meant to be representative of —"

"Shut your lying hole, elf!" said Flargarf.

Raggart laid his dagger back down on the table, and presented his bare chest to Flargarf. "If you would seek the Chiefdom, you are welcome to come and take it."

If they started killing each other, Julian and his friends might be able to escape. It was a second-best resolution, to be sure, but not one that Julian expected he'd lose any sleep over.

Flargarf lowered his head. "I spoke in a fit of passion, Chief. Forgive me. It angers me to see you made a fool of in your own home."

"The elf's explanation is credible," said Raggart. "The one card is marked with the letter A rather than a number. Obviously that holds certain significance." He turned to Julian. "You and your friends are free to leave."

"Great," said Julian. He paused a moment while the bugbears stared at him. "So, I guess we'll just collect our things and be on our way."

Raggart grinned, first at Flargarf, then at Julian. "That was not part of our agreement."

"Come on, man!" said Dave. "You can't just send us out of here unarmed in the middle of the night. That's the same as killing us."

"I am confident that Zabir will recognize the difference."

"Can I at least have my cards?" asked Julian.

"You cannot. We have enjoyed this game of yours, and wish to play more."

"Do you know how long it took me to make those?"

"Dude, fuck your cards," said Cooper. "Let's get the fuck out of here."

"And go where?" asked Dave. "We don't even know where we are, much less how to get back to Cardinia."

Raggart grinned. "The way is not difficult. Travel south until you reach a well-worn path in the woods. Follow it eastward until —"

"But that leads to —" Flargarf interrupted, but was promptly shut up with a glare from Raggart.

"That leads to the coast," Raggart continued. "From there, it's an easy southward stroll to Cardinia."

Flargarf genuflected before Raggart. "I am humbled by your wisdom." His eyes flickered briefly toward Julian before he added, "... and mercy."

"Now go," said Raggart. "And may Zabir guide you swiftly to your destination."

Julian backed cautiously away from the table, lest the bugbears have any last minute tricks up their sleeves, but they merely watched as he, Dave, and Cooper regrouped on the exit side of the table. "Thank you. You're being a very good sport about all this."

Cooper picked Tim up off the floor and took the lead toward the cave entrance. After a few tense minutes, they found themselves in the safety of the dark, monster-infested forest.

"Well done, sir," said Ravenus. "You really saved our biscuits back there."

"Thank you, Ravenus. It's nice to hear that someone appreciates my effort."

"Shall I scout the area?"

"Not this time, buddy. It's probably safer to stay close together, at least until we find the path." Julian looked around. The forest was dense with foliage, limiting visibility in every direction. "Hey. Do either of you guys have any idea which way south is?"

Cooper and Dave shook their heads.

"Does anyone have any ranks in the Survival skill?" asked Dave.

Julian and Cooper shook their heads.

"That's a pretty big party oversight on our part." Dave frowned at the ground and stroked his bushy beard. He looked up. "We could attempt an untrained Survival check."

"I don't even know what that means," said Julian.

"Some skills require you to be trained in order to be able to use them at all," Dave explained. "Languages, for example. If Cooper spent one skill point to learn the Elven language, he could understand everything Ravenus says."

"Fuck that," said Cooper.

"But as long as he continues being a stubborn asshole, he has no chance of understanding anything your familiar says. Other skills aren't quite so cut and dry. You don't have to be Bear Grylls to eat a bug. You'll probably still die if left on your own in the wilderness, but you've got a chance."

"We're not trying to survive for a long time in the wilderness," said Julian. "We're just trying to figure out which way south is."

"Exactly," said Dave. "Which is related to Survival, but probably comes with a lot smaller Difficulty Class modifier."

Julian frowned. "You're losing me again."

"It might be easy enough that we've got a shot at it."

"Okay," said Julian. "So how do we do it?"

Dave scratched his head. "I don't actually know. I guess we just focus on finding south." He put his index fingers on his temples. "Which way is south?"

Julian and Cooper followed Dave's example. "Which way is south?"

Julian looked for clues, but came up with nothing.

"That way," said Dave and Cooper simultaneously, pointing in roughly similar directions.

"How could you possibly..." Julian looked in the direction both of them were sort of pointing in, but nothing looked any different than anything else. "What are you basing this on?"

"What do you mean?" asked Dave.

"I mean, did you look at the way the leaves were facing? Or did you sense magnetic fields or something?"

"No. I just really feel like south is that way."

"Based on nothing? There's a word for that. It's called guessing."

"It's not based on nothing," said Dave. "It's based on our Survival checks. I got a strong sense in my mind that south is that way."

"I got it, too," said Cooper. "It was pretty awesome."

"Why didn't I get it?" asked Julian.

Cooper shrugged. "Shitty roll."

He stomped through the forest at a snail's pace, ripping apart vines and tearing off small branches with one hand, and holding Tim in place over his shoulder with the other. Julian and Dave followed in the wake of his slow destruction.

After an hour and several dozen yards of travel, they came upon the path Raggart had mentioned. It fit the description anyway, insofar as it ran perpendicular to the direction they had been traveling in.

"Thank fuck," said Cooper. "I need to take a rest." He set Tim gently on the ground.

Tim's eyes were open. "You can rest on horseback. We should probably hoof it from here."

Cooper wiped about a gallon of sweat off his face while scratching his ass against the trunk of a tree. "How long have you been awake?"

"I never went to sleep. I was faking it, hoping the bugbears would forget I was there."

"Dude! Do you know how much fucking easier that would have been with two arms available?"

Tim turned up his palms innocently. "I can't see in the dark."

"Hang on," said Dave. "You were hoping the bugbears would forget you were there? What was your plan, exactly? Were you just going to fuck off while the rest of us got chopped up and chucked in the stewpot?"

"I was going to assess the situation and act accordingly." Tim turned to Julian. "Let's giddy up, huh? Conjure up some of those magic horses so we can get the fuck out of here. We'll be safer when we reach the coast."

"I only have a limited number of spells," said Julian. "The bugbears took my bag with all my backup scrolls in it." He clenched his fists in frustration. "And my cards."

Cooper stopped rubbing his ass against the tree trunk and looked at Julian. "Who gives a shit about your stupid cards? The rest of us were trying to get out of there with our lives, and you were trying to negotiate for a deck of goddamn playing cards."

"Seriously," said Tim, facing a tree and unlacing his pants. "What's the deal, Kenny Rogers? Know when to run away. Know when to — however the fuck it goes."

"I spent weeks making them," said Julian.

Over the sound of urine splattering against bark, Tim sighed like he was about to lay down a hard truth. "Maybe outsource that shit next time. They were usable, but hardly works of art. The Queen of Diamonds' eyes were facing two different directions, and the Jack of Clubs' mustache looked like he had a squid trying to escape out of his nose."

"Hmph," said Dave. "As if you could have done any better, Picasso. Remember that pig anatomy poster you drew for your ninth grade biology project?"

Tim gave Dave a sideways glare. "I did that on the fucking bus on the way to school, dumbass." He turned back to focus on his stream of urine. "I'm not saying your cards were terrible. I'm just saying that, given a span of weeks, I could have drawn a better deck of cards with a crayon glued to my dick."

"It wasn't just the drawing," said Julian. "I put an Arcane Mark on the back of each card so that I could cheat."

Tim turned his entire body sideways to look back at Julian. His piss stream found Dave's boots. "Are you out of your fucking mind?"

Julian had expected some kind of surprised reaction, but thought it would be more along the lines of 'Bravo!' and 'Well done!'. "What's the problem? Those cards just saved our asses."

"You're lucky they were just a couple of bugbear grunts," said Tim. "How hard do you think that bullshit zero-level spell would have been to detect for someone with just a smidge of magic savvy? You try to cheat a wizard, and he will Lightning Bolt your stupid ass, and feed the smoldering pile of guts that used to be you to his familiar. Now how about some horses?"

"If I use up two of my Mount spells, that's two less Magic Missiles I'll have if we run into monsters. I think we should just walk."

"Good point," said Tim. He raised his index finger. "Counterpoint. Dave is slow as fuck."

"I don't think that's a counterpoint," said Dave. "I think that's just you being a dick."

Tim ignored him. "The faster we move through the woods, the fewer Random Encounters we are likely to have, thereby nullifying the potential disadvantage of not hanging on to your two shitty Magic Missiles."

"But —"

"Furthermore, with the rest of us weaponless, the likelihood of us surviving an attack by anything more than a one-legged kobold, even with the awesome power of your two extra Magic Missiles, are slim to none."

Julian looked at Dave and Cooper. "Do you guys agree?"

Dave nodded. Cooper nodded and farted. Julian would have preferred to deliberate a bit more, as he suspected both of their votes were more motivated by laziness than by self-preservation, but the rancid cloud squealing its way out of Cooper's ass made a compelling argument to get out of the area as quickly as possible.

"Horse," said Julian, and immediately repeated the incantation. Two horses popped into existence on the path, one black and the other brown.

Cooper helped Dave onto the brown horse's saddle, and Julian climbed on behind him. It wasn't the most comfortable way to ride, but it was favorable to blowing a third spell.

On the black horse, Tim stood behind Cooper, holding on to his shoulders.

The twisty path limited the usefulness of Cooper and Dave's Darkvision, and roots and branches threatened to trip the horses or knock them off their mounts; they were unable to travel faster than a slow trot.

After an hour of riding, Julian's arms were getting sore from holding on to Dave. He didn't know how much longer he could last. "This forest is starting to creep me out. And I still don't smell any sea air. Halflings have a keen sense of smell, don't they? Can you smell anything, Tim? "

"You're thinking of gnomes," said Tim. "Anyway, I could be snorting saltwater right now, and still wouldn't be able to smell anything but Cooper's perpetual stream of farts."

Cooper glared back. "The more you bitch about it, the better I feel about it. I'm brewing up a nice one for your right now."

"You guys chill out," said Dave. "It looks like we'll be out of the woods after we get past those two big oak trees."

Julian looked over Dave's right shoulder. His Low-Light Vision was no match for Dave's Darkvision, but he could just barely make out the two oaks Dave spoke of. Their interlaced branches formed an arc over the path. As hard as he strained his eyes, he could see nothing of the terrain beyond.

Blinking a few times to relax his eyes, Julian let his gaze fall lazily to the ground, where he caught a flicker of movement in his periphery. Whatever had moved was long and serpentine.

"Snake!" Julian shrieked. He was a little embarrassed for reacting like that for something as mundane as a snake while they were in a world where they'd faced off against much more dangerous creatures than that. And then he was more embarrassed when a closer inspection revealed that what he'd saw was, in fact, only a vine. "Sorry. False alarm."

He could have sworn he saw it move. It was just a combination of hunger, thirst, exhaustion, and general paranoia playing tricks with his mind. It was an odd-looking species of vine. At its thickest, it was about as big around as Julian's upper arm. Smaller vines grew out from the main shaft with leaves which, with a little imagination, looked like gnarled human hands.

"What kind of vines do you suppose these —" As he turned to the others, he noticed Tim was missing from the back of Cooper's horse. "What happened to Tim?" When he looked back, he found Tim ten feet back, suspended from one of the lower-hanging oak branches by one of those strange vines wrapped around his neck. "Tim!"

Before anyone had a chance to react, both horses started screaming. Julian looked down at Cooper's horse. Vines were slithering up its legs, immobilizing it. He could safely assume the horse that he and Dave were riding was getting the same treatment. That assumption was confirmed when he felt a snakelike tendril brush against his leg.

"Master," cried Ravenus as he launched himself from Julian's shoulder. "Be careful!"

"Branches!" Julian shouted as he grabbed the oak branch they were passing under. He jerked his feet up and pulled himself onto the branch. There were a few vines in the trees, such as the one which currently had Tim, but it was nothing like the ground, which was now a slithering, writhing mass of vegetation.

Cooper had no trouble pulling himself out of harm's way, but Dave's arms were too short to reach a branch.

"Help!" cried Dave, losing elevation as his horse succumbed to the tangle of vines.

Julian and Cooper each grabbed one of Dave's outstretched arms and started to pull. Dave was a solid mass of dwarf, to be sure, and wore metal armor which weighed him down even more, but he felt somehow heavier than he should. When Julian looked down, he discovered the reason they were having such a hard time pulling him up. A vine had coiled itself around Dave's right leg.

"Shit!" said Julian.

"You hold Dave," said Cooper. "I've got to go save Tim."

"What are you talking about?" cried Julian. "I'm like eighty-five pounds soaking wet!"

"Don't let me go!" said Dave. He was sweating through the leopard fur on his wrist, and Julian's tenuous grip was growing even more tenuous.

"I'm okay!" shouted Tim. "Help Dave."

Julian looked back. Tim was still suspended from the tree, but now on his terms. He was holding on to the dead, severed vine with one hand, and holding a shortsword in his other.

"Where the hell did you get that?" asked Julian.

"I swiped it from the bugbears while the rest of you were jerking each other off. Here, catch." Tim tossed the sword to Julian, who let go of Dave to catch it.

It was a clumsy catch, but Julian managed to grip the handle without losing any fingers. Holding it in his own hand, he realized that it was a large dagger. It had only looked like a shortsword in proportion to Tim.

The horses stopped screaming, which meant that the vines had finally strangled them to death. Since magically summoned horses disappear when they die, this also meant that Dave had lost support from below, and a bunch of confused vines groping around for something to grab on to.

"Cut the fucking vines already!" cried Cooper. "I'm losing Dave!"

Julian wrapped his legs around the branch and hung upside down. He wasn't even close to being able to cut the vine wrapped around Dave's right leg, much less the ones which were now threatening to wrap around his left.

"I can't reach him!" said Julian. "You'll have to pull harder!"

"I'm pulling as hard as I fucking can!"

"Idiot!" said Tim, who had climbed onto the branch he'd been hanging from. "Use your Barbarian Rage!"

"Fuck y—" Cooper paused mid-expletive. "Oh, that's actually a good idea. I'M REALLY ANGRY!"

Julian wasn't at an angle where he could see Cooper's body hulking out, but he could see the expression on Dave's face turn from panic to pain plain enough.

"Ow! My fucking arm!" screamed Dave, but he started to rise.

Hanging onto the branch with both legs and one arm, Julian inched a little closer to Dave. As soon as the vine was in striking distance, Julian hacked at it with the big dagger.

"You're doing it wrong," said Tim. "Use the other side!"

Julian was confused. Surely he didn't mean... "You mean the handle?"

Tim slapped his palm against his forehead. "No, dumbass. The other side of the blade. The serrated side. Saw, don't chop."

Julian maneuvered the dagger in his hand until it was facing the opposite way. He sawed at the vine, and found Tim's method to be much more efficient. The blade's teeth cut through the vine in a matter of seconds. Dave, now free of the vine's grip, rose out of sight.

When Julian righted himself on the branch, Cooper was all bulked up, crazy-eyed, and sweaty, but Dave was curiously still out of sight.

"Where's Dave?" asked Julian.

Cooper panted heavily as his body deflated into its usual flabby state. He looked up.

Julian followed Cooper's gaze, and found Dave straddling a branch about ten feet higher than theirs, hugging the tree trunk. "You okay?"

"I'm not really big on heights," said Dave. "And I think my right arm and left leg are a little longer than they're supposed to be, but otherwise I'm good."

With a bit of coaxing, they were able to talk Dave down from his higher branch, and the four of them climbed down a branch on the east-facing side of the tree, where they were able to hop to the ground outside of the forest. There was still no hint of coastline. They were in some kind of valley, the view ahead of them blocked by massive, sheer cliff faces.

Looking back into the tree tunnel, Julian caught the last of the bloodthirsty vines receding back into either side of the path, waiting for the next poor sucker who fancied a quiet walk through the woods.

"That was a close one, eh?" said Ravenus. "Pity about the horses."

Julian shuddered. "Can you imagine if we hadn't been on horseback?"

"Yeah," said Tim. "We'd have been fucked. Can I have my dagger back?"

"Oh, you mean this dagger?" Julian held up the dagger, but didn't offer it to Tim. "You mean the dagger you stole from the monster who wanted to eat us while I was in the middle of negotiating a peaceful resolution?"

"That's the one."

"How do you justify giving me shit about making a marked deck of cards after pulling a stunt like that?"

"That was kind of stupid," said Dave. "If they had caught you, it would have come down to a fight, and the only one of us that would have been armed would have been you."

Tim pointed at Dave. "That dagger just saved your fat ass."

"Just like my cards saved all our asses," said Julian.

"Okay, fine. Great job. Happy? Can I have my dagger now?"

"Sure. That was all I wanted to —"

"My father's dagger!" shouted Raggart's voice from behind them.

"Never mind," said Tim. "You keep it."

When Julian turned around, he found Raggart, Flargarf, and Horrig, approaching cautiously and brandishing long heavy-bladed machetes, the kind that would be ideal for cutting freshly-killed bodies out of a tangle of carnivorous vines. Horrig was also wearing Julian's bag, though their difference in body styles meant that the cross strap had the bag resting just under Horrig's armpit, rather than where Julian wore it at the hip.

"I don't want to seem unappreciative," said Cooper, "but you guys kinda suck at giving directions."

Raggart grinned. "You made better time than I expected. Tell me, how did you escape the assassin vines?"

Julian handed Cooper the dagger, stepped forward, and raised his fists in the air. "With the power of my great sorcery!"

Tim and Cooper laughed through their noses, and Julian discovered what it felt like to fail an Intimidate check.

"Listen," Julian continued. "The only thing different between now and in your cave is that you don't have a horde of bugbears to back you up."

"Do you think I fear death, elf?" asked Raggart.

Julian took a step back. "Well I kind of thought... I mean, it's only natural. Back at the —"

"I would not risk the lives of the women and children of my clan, but I would take my own life before I surrender to an elf."

Julian scrambled to think of a way to help Raggart out of the bravado hole he was digging himself into. "Who said anything about surrender? We aren't even fighting. We each mistakenly took something from the other, and this is just a hostage exchange. You give me my bag, and we'll give you your dagger."

"Like fuck we will!" said Tim.

"Tim," snapped Julian. "Shut up! I'm trying to diplo... mate? Diplomaciate? Diplo—"

"Don't bother," said Raggart. "I shall take my father's dagger out of the half-orc's dead hand."

Cooper stepped forward, brandishing the dagger. "You can take it out of my ASS!"

The bugbears paused briefly to exchange confused glances, then continued pressing forward.

Diplomacy had failed. A fight was inevitable. Julian was down to one first level spell in his head, but if he could get his hands back on his bag, he'd be able to use his back-up scrolls.

"Everyone gang up on the one coming from ten o'clock." Julian couldn't recall ever seeing any clocks in this world, so the bugbears would have no frame of reference. His order might give them a slight edge.

"Is that the one on the left?" asked Cooper.

Julian sighed. "Yes, Cooper."

"What difference does it make who we attack first?" asked Dave, glancing at Horrig. "Hang on... Is this about your stupid cards again?"

"What? Of course not! Why would you even — Wait... Do you hear that?" A strange and beautiful melody flowed down with the breeze from atop the cliffs ahead.

To Julian's surprise, the bugbears lowered their weapons and tilted their heads so that their ears faced upward, toward the source of the sound.

"It's the most beautiful thing I've ever heard," said Horrig, a tear rolling down the long scar on his cheek. He did a complete about-face and started walking toward the cliff.

Raggart's eyes were watery as well, but he shook off the song's enchanting effect when he spotted his subordinate retreating. "Horrig! Where do you think you're going?"

"The song," said Flargarf, who now also turned his back on his leader. "Must... find... the song..."

"Hey!" Julian shouted after Horrig. "Can you at least leave my bag behind?"

Horrig didn't respond. He and Flargarf continued their entranced journey in search of the song's source.

Scrolls or no scrolls, they now had enough of an advantage over Raggart that Julian might have another shot at ending their conflict without violence. He put his hands on his hips and attempted to smile in such a way that expressed confidence without being too cocky.

"It would appear the circumstances have changed," said Julian. "Do you still want to —"

Cooper walked past him, dagger in hand.

"Hey, Coop!" said Julian. "Chill out. We can end this peacefull—"

"Surrender my father's dagger at once!" demanded Raggart. "Or in Zabir's name, I'll —"

Cooper tossed the dagger to Raggart. "Dude. Take it. Just shut up so I can hear the song."

Raggart dropped his machete to catch his prized dagger with both hands, then gawked at Cooper as he walked right by him. "Oh. Um... Thank you."

Cooper squirted out a fart in response.

"Cooper!" cried Julian. "Why the hell did you —" Dave and Tim followed Cooper, mouths hanging open and eyes glazed over. "Guys! What the hell are you doing?"

They continued walking as if Julian hadn't even spoken.

Ravenus was standing on the ground, watching everything in curious oblivion, when suddenly his chest puffed out and his beak opened wide. "What is that?"

"Oh no, Ravenus. Not you too," said Julian. "Come on. Shake it off. It's just music."

"A thousand pardons, sir. I wasn't speaking of the music." Ravenus inhaled deeply. "Can you smell that?"

Julian didn't smell anything out of the ordinary, and didn't make any efforts to sniff the air more acutely. If Ravenus thought it smelled good, there was a good chance it smelled like rotting flesh.

"May I go sir?"

Julian frowned. "Don't go far. And if you see what's singing, come back and report."

"Very good, sir!" Ravenus flew off in the direction of the cliff face, but stayed low to the ground. Julian lost sight of him beyond a drop in elevation.

"I gave you an order!" Raggart barked at Horrig. He made a grab at his subordinate's arm, but was elbowed in the face. "How dare you... Who do you think..." The shocked words honked out from his hands cupped over his face. Horrig paid him no further attention as he continued toward the base of the cliff.

Julian wasn't even going to try the same tactic on Cooper. He frowned at Raggart, who was still wheezing through his bloodied nose. "Do you think we should just follow along and see what's going on at the source?"

"Fools!" said Raggart. "Let them meet what fate awaits them!"

"I don't think you really mean that," said Julian. "Those are your friends."

"They'll be meat for the stewpot soon enough, as will you and yours."

Raggart was talking a big game, but Julian noted the conspicuous lack of stabbing he was doing as they walked together behind their entranced companions.

Julian tried to think of something to ask Raggart. Something slightly personal, but not too intrusive. Just enough for them to do some bonding, so that maybe when they got out of whatever was going on here, they might be able to go their separate ways peacefully.

"So... How many children do you have?"

Raggart grunted and gripped the handle of his dagger more tightly.

Too personal. Best to cut off that line of questioning. "I bet you're a great father."

"My son was born with only two testicles, so we ate him. My wife is no longer able to conceive."

Fuck! Julian focused on trying not to look at Raggart's crotch and finding a change of subject. Something else... Anything... Birds!

"There sure are a lot of birds over there." Straight ahead, just in front of the cliff's face, black birds were hopping and flapping over something still obscured by the topography.

"Indeed there are," said Raggart, sounding much more interested than Julian had anticipated. "Carrion feeders, like the one you pretend to converse with."

"I'm not pretending," said Julian. "We're speaking in Elven."

Raggart snorted. "Of course you are."

"You believe what you want," said Julian. "I've got nothing to prove to a guy who just wants to murder and eat me."

"Fear not, elf. We would not eat you, for fear of contracting your brain disease."

"I don't have a —" Julian stopped. Maybe he could work with

this. Maybe he could convince them that they all had brain diseases. "Sorry. I get confused sometimes since my friends and I escaped from the asylum. So... If you're not going to eat us, what are you going to do with us?"

"We'll boil you in a separate cauldron and feed you to a rival tribe under the guise of peace negotiations."

Shit. Nothing gained there. "I was making that stuff up about the asylum."

"You are a persuasive one, elf. But you have already betrayed your contaminated brain."

"My brain isn't contaminated!" said Julian. "I'm just as edible as your two-balled —" Whoa. Close call. Don't say 'son'. Don't say 'son'. "— mom!" Shit.

Raggart glanced at him briefly before something ahead caught his attention.

The base of the cliff was visible now. Those entranced by the singing were headed toward a steep staircase carved into the cliff, slightly to the right of where the body of a large humanoid creature lay on its back between concentric rings of jagged rocks on the ground, being picked apart by birds.

Ravenus, being larger than the other birds, was easy enough to spot, tearing yellow-grey flesh loose from the creature's shoulder. From the empathic link they shared, Julian sensed his familiar was in a state of gluttonous ecstasy. That made it even worse.

Julian ran toward the corpse. "Ravenus! Get away from there! Ravenus!" He waved his arms and screamed to shoo the other birds away. "Scram! Go on, get out of here!"

The birds ignored him until he got pretty close, at which point they exploded away in every direction, leaving only Ravenus behind.

"Ravenus!" Julian said again.

The bird's head jerked to attention. He turned around and looked up at Julian. "Forgive me, master. I suppose I got carried away."

"Get off of him. You know I don't like you to do this while I'm

around."

Julian glanced over at his friends. They weren't moving particularly fast, but he didn't want to leave their side for long. If there was any information to be gathered here, he'd have to do it quickly. He looked down at the body.

It was bigger than a man's, with a disproportionately large head and arms longer than its legs. It had pointed ears, and an underbite big enough to accommodate the massive teeth of its lower jaw, jutting upward like a spiked fence around his upper lip.

"What is that?" Julian muttered.

"An ogre," said Raggart, who Julian hadn't realized had followed him. "Not dead long. Meat is still good."

The rough, hairy skin was covered in beak and talon marks. The eyes were missing, which came as no surprise to Julian. That was always the first thing Ravenus went for. More surprising was the missing genitalia.

"Did you eat his junk?" Julian asked Ravenus.

"I beg your pardon, sir."

"The things we mammalian guys have between our legs." Julian gestured around his crotch area. "God knows you've seen Tim's enough times."

"The little worm and berries, you mean?"

"Um... yeah. I suppose so."

"No, sir. Those were missing by the time I arrived."

"Ravenus says he didn't eat the dick."

"I should think not," said Raggart. "Your bird is large indeed, but an ogre penis is enough to satisfy a full-grown bugbear."

"Is that right?" It was both a blessing and a tragedy that Cooper wasn't around to ask him how many ogre penises Raggart had been satisfied by.

"Besides, the wound is too even. This was the work of a sharp blade." Raggart stared down at the blade of his father's dagger.

Julian looked over at his friends. They were waiting their turn as Horrig and Flargarf climbed up the first tier of the staircase.

He didn't have long if he was going to keep up with them. "Okay. That's some good CSI stuff you've got going on there. What else can you see? How do you think he died?"

Raggart gave a satisfied grunt and a nod. Of course. He didn't want a buddy. He longed for respect, and deference to his Wisdom.

"The removal of the genitals, and the circular pattern of stones suggest some sort of religious sacrifice," said Raggart. "But I am not learned in such practices."

Julian stepped back and took a wider view of the pattern of concentric circles in which the stones were arranged. He let out a weak laugh. "You know what it looks like to me?"

"What's that?"

Oh shit. "I know how he died. We have to keep the others from —"

"WHAAAAAAAAAAAAAAAAAAAA..." said a voice from above, growing louder and louder.

"Sir, watch out!" cried Ravenus.

Julian didn't bother to look up. He ran as fast as he could to the outermost circle of rocks.

"AAAAAAAAAAAAHHHHHHH—"

SPLAT.

Julian turned around to find another ogre lying face-down right where he'd just been standing. If the first ogre had suffered at all before opportunistic birds had taken his few remaining Hit Points, then this one was luckier. His head had landed on one of the larger rocks, obliterating his skull on impact. His 'worm and berries' were also missing.

"This is no religious ceremony," said Julian. "This is a target." He looked up. Three hundred feet in the air, three creatures with bat-like wings hovered over the edge of the cliff. That's where the song was coming from.

"Harpies," said Raggart. "It's just as I feared. Our friends are compelled to seek the source of the song. They will not listen to reason. They outnumber us by too great a margin. If we try to

restrain them as they climb, we will all surely fall to our deaths. There is another route up this mountain, but it is much longer. Would that we had a horse, we could —"

"Horse!" said Julian. A strong brown steed appeared before them.

Raggart looked at him. "Mighty sorcerer indeed." He didn't smile, but Julian felt a mutual respect building between them.

Julian opted to hold off on telling him that he'd just spent his last spell for the day... not counting the backup scrolls that Horrig still held in his bag.

When doubling up on a horse, the heavier person gets to sit in the saddle. They are the anchor. Being an elf, this usually meant that Julian was going to be the one with the sore arms and ass.

Raggart rode in the saddle, and Julian wrapped his arms around him from behind.

"Shall I scout ahead, sir?" Ravenus asked as they prepared to depart.

"No," said Julian. "Those things are dangerous, and they can fly. Why don't you go keep an eye on the others? Don't try to interfere. Just watch over them and report back if there's anything you think I need to know."

"Very good, sir."

Julian didn't have a good view of the path they took. He was too preoccupied with hugging a monster who wanted to feed him to his enemies to pay much attention to his surroundings. All he could tell for certain was that they were riding fast, gradually ascending along a gradual clockwise curve, and that bugbear hair was prickly and smelled like fermented garbage.

Some time between forty-five minutes to an hour later, the rhythm of hooves slowed as the pounding of horse ass against his balls grew less and less severe. They must have been close, because the harpy's song was loud and clear, so much so that Julian didn't feel the need to be particularly quiet.

"Are we planning to fight the harpies?" asked Julian.

"Until not one of their wretched hearts still beat." Raggart stopped the horse and dismounted. "I've never tasted harpy before." He licked his lips.

"Do you have a plan of attack?"

"I shall hack away at them until they no longer continue to live."

Julian frowned. "That's nice and uncomplicated."

"These beasts are far too dangerous to try to capture alive."

"That wasn't my primary concern."

Raggart looked at Julian, inviting him to continue.

"I'm more worried that they outnumber us at least three to one, and I'm not much good in a fight."

"I have seen you conjure up a living horse with your sorcery. Surely you can melt their faces off."

Julian wondered briefly if Melt Face Off was actually a spell in the game, then focused his attention on the task of avoiding a suicide mission without having to admit that he was both unarmed and out of spells. "I was thinking more along the lines of a diplomatic approach. Get a lay of the land, so to speak, maybe find a tactical advantage before we dive headlong into stabbing and face-melting."

"Your methods are unconventional, elf. But you have proved yourself both cunning and capable. I shall follow your lead... for now."

"Okay, good. Now here's how I think we should—" Julian heard voices other than the harpy song. It was the other two bugbears.

"Me first!"

"No, me!"

"Shut up! I can't hear the song!"

"You shut up!"

"Okay," said Julian. "We come out non-threateningly, as if we were also entranced by the song."

Raggart nodded.

Julian chanced a peek over the rock he was hiding behind. The mountaintop was wide, flat and rocky, spotted here and there with dried pools of blood. He didn't see any harpies, but he saw

where Horrig and Flargarf were scrambling onto the scene. Horrig was up first, and Julian noticed he was pitching a major tent under his hide pants.

"There you are, sir."

Julian ducked back behind his rock, trying to stifle a heart attack. "Ravenus! Keep it down." He looked up at Raggart. "This isn't going to work."

"Why not?"

"They're not going to believe we're entranced if we don't have erections."

"Not a problem," said Raggart. He closed his eyes. "I shall recall the time I deflowered my niece."

Julian grimaced. "That's... um... lovely."

"At the time, it was. But we were caught, and she was deemed unfit for marriage. We ate her."

Raggart's short tale of incest, murder, and cannibalism threw any chance of Julian's ability to conjure up an erection on the spot right out the window. Desperate times. Desperate measures. He looked down at his familiar.

"Ravenus. I need a favor."

"Anything, master!"

"I need you to be my... worm and berries."

Ravenus stood a little straighter, staring at Julian's crotch. "You mean your... junk, sir?"

"Correct."

"I'm flattered, sir. But I don't even know if we're compatible. Physically, I mean."

"What? No! I just need you to perch on my belt and keep still under my serape, providing the illusion that my junk is larger than it actually is."

"Are you attempting to seduce the harpies, sir? Once you get a close look at them, you may have a change of heart."

"Just get in here and hold still until I tell you otherwise." Julian pulled back one side of his serape.

"My my, gentlemen," said a voice that Julian assumed was

one of the harpies that wasn't the one singing. "What a strapping bunch of visitors we have here today." Her voice was raspier than the singer's. Maybe it was her grandmother or something. "Do you think we're... pretty?"

Eager responses came from everyone.

"Oh yes!"

"Absolutely!"

"Lady, I've got more blood in my dick than in my head right now."

Julian waved Ravenus forward. "Hurry up!"

Ravenus hopped onto Julian's crotch and gripped his belt with his talons. Julian stood up and covered Ravenus with his serape.

"That's no good. They'll never believe my dick's that big. Here. Go between my legs so that only your head is poking out." Julian reached down and helped Ravenus into position.

"Shall I grip you by the junk, sir?"

"Hell no!" said Julian. "You keep those talons away from my junk. I'll just hold you snug between my thighs." Every part of that sounded wrong.

"But there are more of you than there are of us," said the raspy harpy. "How will we ever choose who gets to mate with us?"

Shit was about to go down. It was time for Julian and Raggart to make their move. Julian looked at Raggart, who was still concentrating, but already had a passable bulge going on. "You about ready?"

Raggart's eyes were shut tight. His fists were clenched. "Don't worry. They'll never find us. The danger is what makes it exciting."

Julian cleared his throat.

Raggart awoke from his memory. "Oh. Yes. Let's go."

Julian spread his arms and looked down at his crotch. "How do I look?"

Raggart also looked at Julian's crotch, but seemed uncomfortable. "Um... great." He must have been pretty deep into that memory, but the awkwardness of the moment confirmed in Ju-

lian's mind that Ravenus was doing a satisfactory job of passing for a penis.

"All right," said Julian. "Remember. We're madly, desperately in love with them." He turned around, grabbed his horse's lead rope, and started walking. With Ravenus between his legs, he had to walk like he was holding in a fart.

"What's wrong with your legs?" asked Raggart.

"Don't worry about it."

He shuffled out from the rock and found Tim, Cooper, and the two bugbears standing at attention. Okay Julian. Time to put that Charisma score to the test. "Oh, what sweet, beautiful music is this? I am entranced by the —"

These were truly the most horrifying creatures Julian had ever seen. They offended his eyes in every way imaginable. The singing one's face was completely covered in brown, dry blood, crusted and cracked all the way down her neck to the tops of her sagging, old-lady breasts. Her hair was a tangled mess, also caked with dried blood. Her bat wings were folded back, as she stood on scaly reptilian legs. Around her neck she wore a long necklace which consisted of a thin hempen cord sewn through a collection of dried, shriveled penises of varying lengths and states of decomposition.

The other two were pretty much the same, the main differences being the fresh red blood covering the lower halves of their faces, and the recently-severed giant ogre penises on each of their necklaces.

"My my, Lucinda," said the raspy harpy. "Two more players. We shall have to think of a new game."

Raggart whispered to himself. "The danger is what makes it exciting. The danger is what makes it exciting. The danger is what makes it exciting." He was understandably having difficulty maintaining his erection.

The harpy Julian assumed was named Lucinda clapped her hands together. "Oh fun! I love new games! And have you ever seen an elf so well-endowed? I must have that one for my collection."

Julian's body involuntarily stiffened, including his thighs.

"KWAA!" cried Julian's junk.

Julian cleared his throat. "Excuse me."

"I know a game," said Horrig. "It's a card game called 'Pok'Har'.

The raspy harpy sneered at him. "I was thinking of something more along the lines of clawing all your eyes out and forcing you to blindly fight to the death."

"Yes!" said Cooper. "That sounds fucking awesome!"

The song, which the third harpy had been singing this whole time until it was unnoticeable background noise, came to a sudden halt.

Flargarf and Horrig screamed something in their native Goblin tongue as the two harpies who hadn't been singing screeched and flew backward, just out of everyone's immediate reach.

"Fuck!" cried Cooper.

"Jesus Christ!" shouted Tim. "Couldn't you have at least made good on your promise to claw our eyes out?"

While Julian's eyes were focused on everyone else's erections withering like time-lapse photography of dying flowers, he didn't notice everyone staring at his seemingly still-raging boner... until he did. He relaxed his thighs, and his junk fell to the ground with a muffled grunt.

"Matilda!" snapped the raspy harpy. "Why have you stopped singing?"

Matilda walked toward Horrig like a Jesus lizard. "I want to know more about this 'Pok'Har'. Do you have a deck of cards with you, bugbear?"

"Uh... uh... of course I do," said Horrig. He pulled Julian's deck out of Julian's bag, glancing briefly at Julian to see if he was going to raise any objections.

Julian nodded his encouragement, then glanced over to see if Tim was appreciating the value of his cards. He must have been doing a poor job of containing his smugness, as Tim responded with a jerk-off gesture.

Horrig nervously licked his big lips before turning back to Matilda. "What say we make this interesting?"

Lucinda hovered low over the ground. "How do you mean?"

Horrig swallowed hard. "Every time one of us wins a round, the winner is free to go. Every time one of you wins a hand, you get to choose one of us to do with as you will."

Julian would have used different terms, but Horrig was desperate and perhaps not as gifted a negotiator. He was doing a pretty good job. If Julian tried to step in now, it might stink of conspiracy. Unbeknownst to Horrig, he might be setting up Julian and his friends with a heavy advantage. If they were bright enough to look to him before discarding, he'd be able to tip them off.

The raspy harpy scoffed. "Your terms are too one-sided. You offer us nothing we cannot take for ourselves. Continue your song, Matilda."

Shit. Julian balled his fists and willed himself to resist the enchanting song.

"I want to learn the game, mother!"

The two harpies took to the air, circling around one another, hissing and screeching in some sort of dominance ritual. Finally, they descended and mom gave in to her daughter's wishes.

"Very well," said the mother. "Let me see those cards."

Horrig held out the deck in his trembling hand.

The mother harpy snatched it away and began observing individual cards. "Did a child draw these while being chased by a pack of wolves?"

Everyone's a fucking critic.

"Apologies, ma'am," said Horrig. "I'm no artist. The beauty of these cards cannot hope to match your own."

Well, well. Perhaps ol' Horrig has taken a few ranks in Diplomacy too.

The mother harpy's lips tightened, as if she was trying to mask her satisfaction. "I suppose they are serviceable." She pulled on a chain around her neck until a glass pendant came up from between her breasts.

She held the pendant to one eye, squinted through it at a card, then flipped the card over and squinted at the back. "What's this?"

Shit.

The mother harpy flipped through several more cards, observing the fronts and backs, before finally flinging the entire deck to the ground. "Cheater!"

"What?" said Matilda and Horrig.

"The bugbear takes us for fools! The cards are marked!"

Horrig stood dumbfounded.

Flargarf glared at Julian. "I knew it!"

Julian could feel Raggart's eyes burning a hole in the back of his head. He was glad there was a horse between them.

The mother harpy flapped her wings slowly, descending toward Horrig like an Angel of Death. "We have penalties for those who would deceive us."

Julian heard Tim clear his throat, but didn't give him the satisfaction of looking his way.

"It wasn't me!" cried Horrig. "They belong to the elf! This is his bag!" He threw Julian's bag like it was crawling with spiders. It landed at Julian's feet.

Julian looked down at the bag, then up at the mother harpy, who was waiting for a response to the accusation.

Sorry, Horrig.

"I've never seen this bag or those cards in my life."

The mother harpy looked back at Horrig. "More lies!" She grabbed him by his upper arms, restrained them against his body, and flapped her wings harder. "Time for this bird to leave the nest."

Lucinda and Matilda screeched gleefully as Horrig's urine traced a line past the cliff's edge.

"Filthy cheater!"

"Make him fly, mother!"

Julian started to feel a tug of guilt. If it meant he and his

friends survive, he might have been able to just sit back and let it happen. But Horrig's death would just mean one less ally against the harpies, now that a fight was looking all but inevitable.

"Stop!" cried Julian. The harpies all looked at him. "Horrig was telling the truth. I made those cards."

The mother harpy glared at Julian and screeched, but didn't move back to the edge of the cliff. Time to add a little Bluff to the Diplomacy.

"I only ever intended to use them in the event of an emergency. Judge me if you will, but from one parent to another, is a little deception such a bad thing if it means I get to see my daughters again?"

The mother harpy's grimace wavered. "You have daughters?"

No.

"Two beautiful baby girls, just like yours... just like Horrig's." Julian gestured at the harpy's terrified captive. "His youngest is only a few weeks old. She's adorable."

The mother harpy frowned at Horrig, then looked back at Julian. "No one appreciates how hard it is to raise two daughters all by yourself."

"What happened to your... to their father?"

She looked down at her necklace of shriveled dicks. "A human father has nothing to teach a harpy chick. Once I had his seed inside me, I unmanned and ate him."

"Well that's... resourceful?" Come on, Julian. You can do better than that. "We have offended you, but I beg you to show mercy on our baby girls."

"I would never harm a child," said the mother harpy. "What kind of monster do you take me for?"

"Hold on," said Cooper. "I know this one." He pressed his fat lips together for a moment while his tiny half-orc brain went into overdrive. "Medium monstrous humanoid!"

Tim punched Cooper in the hamstring and whispered, "Dude, shut the fuck up!"

Julian was finally beginning to see some humanity through

the crusty mask of dried blood on the harpy mother's face, and he knew he'd better start talking before Cooper made her start thinking about murder again. "Don't you think you'd be harming Horrig's children by taking their father from them?"

The mother harpy thought for a moment, then finally sighed. "You have touched my heart, elf. All too often, I teach my girls the arts of seduction, maiming, torturing, and killing. Rarely do I teach them about compassion and mercy. As an example for my daughters, I shall set you and your friends free."

A wave of relief washed over Julian. Finally, he had the courage to look back at Raggart, who gave him a grudging nod.

Horrig was breathing heavily as the mother harpy flew him back toward the cliff's edge, and he wasn't the only one. Someone behind Julian was breathing like they'd just run a marathon in under an hour.

"I..." *pant* "HOLD..." *pant* "THEE!" *pant pant pant*

Julian turned around. "Dave?" He'd completely forgotten that Dave had been missing all this time. He must have had a hard time climbing the mountain with his fat little dwarf legs.

"NOOOOOOOOoooooooooo..."

Julian turned back to the cliff's edge. "Horrig?" But Horrig and the mother harpy were nowhere to be seen. From the fading of Horrig's scream, he had a pretty good idea which way they'd gone.

"Mother!" cried Matilda. Lucinda merely screeched in horror as the both of them dove out of sight after their falling mother.

Julian, Cooper, and Raggart ran toward the cliff's edge to see if there was any chance that the harpy daughters would be able to save their mother and Horrig, but the abrupt end to Horrig's scream told them all they needed to know before they made it that far.

"Dave!" said Tim. "What the hell have you done?"

"What's wrong?" asked Dave. "I used a Hold Person spell. I thought we were in a fight."

"Well we're sure as shit in one now!"

"Yah!" shouted Flargarf. He was sitting on Julian's horse, now looking far less confident than his 'Yah!' had sounded. The horse wasn't going anywhere.

"Yah!" Flargarf shouted again, with more than a hint of desperation in his voice as he kicked at the stubbornly immobile horse's sides.

Raggart shoved Julian aside as he stomped back toward the horse. "You stinking coward! You would leave me here to die with this band of idiots and bird fuckers?"

"It wasn't like that," said Julian. "I needed Ravenus to be my —"

"EEEEELLLLLLLFFFF!" shouted one of the daughter harpies, her voice getting louder as she drew near.

Shit! Dave killed their mom. Why were they blaming Julian? Unless they thought he'd orchestrated the whole thing. Shit!

Julian spotted his bag on the ground next to the horse and made a mad dash for it. As he got close, Flargarf, still flicking the horse's reins and kicking its sides, drew one of his long machetes. His terrified eyes were focused on a point behind Julian.

One of the harpies screeched behind him. She sounded pissed.

Julian scooped up his bag and ran around to the other side of the horse, hoping that Flargarf could keep her busy while he opened up a scroll tube.

He hadn't yet gotten around to labeling his scroll tubes, so he might have to get creative. As he unscrewed the cap, he hoped for a Magic Missile or a Web, or really anything but a Ventriloquism. He unrolled the parchment inside and read the name of the spell.

Animate Rope

Not Ventriloquism, but almost as useless in a fight.

The harpy howled. Julian looked up from his scroll. Matilda was hovering above Flargarf, bleeding from a fresh cut in her left tit. In a mad rage, she grabbed him by both ears and shoved her nicotine-yellow thumbnails into his eyes.

Julian winced as Flargarf's machete fell out of his hand and onto the blood-spattered ground. He had a terrible, terrible idea. He licked his lips as he looked over the spell, then read the incantation aloud.

"Rope! Grab!"

The horse's lead rope wrapped itself tightly around Matilda's scaly right leg, between calf and talon.

Sorry, horse. "Run!" cried Julian. The horse bolted off so fast that Flargarf would almost certainly have fallen off if Matilda hadn't had such a firm grip on his eye sockets.

Matilda got in a few desperate (but ultimately futile) wing flaps, before she, Flargarf, and Baxter (Julian decided the horse should have a name before he died) sailed off the edge of the cliff together.

Lucinda screeched helplessly as her sister fell to her death, then locked her eyes on Julian.

Cooper, Dave, Tim, and even Raggart took defensive positions in front of Julian.

"Hurry, sorcerer," said Raggart. "Find another spell. The rest of you, defend him." He passed one of his own machetes to Cooper, and his father's dagger to Tim. Dave picked up Flargarf's machete, still soaked in tit-blood, off the ground. There were now four of them, not counting Julian, against one harpy. If she moved in to attack, they stood a pretty good chance.

Julian opened up another scroll tube.

Mage Hand

Shit. There wasn't much he could think to do with that one. Hopefully, the others could hold her at bay while he found a better —

Lucinda, hovering above them all, began to sing again. Julian felt a flutter in his heart. His Willpower was being tested.

Julian dropped his bag and covered his ears. "It's just a song. It's just a song." But his elven ears were far too sensitive, and the

harpy's music saturated the air around him.

"Sir," said Ravenus, looking up at Julian from on the ground. "Are you feeling all right?"

That's a good bird, Ravenus. Keep distracting me. "Yeah, great. You?"

"I'm beginning to feel a bit woozy, sir."

Julian knew what he was talking about. His own blood was beginning to flow out of his head and into his dick. He was losing the battle.

"This is, like, my new favorite song," said Tim.

Damn. She got Tim again.

"It moves my heart," said Dave.

"It's the most beautiful thing I've ever heard," said Cooper. The long, soft fart that wafted out only seemed to compliment the melody.

"It's beauty is only matched by your own," said Raggart.

Julian could resist no longer. He looked up.

Lucinda was radiant in her nakedness, hovering above them like a winged goddess, her sweet breath caressing her vocal cords like gentle fingers dancing over the strings of a harp.

"I need you," Julian heard himself say, as if in a lucid dream.

Lucinda smiled at him as she slowly descended toward him, still singing her beautiful song.

The others crowded near him, but Lucinda waved them all back. Julian's heart beat harder, knowing she wanted him, and only him.

When she reached the ground, she ran a fingernail down Julian's cheek. It felt like the gentlest thing ever, but at the same time he was aware that she'd drawn blood. He didn't care. He'd give her all the blood he had and more.

Julian inhaled deeply to calm his nerves. "I would be honored if you would take my..."

Lucinda nodded for him to continue.

"... my member, and wear it around your neck so that you may never forget me. I want to bleed until my spirit parts from my body, riding to the next life on the sound of your voice."

Lucinda smiled and held up a small, slightly rusted, hooked knife.

Julian's penis grew even harder. He couldn't wait. "Take my testicles, too. Everything that makes me a man now belongs to you."

"And if you have any use for my cloaca," said Ravenus, "by all means, have at it."

Lucinda gestured for Julian to lift up his robes.

Julian hurried to comply. He couldn't wait for the bite of rusty steel against his junk. "Your song shall transport me between worlds."

"This Justin Bieber bullshit?" said Tim, from behind Lucinda. "Please."

What an odd, roundabout compliment... Why would he...?

A look of sudden confusion showed on Lucinda's face as well.

"I made my Saving Throw, bitch. Sneak Attack!"

Before Julian knew what was happening, Lucinda hit a note that was wildly off-key. Julian dropped to his knees, shutting his eyes and clapping his hands over his ears. Certainly not the caliber of singing a guy would want to lose his dick over.

When Julian opened his eyes again, Lucinda was hideous. But she always had been, even when I... Why did I think she... Was I just about to let her...

Lucinda spun around to rake her claws across Tim's face. She drew some blood, but it didn't look half as bad as the bleeding dagger wound he'd left in her back.

Cooper, Dave, and Raggart were still coming out of their enchantment when Lucinda started flapping her wings again.

Julian knew he wasn't heavy enough to weigh her down, but he couldn't risk letting her escape to start singing again. He lunged at her and wrapped his hands around one of her reptilian chicken legs.

She tore through his sleeve with her free talon, into his forearm. Julian was riding on enough adrenaline such that the pain

didn't yet register, but he could see the blood soaking through his shirt. He wouldn't be able to withstand many of those before letting go.

Holding firm with his good arm, he grabbed at her other ankle with his injured arm. This kept him safe from her talons, but it did little to improve his lack of contact with the ground.

Tim made an impressive jump to grab at Julian's foot, but came up short, swiping the air just below him.

"I'm coming for you, sir!" said Ravenus, rocketing in a trajectory that would intersect with Lucinda's face.

"No, Ravenus!" said Julian. "Back off. She's too dangerous for you to handle. I've got this." With little regard for how Ravenus might take it, he then shouted, "Cooper!"

Cooper shook his big, meaty head and looked from side to side.

"Up here!"

Cooper looked up. "Julian?"

It didn't matter. As high as they'd flown, Cooper appeared about as big as Tim. Julian was on his own.

He wished he hadn't blown through all his spells already. His bag, with all of his backup scrolls, was barely visible from this high up.

Hold on... He hadn't blown through all his spells. Only the first-level ones. Were there any 0-level spells that would be of any use? The damage-inflicting spells wouldn't inflict enough damage to be worth it. What did that leave?

Read Magic. No.

Detect Magic. No.

Dancing Lights. No.

Ghost Sound. No.

Touch of Fatigue. No... Wait a minute... Yes. Hell yes!

"Touch of Fatigue!"

A trickle of magic flowed out of Julian's hands into Lucinda's legs. She started to screech an objection, but it quickly morphed into a yawn. Her wing flaps became more labored, and they began to descend.

When they were low enough so that Julian could let go, he held on even tighter. Her scaly legs were getting slippery with sweat, but he couldn't risk letting her go. Fortunately, she was panting too hard to be able to sing.

Finally, they were low enough for Cooper to grab Julian by the leg and pull them down to the ground.

When Cooper grabbed Lucinda by the throat, Julian let go of her legs.

She weakly attempted to scratch and claw at Cooper, but his outstretched arm was longer than hers were.

"What should I do with her?" asked Cooper.

"Kill her!" said Tim, albeit from a safe distance.

Cooper frowned.

Dave seemed to sense Cooper's moral quandary. "At least punch her unconscious so we can tie her up."

"But she's a girl."

"Dude, she was going to cut your dick off!"

"It doesn't feel right to punch a girl in the face."

The face in question was turning blue through its brown, crusty exterior as both of Lucinda's hands were trying in vain to pry her neck loose from Cooper's grip.

"You're strangling her to death right now," said Dave. "I don't know what your own code of chivalry says, but I can't see how straight up murder is preferable to just knocking the bitch out.

Cooper looked to Julian. Julian nodded.

"Okay." Cooper punched Lucinda in the face until her arms went limp.

"It's just subdual damage," said Dave. "She'll get those Hit Points back when she wakes up."

"We should stuff her mouth with something," said Tim. "Just in case she wakes up and starts singing before we're far enough away. Cooper, tear me off a piece of your loincloth."

"Which piece?"

"The piece with the most shit caked into it."

Cooper ripped off a piece of loincloth which had been cov-

ering his ass, leaving one cheek exposed to the elements. The lesion-marred fur suggested that whatever animal it had come from was only slightly better off in life than it was now in death, covered in half-orc shit.

Tim pulled his shirtsleeves up over his hands before stuffing the rolled up ball of hide into the harpy's mouth. When it was in as deep as he could get it, he pulled a rope out of Julian's bag and tied her arms behind her around a thick tree.

"Are you quite finished with your shameful display of compassion?" asked Raggart.

Tim shrugged. "Pretty much. Now, are we anywhere near the coast, or was that whole story bullshit?"

"Hand over my father's dagger, halfling."

"Ha ha," said Tim. "How about no."

"Come on," said Julian. "It belonged to his father."

"Fuck his father. Those assholes probably ate the old bastard anyway."

"It is our custom," said Raggart. "It matters not. I shall take back my father's dagger once I have destroyed you all." He held up his long machete. "Prepare to die."

Julian backed up. "Hold on, man. You can't be serious. After all we've just been through?"

"I must avenge my fallen comrades, murdered by your sorcery."

"We were only defending ourselves," said Julian. "Be reasonable about this. We outnumber you four to one. Surely we've all seen enough death for one day."

"You won't talk your way out of this one, elf. Today is the day you die."

"Fuck this," said Tim. "Dave?"

Dave nodded. "I hold thee."

Raggart froze as still as a statue, his eyes boiling with impotent rage. Cooper started dragging his body toward another tree.

"No," said Julian. "We should tie them to each other."

"Why?" asked Dave.

"If we just tie them both to trees, the first one to get free will just murder the other one."

Tim shrugged. "And we should give a fuck because..."

"If they're tied to one another, they'll have to work as a team to get free. Maybe through working together, they'll earn each other's respect, and go on to form a lasting friendship."

Dave snorted. "You can't possibly still be this naive. They'll start beating the shit out of each other as soon as they get a free hand."

"Then it'll be as fair a fight as we can grant each of them. Let's get the hell out of here."

The End

The Unwashed Asses

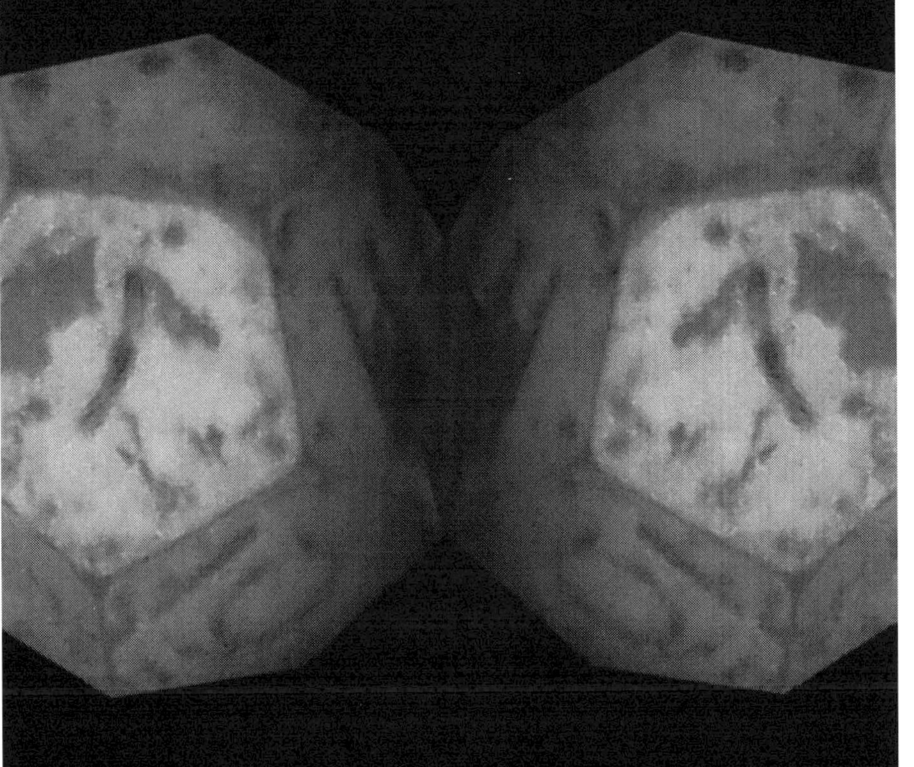

ROBERT BEVAN

THE UNWASHED ASSES

(Original Publication Date: April 13, 2016)

Cooper's asshole itched something fierce. It was too deep an itch to scratch through the loincloth. He had to get his claws right up in there to properly meet the demand, but he couldn't do that while Dave was walking behind him. And he couldn't walk slower than Dave without everyone wondering what was wrong with him. There was only one option.

"Holy shit!" shouted Cooper, doing his best to look amazed as he peered ahead of the group into the forest. "It's El Dorito!" With that, he bolted forward as fast as his massive half-orc legs would carry him.

"Cooper, wait!" cried Tim.

"El Dorito?" asked Julian.

Neither of them would be able to keep up with Cooper's Base Movement Speed of 40, or even more due to him running down the side of a hill.

Cooper pounded the forest floor, ducking under branches and weaving around tree trunks until he thought he had enough of a lead to get a good scratch in, and maybe a couple soothing bonus scratches. He looked back to see if anyone was tailing him. The coast was clear. Just to be safe, he'd put a little more distance between himself and —

"Son of a bitch!" The pain in Cooper's right ear pulsed in his head as he lay on the ground.

He looked up at a pine branch hanging just about ear-height, missing a small scrap of bark and stained with a bit of dark red blood. His blood. "Fuck you, tree."

"Cooper?" Julian called out. "Are you okay?" He was still a pretty good distance away, but he must have heard Cooper swearing with his freakishly long elf ears.

As hard as his head was throbbing, his asshole itched even worse. Now was the time.

He stood up and squatted for optimal reach, lifted the back of his loincloth with his left hand, and plunged the clawed fingers of his right hand into his hole like a sarlacc toothbrush.

The relief was instant and glorious.

"Unnnnggggg," Cooper moaned. "Sooo worth it."

He blissfully scratched his ass until it was causing more pain than relief. Removing his hand, he found he was clutching a fistful of his own shit. When the hell had he last eaten corn?

"Shit, that's disgusting." That last fart had been a wet one, but he didn't think he'd actually —

A bird cawed loudly behind him.

Cooper turned around quickly, but kept his shit-filled hand behind his back. Ravenus was sitting on the tree branch that had assaulted him.

"What the fuck are you doing here?" said Cooper, despite knowing that the bird couldn't understand him. It didn't matter. He already knew the answer to the question. Julian had sent Ravenus after him.

Ravenus lifted his wings and squawked incomprehensibly.

"What's that?" said Cooper. "You don't understand me? Well maybe you'll understand this." He flung his handful of shit in Ravenus's direction, catching him squarely in the chest and face.

Ravenus fell off the branch and writhed on the ground, trying to flap away the greenish-brown paste gluing his feathers together.

"Oh shit, man. I'm sorry," said Cooper. "I didn't expect it to actually hit you that... directly."

"Ravenus!" Julian called out. He was closer now. "What's wrong?"

Fuck! Julian had that goddamn empathic link with Ravenus. He must have sensed the bird's reaction to suddenly being covered in half-orc shit.

Cooper looked down at the shit on his hand. He had to get rid of the evidence. He wrapped his hand around the smooth grey trunk of a young tree and rubbed up and down vigorously.

"Here they are," said Tim, jogging out from behind some undergrowth. "Cooper, are you jerking off that tree?"

The choice between making up a plausible lie and accepting the one that was just handed to him was no choice at all.

"Um... yes."

Tim closed his eyes and put his fingertips to his temples. "Why?"

Shit. Cooper hadn't anticipated this thorough an interrogation. Think fast. "You ever hear of a little place called Canada? This is how they make maple syrup."

"Ravenus!" cried Julian, kneeling over his bird, but stopping short of touching him. "What happened to you?"

Ravenus squawked and cawed.

"Don't listen to him," said Cooper. "He's a goddamn liar!"

Julian turned back to look at Cooper. "All he said was that he spotted a pool of clean water on his way here that he could wash himself off in."

Shit. No turning back now. "And I'm telling you that's a load of horseshit."

Julian ignored him, scraping some of the bigger gobs of shit off Ravenus's feathers with a twig.

Tim frowned at the greenish-brown section of tree trunk, then up at Cooper. "Maybe a bath isn't such a bad idea."

The little fucker must be using his Sense Motive skill. He could see right through the fortress of deceit Cooper had constructed around himself.

Cooper frowned. "You can't wash away a Charisma score of 4."

"Well maybe you could just wash your ass."

"You guys do what you want," said Julian. "But Ravenus needs a bath." He looked down at his bird. "Can you lead us to the pool?"

Ravenus whistled and chirped.

Julian stepped back and held one side of his serape up over his face Dracula-style. "He says we should shield ourselves. When he starts flapping, the shit will probably spray in every direction.

Tim took a defensive position behind Cooper. Cooper didn't even bother shielding himself, except to close his eyes, when Ravenus started flapping.

The bird wasn't wrong. Cooper felt the splatter of hundreds of tiny shit-gobs pelting him as Ravenus attempted to take flight.

"Hey guys. I'm here," said Dave, huffing and puffing like he'd just outrun a pack of wolves. "Where are the Dorit— Oh shit! What the fuck is — Oh God, stop already! Ugh, it's in my mouth!"

Seeing that was worth risking a little shit in the eyes. Cooper opened his eyes.

Dave had entered the clearing right next to where Ravenus was flapping. He looked like he'd just been standing next to a shit-grenade. His beard and leopard-furred forearm were caked in it. Cooper didn't know that much shit could fit in his hand.

Julian lowered his serape and pointed a thumb behind his shoulder. "Ravenus went that way."

Cooper led the way, ripping through vines, brambles, and small branches with the force of his girth, clearing a path for the others.

About ten minutes later, they came upon Ravenus, splashing in the edge of a crystal clear pool of water. His feathers were shiny black, with no trace of half-orc shit. There wasn't even a floating circle of filth around him.

"This is lovely," said Julian, pulling his serape up over his head.

"A little too lovely if you ask me," said Dave. "It doesn't really fit with the tone of this dreary forest."

Tim jumped in to where the water came up to his knees. Somehow, he'd managed to get completely undressed in the time it took Dave to bitch about how lovely the water was.

Naked but for his hip flask, Tim dropped to his bare ass. The pristine surface of the water barely rippled, and did nothing to hide his tiny halfling dick.

He took a swig from his flask. "Guys, you need to get in here. It's fucking heated. And the ground feels like I'm walking on baby asses." He squinted downward. "I can almost see through it."

Julian kept his pants on as he stepped into the water. When he got up to mid-shin, he sighed in a way that sounded like what Cooper finally being able to scratch his ass had felt like.

After staring thoughtfully at his feet for a moment, Julian dipped one hand into the water, then pulled it back out. "Look at this," he said, holding his hands side by side. "I didn't even realize how filthy I was."

The hand he had dipped in the water was pale white, making the rest of him look like a darker race.

Tim leaned back, submerging himself completely underwater, except for the hand holding his flask. When he resurfaced, he looked like a freshly-scrubbed, hairy-chested toddler wearing a brown glove.

"This isn't natural," said Dave. "We're in a forest. The water shouldn't be that clean. There should be bears and wolves pissing in it all the time."

"It must have some kind of magical cleansing properties or something," said Julian.

"I'm pissing in it right now," said Tim, staring a his crotch. He looked up and shrugged. "You can't even tell."

Julian grabbed Ravenus and waded to the opposite side of the pool.

Dave shook his head. "You're not really selling me on the idea as well as you think you might be."

Tim sucked down some more stonepiss from his flask. "I don't give a fuck if you come in here or not. You can stay covered in Cooper's shit for the rest of your life for all I care. Why don't you go give him a good salad-toss right now?"

"Come on, man," said Julian. "I don't need that image in my

head."

Dave started to unbuckle his armor. "Fine. I'll come in."

"I honestly wasn't trying to convince you," said Tim. "Whoa! Hold on." He was now looking at Cooper.

Cooper stopped pulling down his loincloth. "What?"

"What are you doing?"

Cooper considered that there might be more to the question than the very very obvious, but he was in no mood for riddles. "I'm getting undressed."

"Well could you maybe... not?"

"Why the fuck not?" asked Cooper. "Nobody objected to you flapping your little wang all over the place."

Tim frowned as though what he said next wouldn't be well-received. "I meant, could you not get in the pool."

"It was your fucking idea, shithead! You told me I should wash my ass."

"I mean, just not yet." Tim took a swig from his flask. "Look, Coop. Julian's probably right about the magical cleansing properties of this pool. But we don't know how strong that magic is. Your shit is some pretty powerful... well... shit. If it's strong enough to break the spell or whatever, then that's no good for anyone."

"What about Dave? He's covered in the same shit I am."

"Dave has a thin spattering. You're coated in, like, a half-inch layer from head to toe, probably thicker around the ass and thigh areas. All I'm saying is, let the rest of us bathe first, then you get the whole pool to yourself. Doesn't that sound nice?"

Cooper folded his arms and sat down hard on a fallen tree. "I hope a fish bites your tiny dick off."

Dave, now completely naked, waddled his fat, wrinkly dwarven ass into the pool. "Oh man, you guys were right. This is amazing."

He swam out to the middle of the pool, his head and ass moving in unison above the surface of the water like three pasty and/or hairy islands. When he stood, he was up to his neck in water. He gargled the mouthful that he'd taken in, then spit it out.

"I've never tasted water so sweet. It's like liquid flower petals."

"You realize, of course," said Julian, "that this pool is contaminated with our collective filth."

"And I pissed in it," added Tim.

Dave sucked up some more water, swished it around in his mouth, and spit it out again. "It's still a lot less concentrated than the actual shit that was in my mouth."

Cooper sat angrily thinking about how everyone was complaining about the tiny bit of filth in their clear spring water while he was staring at a puddle of his own urine pool around his feet. He had been weighing the pros and cons of taking a big steamy leak in the pool when his bladder suddenly took that option off the table.

"Whoa!" said Dave. "What the hell is this?"

Cooper looked up. The water at the center of the pool was bubbling, but way too much for it to be a fart that Dave was trying to make an excuse for.

"Sweet!" said Tim. "Somebody turned on the jets."

Julian frowned. "This isn't actually a Jacuzzi. We should get out of here."

As Cooper observed, the water became murkier. He noticed that he could no longer see anyone's junk.

"It's getting thicker!" cried Dave. "Wait... what's going on?" His body was beginning to rotate. As he tried to freestyle swim his way out of the center of the pool, he only managed to throw back a blob of translucent sludge at Tim, who was now revolving slowly around Dave.

"What the fuck is going on?" asked Cooper. The water had become the consistency of glue, and was beginning to funnel in the center.

"How the hell should we know?" asked Tim. "Help us!"

"We're whirlpooling!" said Julian. With what looked like a massive amount of effort, he lifted his arms out of the swirling liquid, grabbed Ravenus, cocked him back over his head, and

threw him at Cooper, hitting him square in the face.

It felt like a big ball of Jell-O when it hit him, but re-liquefied upon impact, running down his face and chest like normal water. With the tip of his tongue, he sampled a bit that had spattered onto his upper lip. No mistaking the taste either. It was water all right. He didn't taste anything like flower petals, or whatever bullshit Dave had said. In fact, it tasted a little bit dirty, with just a hint of piss.

"Cooper!" shouted Tim. "What the fuck are you doing?"

Fuck!

"I don't know. What should I do?" They were swirling around faster now.

"Noooo!" cried Dave, his head barely above the surface. "I can't braaghhblaagglpppt!"

Cooper wouldn't be able to reach any of them without getting in. But as soon as he stepped forward, Tim shouted at him again.

"No! Don't come in!"

"Seriously, dude?" said Cooper. "Now you're just being an asshole."

"There's a rope in my bag. Throw it to me."

Cooper nodded. "Good call." He grabbed Tim's bag and turned back to the pool. "Ready? Catch!"

"What? No!"

Cooper hurled the bag at Tim. His failure to account for the motion of the whirlpool landed the bag out of both Tim and Julian's reach. Dave had completely disappeared under the surface.

"You fucking moron!" said Tim. "I meant one end of the rope. Not the whole goddamn bag!"

"I'm sorry!" said Cooper. "You should have been more specific."

"Fuck yuhggbgliglub..." Tim's head disappeared under the surface, leaving only his right hand raised, middle finger extended, orbiting the center of the pool at an increasingly high speed.

The whirlpool coned deeper downward into the earth.

"Cooper!" said Julian as he spiraled down into the center.

"Take care of Ravenus!"

Ravenus screeched as Julian's head submerged.

"What? Your fucking bird? I don't even... Fuck this!" Cooper raced toward the swirling vortex and dove straight for the center. While he was in midair, the translucent sludge instantaneously changed back into a clear, still pool. He bellyflopped on the surface, but it didn't even sting. The water was warm and soothing, almost to the point of making him forget that his friends had all just drowned.

He shook off the tranquility of the pool when he saw Ravenus waddling toward it.

"Stop! It's too dangerous. Julian told me to take care of you. If I'm just following him to his death, I can at least grant his dying request."

Ravenus paused for a moment, then started toward the pool again. Of course. The stupid bird didn't understand English. He only knew that bullshit they spoke in England. Maybe pantomiming would work.

Cooper put out his palm toward Ravenus. "Stop!" Ravenus stopped.

Okay. Now they were getting somewhere.

Cooper pinched the tips of his ears and pulled them upward. "Julian." He dragged a thumb across his neck. "Dead." He shrugged. "Maybe."

Ravenus shook his head.

"How the fuck do you know?" Cooper thought about how he could best convey that question best through pantomime. It came to him in a flash of brilliance. He shrugged. "How..." He raised his middle finger at Ravenus. "... the FUCK do YOU..." He pointed at his own head. "...know?" Perhaps he was diluting the meaning of a shrug, but it should have been clear in context.

Ravenus stubbornly continued waddling toward him.

"Goddammit, Ravenus! Don't you understand sign language? I said FUCK OFF!" Cooper cocked back his arm, his palm halfway submerged in the water, and prepared to send a tsunami of a splash at the bird. When he shoved his hand forward, however, the water barely rippled around it.

"What the fuck?" This was not how water was supposed to behave. Of course, it also wasn't supposed to coalesce into slime and swallow his friends. So maybe, in a big picture sort of way, the splash thing wasn't so weird.

It didn't matter. If Julian could throw Ravenus out of the pool, Cooper could launch that feathered shitball into the stratosphere.

He started wading toward the bird. Each step was more laborious than the last. Ravenus was veering to the left like he was out of alignment, or like one of them was drunk.

Ravenus hopped into the water, which Cooper now noticed was beginning to thicken. The bird wasn't veering. He was. Now both of them were swirling in a vat of lube, orbiting the center which was funneling downward again.

Cooper gave up on trying to save Ravenus. If the bird wanted to die with him, so be it. He relaxed and let himself float like a fibrous turd in a bus station toilet. When the rotations became faster and close enough to the center, he took a deep breath.

A few seconds after the thick liquid engulfed him completely, Cooper felt the sensation of falling through air. His eyes were glued together with slime, but he was able to open his mouth to take one more breath before he bellyflopped again. This time it stung like water was supposed to sting.

Underwater, he rubbed the slime out of his eyes. When he opened them, some kind of scaly green fish-man was swimming right at him. He barely had time to scream out a torrent of bubbles and punch the fucker in its slimy face.

A mixture of snot and blood squirted out of the creature's nostrils and hung suspended in the water like astronaut puke.

The fish-man covered his face with webbed hands. Cooper started to swim forward to ride the advantage he'd just created, but more webbed hands grabbed his arms and legs from behind.

Cooper was a strong swimmer. Because Swim was one of the few Strength-based skills in the game, he'd dumped as many skill points into it as he could. But in spite of that, his efforts to struggle free were in vain. These slimy assholes were strong as fuck, and made for the water. Even with his Barbarian Rage, he didn't think he'd be able to break free. He would wait and see if they tried to drown him before testing that theory.

Fortunately, the fish-men dragged him up toward the surface.

As Cooper sucked in his fill of stagnant subterranean air, the fish-men let go of his limbs and surfaced around him. The message was clear. He wasn't going anywhere.

Also clear were these things' horrible faces. Through the haze of murky water, the dude Cooper had punched looked like your run-of-the-mill fish-man monster. But in the sharp clarity of viewing them in open air, and the dim light shining through the watery anus in the ceiling, the mucus coating that Cooper had felt on his fist glimmered on their deformed fish faces. They looked like burn victims whose skin was overcompensating. The one he had punched was identifiable by the two streams of blood still running from its nostrils to its big fish lips.

"Hey, um... Swamp Thing. Sorry about that. You startled me. No hard feelings?"

The fish-man responded in a language that sounded like Charlie Brown's teacher.

"I don't know what you're —" Something like a giant wet turd landed on Cooper's head. "What the fuck?"

The fish-men laughed while Cooper wiped the slimy mass off his head. In the water before him, a slime-encapsulated Ravenus writhed and flapped while the gelatinous coating dissolved.

"Oh, hey Ravenus," said Cooper. "What's up?"

Having shed most of the slime, Ravenus looked around at their captors, then flapped and squawked more vigorously.

After the fish-men exchanged a few words in their nasally fish language, the one Cooper had punched licked his big fish lips while gawking at Ravenus with hungry eyes.

Cooper had just enough time to grab Ravenus and throw him up in the air before the fish-man caught him. "Fly, Ravenus! Find

Jul—"

FWUMP!

Cooper's face felt like it had been hit by a flying log covered in snot. "Mother fucker!" Two images of Swamp Thing merged into one as Cooper wiped blood from under his nose. "What the fuck was that for?"

Swamp Thing shouted nonsense while pointing at his own nose.

"Oh, I see how it is. I hit you, so you gotta hit me. That's real fucking mature. Haven't you ever heard of 'Turn the other cheek', asshole?" Cooper felt a familiar tug in his guts. All the stress from worrying about his friends and getting captured by fish monsters, in addition to the strain of treading water for so long, was giving him gas.

As a torrent of relief flowed out of Cooper's ass, the surface of the water erupted with bubbles like it was being carpet bombed.

The fish-men scowled and backed away from him, though not far enough for him to escape.

"Sorry, guys," said Cooper. "I was... um... turning my other cheeks."

Swamp Thing honked out some orders, and two of the other fish-men broke off from the group. They swam toward the edge of the pool where four wooden pails were sitting. They each filled two of the pails and walked off down a wide corridor.

The rest of the group closed in a tighter circle around Cooper. Swamp Thing swam backwards toward the opposite edge of the pool from where the buckets had been, and gestured for Cooper to follow him.

Not having to tread water anymore sounded just fine to Cooper, so he raised no argument. The others followed close behind him.

Outside of the pool, Cooper had a better view of his surroundings. The main chamber was an irregular blob in shape, carved out of layered clay and earth. At the top, of course, there was some kind of pulsating sphincter which fed would-be bathers into the large, rectangular pool below. Tunnels lined the base of the walls. One of the tunnels, the one the two bucket-carrying fish-men retreated into, was significantly larger than all of the others, large enough to drive a bus through. The other tunnels were much smaller, and all seemed to lead downward, unlike the larger tunnel which seemed to stay level with the main chamber. On the whole, the place looked much like what Cooper imagined the inside of an ant colony must look like, except bigger... and with a swimming pool. Maybe a luxury ant colony.

Swamp Thing led Cooper toward one of the smaller tunnels. The fish-men were noticeably less graceful on land than they were in the water. They plodded along with their big webbed feet flopping on the ground, like men trying to walk in swim fins.

The tunnel was only wide enough for them to walk single file. It sloped downward at an angle that might have made a cool water slide, but would likely only rub his ass raw if he tried to slide on it dry. Cooper briefly considered the tactical advantage of walking single file. If he caught Swamp Thing by surprise with a kick in the nuts, sending him tumbling down the tunnel a bit, he would only have to face the other four one at a time. But then Swamp Thing would, in a best-case scenario, only be out of the fight for a couple of rounds, and then return with sore nuts. That dude was a big believer in retaliation. For the sake of his own nuts, he decided to hold off for a while, and use this opportunity to observe and consider alternative strategies.

They walked for a long time down the earthen-walled tunnel. It probably wasn't as far as it seemed, though. These web-footed assholes could swim like motherfuckers, but were at least as slow as Dave on land. Cooper was tempted to punch one just to break up the monotony of their flopping footsteps.

Wait. Wait. Wait.

Eventually they came to a small cell. The entrance was an iron gate held into place by what appeared to be a big stone doughnut. It didn't seem to have much more thought or care put into it than the scraped out walls of the tunnel, but it looked solid enough.

Probably the work of a Stone Shape spell. He might be able to dig his way around it, but there was no way to tell how far the stone was embedded in the earth.

Swamp Thing pulled a key off his chest that, along with the thin rope that it hung from around his neck, had been hidden by his constant secretion of mucus. After shaking most of the slime off, he inserted the key into the gate lock, opened the gate barely wide enough for Cooper to slip through, puckered his big fish lips, and looked expectantly at Cooper.

Go in the easy way, or have his fishfucker thugs force him in? No point in getting the shit beat out of him now. Not until he'd come up with a plan. He stepped through the open gate, into an empty cell that was barely big enough for him to lie down in.

As Swamp Thing locked the gate, Cooper noticed that there wasn't even a bucket for him to shit in. They were prepared to house prisoners, but not for any extended length of time. Cooper was proud of himself for coming up with this conclusion, but felt it didn't bode well for him or his friends.

Swamp Thing slipped the key rope back over his head, and it was almost immediately engulfed in mucus again.

Cooper gave the bars a token shake. "What are you going to do with me? What have you done with my friends? Where am I supposed to shit?"

Swamp Thing spit a stream of brownish-green slime-water at Cooper's face. He and the others shared a laugh and started walking back toward the large chamber.

The limit for how much shit he was willing to take from these assholes having been reached, Cooper employed his Barbarian Rage.

"I'm really angry!"

The flopping of the fish-men's feet was drowned out by the rush of blood flowing through Cooper's ears. His vision turned pink as his hands grew larger around the shrinking cell door.

"UnnnngggggGraah!" The hinges popped in rapid succession, and Cooper found himself standing outside of the cell, door in his hands, face-to-face with a wide-eyed Swamp Thing.

"Wrrraaaahhh!" said Cooper as he shoved the bottom of the door into Swamp Thing's chest, impaling him with two of the iron bars. If the scaly bastard survived being run through with a door, he surely didn't fare so well after Cooper trampled over him, and the door, on his way to confront the rest of them.

The first one was waiting for him, fist cocked, ready to deliver a slime-cannon to Cooper's face. Cooper took a knee and ducked under the blow. He brought his own fist up to meet the fish-man's nutsack. Or was it a fish-woman's nutsack? Because there was no nutsack. His fist was just sort of... in there. Was he fisting a fish-chick? Maybe they had cloacas. Either way, it was awkward.

Keep your head in the game. Don't lose the Rage.

Cooper's opponent grabbed him by both ears and bit him on top of the head. Motherfucker had a lot of teeth in that big mouth.

"Yeeeooooowww!" Cooper screamed as he removed his hand from the fish-person's orifice. Rather than try to rip his head from its grasp outright, he rolled backward. It let go as it fell behind him, but now he was flanked, a situation he had been meaning to avoid.

His violated opponent on the ground for the time being, Cooper focused his attention on the next one in line. It lunged at him, both webbed hands and mouth open. Cooper opened his own hand and palmed the creature in the face. He was packing a lot more slime than he'd expected. It was a mix of green and red and brown, like someone took a dump in the Christmas Jell-O.

The fish-monster reeled back, not so much from the force of Cooper's slap, he expected, but from the horror of what was seeping into its eyes, nostrils, and mouth.

The immediate threat temporarily blinded by... whatever, Cooper turned back to find the creature he'd inadvertently entered was back up on its feet and crouched to spring.

Even in his Rage and with the threat of impending death, Cooper wanted to avoid punching a girl in the face if he could. When it sprang at him, Cooper grabbed it by the throat and hurled it backward.

"Learn how to wipe!"

The creature howled in agony as the top bars of the cage door burst out of its belly and chest. It flapped its webbed appendages until they went limp.

It was time to stop fucking around. His friends were still around here somewhere. Cooper turned around, once again only threatened on one side. His immediate threat was sobbing while trying to scrape the vag-shit out of its eyes.

"FUCK YOU!" shouted Cooper. He kicked it in the gut, sending it flying into the fish-monster behind it.

The last fish-person in line turned tail and ran, it's webbed feet flopping loudly on the dirt floor of the tunnel. In hot pursuit, Cooper trampled the two on the ground, but one of them grabbed his ankle, tripping him. He hit the ground hard, then looked back to see the fish-monster without shit all over its face climbing up his left leg.

Cooper didn't have time for this shit. If he let one of these fuckers get away, they might raise an alarm, calling forth a whole army of watery assholes. With his right leg, he drove his foot down hard, relishing the crunch of face beneath his heel. His left leg was suddenly free of the creature's grasp.

His fears of the creature's escape proved unfounded. These things couldn't run for shit on land. Cooper caught up with the fleeing fish-person just as the opening of the tunnel came into view. He tackled it and punched it in the back of the head until it stopped moving.

With the immediate threat neutralized, Cooper's Barbarian Rage subsided, and his bulging muscles deflated back into flab. He felt for the creature's pulse through the mucus on its neck. Its heart was still beating. He hadn't killed it.

Cooper had two choices. He could kill this thing dead and go look for his friends on his own, or he could keep it alive and beat some answers out of it. The interrogation option felt more ethical. He grabbed the fish-person by the foot and dragged it toward the pool outside of the tunnel.

Barbarian Rage had sapped a lot of his energy, and Cooper was a sweaty exhausted mess by the time he made it to the pool.

"No time to rest," Cooper grumbled to himself. His friends needed him.

Positioning the unconscious fish-monster face down at the edge of the pool, Cooper sat on its back and dunked its face in the water. After a few seconds, he pulled the head up by its slimy hair.

The fish-person's eyes were wide open.

"Ready to talk, asshole?" said Cooper.

"Wha wahh waaa whaa wa," said the fish-monster.

"English, motherfucker!" Cooper shoved the creature's head back down into the water. After counting slowly to ten, he pulled the head back again. "Where the fuck are my friends?"

"Whaa wa waa wha wa!"

"I can't understand your crazy fish language!" Cooper shoved its head underwater again. "One Mississippi, two Mississippi, three Mississ—"

"Cooper!" Tim's voice came from behind him.

Cooper turned around. "Tim?"

Tim was naked and sopping wet. "What the fuck are you doing?"

"I have a prisoner. I was interrogating him."

"It's not going to do you any good," said Tim. "He doesn't speak the Common tongue. And besides that, he's amphibious."

Cooper concentrated for a moment. "He's neither right nor left handed?"

"No, dumbass. That's ambidextrous."

"He's into dudes?"

"Jesus, Cooper." Tim's voice was starting to take on that familiar 'Please punch me in the throat' tone. "He can breathe underwater."

"What?" Cooper pulled the creature's head out of the water again. Its face betrayed less distress than Cooper thought ap-

propriate, considering that he'd lost track of time while he was talking to Tim. "That's cheating!"

"Hey guys," said Julian, emerging from the tunnel adjacent to the one Tim had come from. He had Ravenus with him and, for reasons beyond any Cooper could guess, also a horse. "What's going on?"

"Don't 'What's gong on?' me," said Tim. "Why the hell did you summon a horse down here?"

"This is Gilbert," said Julian. "He kicked open the cell door for me."

Tim nodded. "That was actually pretty resourceful. Well done."

"How did you get out?"

"I picked the lock. As soon as those fishface fuckers started closing in on us, I grabbed my lock picks out of the bag that Cooper was stupid enough to throw at me."

"You're welcome," said Cooper. "How did either one of you two pansies fight your way through the guards?"

Tim and Julian looked at each other, then back at Cooper.

"I didn't," said Tim. "I waited for them to leave."

"Me too," said Julian. "Those things are strong as hell, and we're unarmed. What did you fight them with?"

"The cell door."

Tim looked down at the fish-person pinned under Cooper. "Can you hurry up and kill this one so we can get the hell out of here?"

"I'm not going to kill it. Can't we just tie it up or something?"

"With what? Our dicks?"

"Certainly not yours." The tip of Tim's halfling dick barely poked out from his massive pube nest.

"Fuck you," said Tim.

"Shut up," said Julian.

Tim gave him the finger. "Fuck you too."

"No, seriously. Shut up for a second. I think I hear something." Julian cupped a hand next to one of his ridiculously long elf ears.

"Two more," he whispered. "Coming this way from the big tunnel." Silently, he gestured for Cooper to travel counter-clockwise around the pool while he and Tim went the other way, and they'd meet on either side of the tunnel's opening. He was much better at improvisational sign language than Cooper was.

"What about this asshole?" asked Tim, pointing down to Cooper's captive.

Cooper gave it a solid punch in the back of the head. It hadn't been struggling, but the sudden lack of tension in its muscles led Cooper to believe it was genuinely unconscious. He let the head drop back down into the water.

"He'll be okay, right? On account of him being an Albanian?"

Julian squinted at him. "A what?"

"Amphibian," said Tim. "He's fine. Let's go."

Cooper didn't worry about being too quiet. He figured no one could bitch at him as long as he made less noise than Julian's goddamn horse. It was only when they had met on the other side of the pool at their respective sides of the large tunnel's entrance, and everyone stopped moving, that Cooper was finally able to hear the flopping of wet webbed feet against hard-packed earth. This was Julian's plan. Cooper looked to him for further instructions.

Julian pointed at Cooper, then punched the air. He pointed at himself, then threw his hands forward in a gesture which suggested a magical spell way more powerful than any he could perform. He pointed at Tim, then shrugged. Tim responded with a jerking off gesture, equally generous with regard to what he had to work with.

Julian's horse seemed to be picking up on the increasing tension in the air. It pawed its hooves on the ground restlessly and grunted and snorted.

"Okay, Tim," said Julian. "Your job can be keeping Gilbert calm."

"Do I look like the fucking horse whisperer to you? Why don't you just dispel it?"

"That would be wasteful. Now be quiet and stroke his mane. He likes that."

"I'm only three goddamn feet tall. All I could stroke is his dick."

Cooper nodded to himself. It was a solid plan. Surely there was no sight more distracting than a naked midget jerking off a horse. The fish-men would be caught entirely off guard. He would put the first one in a choke hold while Julian — Wait... What the fuck were they doing now?

Julian picked up Tim and placed him on the horse's saddle. When he turned around again, Cooper waved for his attention.

Julian mouthed the word, "What?"

The flopping footsteps were getting closer. Cooper didn't have time to carefully think through a pantomime. He did his best. He started with a shrug, then a jerking off gesture with his left hand, and finally a choke hold with his right arm.

By the look on Julian's face, he guessed his attempt at non-verbal communication had once again failed. He couldn't blame Julian. Now that he considered it, he probably looked like he was trying to give a reach around to an unwilling bear.

Ah well. At least the horse seemed to have calmed down.

Flop. Flop. Flop. The footsteps were very close now.

Julian nodded at Cooper. Cooper nodded back. Julian held up one finger, then two. With the third finger, he jumped in front of the tunnel entrance.

"Magic Miss—" His spell was interrupted by a bucket to the face. Magic sparked and crackled ineffectively from his right hand.

Cooper, only now realizing the significance of Julian's counting, lunged for the fish-person who had bucketed Julian. He was intercepted mid-lunge with a bucket in his own face.

"Son of a bitch, that hurts!" said Cooper. It couldn't have done more than a couple Hit Points' worth of damage to him, but goddamn. What kind of assholes fight exclusively with buckets?

"Waa wa wha wa wa!" said the fish-person who had hit Julian.

Tim whistled. "Hey! Shithead!"

"Wha wa?" said the fish-person, turning around to face Tim just before receiving two hooves to the chest. With a simultaneous squelch and crunch, the creature flew backwards. The bucket in its left hand connected with Cooper's ear.

"Goddammit!" Cooper shouted.

The standing fish-man held his buckets in front of him defensively. "Please! Wait!" he said in a croaky voice.

"Give me that!" said Cooper, ripping one of the buckets out of the creature's webbed hand. He pounded it over the head with the bucket repeatedly as he shouted, "How. Do. You. Fucking. Like. That. Asshole!"

"Cooper!" cried Julian. "Stop!"

Cooper stopped, not because Julian had told him to, but because his bucket was smashed to pieces.

Julian forced himself between Cooper and the cowering fish-person.

"Get out of the way," said Cooper. "He's still got one more bucket. I want to beat the shit out of him some more."

"Didn't you hear him?" asked Julian. "He said 'Please! Wait!'."

"Who gives a shit? You can't call 'Time Out' in the middle of a fight."

"No, you dolt! Think for a minute. He speaks the... What do you call it in the game? The International Language?"

Cooper scratched his head. "Love?"

"The Common Tongue," said Tim. "Good call, Julian." He hopped down from the horse and stood before the creature. It was bleeding more than its bucket wounds should have accounted for, and in places he hadn't even been hit. Its mucus coating was thin to the point of being nonexistent, and the skin underneath was pale and cracked. "Cooper, what the hell did you do to it?"

"I didn't do anything! Well, aside from beat it with a bucket, but —"

"Waaa...teeerr," the fish-person croaked weakly.

"You're thirsty?" asked Cooper.

"My... skin. It's too... dry."

"His skin needs moisture," said Julian. "Like a beached whale. We need to get him to the pool."

"Not so fast," said Tim. "First he can answer some questions. Who are you? And why did you lock us up?"

"We are scum. We obey the master's commands."

Julian pulled Tim and Cooper away from the creature. "This guy's been through a lot. Maybe we should go easy on him."

"He tried to kill me with a bucket!" said Cooper.

"I think you got adequate revenge for that. He's obviously in some kind of abusive Theon Greyjoy Stockholm Syndrome type of relationship with his so-called master. He called himself scum."

Tim rolled his eyes. "That's skum, spelled with a 'k'."

"No it isn't," said Julian. "Where the hell did you go to school?"

"It's a type of creature, dumbass. It's in the Monster Manual."

"Oh." Julian frowned. "Well I still think we should put him in the water. What we're doing here is torture. Aren't we too good of people for that."

Cooper thought of his previous attempt at interrogation. "Maybe not too good for, but also not good at."

"Just pick him up and drop him in the pool before —"

"We're too late," said Tim.

Cooper and Julian looked back. The two skum were sprawled on the ground, their skin as dry and thin as paper. The one who had gotten kicked by the horse was missing its eyes, and Ravenus was perched on the head of the one who had spoken English.

"Ravenus!" said Julian. "Don't you dare!"

Ravenus squawked and flapped his wings.

"You don't know that. He might only be unconscious."

Tim knelt down next to the dead-looking skum and slapped it lightly on the face. "Come on, man. Wake up! If Dave can bring his Hit Points to more than zero, he might be able to... Hey, where the hell is Dave?" He looked up at Cooper and Julian. "Oh shit. Did we forget about Dave?"

Julian looked down at his feet. "I um... thought we were looking for him."

Cooper scratched his ass. "If I'm honest, I forgot about Dave."

"This is no use," said Tim. "Cooper. Pick him up and throw him in the pool."

Cooper bent over and slid his forearms under the skum's neck and knees, picking him up forklift style. The body was cool and surprisingly dry. He walked over to the edge of the pool and launched the body in a somersaulting arc into the middle of the pool, where it landed face down with a moderate splash.

"Jesus, Cooper!" cried Tim. "I didn't mean you should literally throw him. We're trying to see if he's got any life left in him."

"Well I didn't know that. I thought we were just dumping a body."

Tim frowned, looking at the floating skum lying still on top of the water. "From the looks of it, I guess we were."

"Should I do the other one too?" asked Cooper.

"No. Let's go find Dave."

Ravenus cawed excitedly.

Julian sighed. "Fine, whatever. But I'm not going in there to flip the body over for you." He turned away as Ravenus flew toward the floating corpse. "I can't look at this. Should we search all the smaller tunnels first, or start with the big one?"

Tim put his hands behind his head and stretched backwards as he pissed into the pool. "Floppy McBirdfood said something about a master. If there's a Big Bad in this sewer, I'm betting his lair is down the big tunnel."

"But there are dozens of tunnels to search," said Julian. "What if Dave's getting raped by fish monsters the whole time?"

"They're skum."

"I can't bring myself to call them that."

"You just called them fucking rapists!" said Tim, shaking the last drops of pee from his dick.

"I didn't say they were raping him. I said they could be, or even worse."

Cooper picked up pissing in the pool where Tim left off. He watched Ravenus trying to peck a hole through the back of the dead skum's head. "What's worse than getting raped by fish monsters?"

"How about getting murdered and eaten by fish monsters?" Julian's tone was growing impatient.

"I don't know," said Cooper. "Given the choice, I think I'd rather —"

"Fine!" said Julian. "Can we settle on 'differently just as bad?' My point is that Dave could be in serious danger right now, while you guys are wasting time pissing in a pool."

"Or more likely," said Tim, "he's just sitting in a cell like the rest of us were, but lacks the brute strength, brains, or Gordon the Magical Fucking Horse to free himself."

"It's Gilbert."

"Whatever. If we have to go up against a boss monster, I'd rather do it with the healer in the party." Tim looked at Cooper. "What do you think?"

Cooper shrugged. "Those skum are pretty tough in the water, but not so much on land. Hell, if shit gets too thick, we can just outrun them. Out of the water, they're as slow as —" Tim had been making a lot of sense, and Cooper didn't want to lend any more weight to Julian's argument than he'd intended to.

"Cooper?" said Julian. "What were you going to say?" His encouraging tone suggested he knew exactly what Cooper was going to say.

Cooper hung his head. "Dave."

"There you have it," said Julian. "We could take a peek down the big tunnel at minimal risk to ourselves, or we could waste a bunch of time in the little tunnels while Dave is potentially being violated and/or murdered."

"Logically, what you propose sounds like a tremendously stupid idea," said Tim. "So why does it suddenly seem so reasonable to me? Wait a minute... You're using Diplomacy on me again, aren't you?" He clapped his hands over his ears and shut his eyes.

"Get the fuck out of my head!"

Julian smiled. "I guess that's that, then. Cooper, would you care to lead the way?"

Cooper picked up Tim and put him back on the horse's saddle.

After about five minutes of walking along the wide earthen corridor, they came to the first of a series of hard-packed steps. Each was about half a foot tall, and four feet deep. They made for an easy, gradual climb.

Ten minutes into Tim's constant bitching about how he couldn't see, Julian raised a more puzzling question.

"How high have we climbed? How are we even still underground at this point?"

"We must be climbing up into that hill Cooper ran down," said Tim. "Do you have any Light spells?"

"I can cast it on a fixed point in space. But if we want it to travel with us, I need to cast it on an inanimate object."

"Cast it on your pants," said Tim.

"I don't want light shining out of my crotch. What if I need to hide?"

Cooper, who could see just fine with his Darkvision, clawed a small chunk of rock out of the dirt wall. "Here."

The passage had apparently grown too dark for even Julian's Low Light Vision; he waved his hand around like a jackass before finally connecting with Cooper's.

"Light," said Julian. The light from the rock was blinding at first, but the spots in his vision slowly faded, mingling with the new light's reflection sparkling on the water just ahead of them.

"This is a dead end?" asked Tim.

"We could swim," suggested Cooper.

"This water could be crawling with skum, and I can see the other side from here. Why didn't you tell us we were at a dead end, so Julian wouldn't have to blow a spell?"

"Why don't you blow me?"

"Take it easy, guys," said Julian. "It's just a zero-level spell. I've got plenty." He stroked his horse's mane. "Take a drink, Gilbert." He held his enchanted chunk of rock out over the water, shining it left, then right. "Doesn't look like there's anything here." He walked back and shone his light back down the tunnel. "From what I could tell, this is the only tunnel leading upward. The rest of them led deeper underground. We can take each tunnel, clockwise one at a time, until we find —"

"JESUS!" cried Tim.

When Cooper looked back, the horse was struggling to stand, its head completely engulfed by a massive three-eyed fish.

Tim jumped off the back of the horse just in time to avoid being grabbed by one of the four tentacles reaching for him from the creature's sides. They struck the horse instead, and it disappeared instantly.

The fish's lamprey-like mouth closed around nothing as it fell, smacking the bottom of its head against the dirt at the side of the pool.

"Gilbert!" cried Julian.

"Who gives a shit about your horse?" said Cooper. "What the fuck is that thing?"

The fish retreated backwards into the water, which had suddenly become thick, opaque, and rancid. Its three eyes peeked above the surface, staring at them.

"You dare bring a false offering to Bal'Horzahg?" Whatever had spoken hadn't done so in the conventional sense. The words had bypassed Cooper's ears and been directly transmitted into his brain somehow.

Had the others heard it?

Tim clapped his hands over his ears. "Get the fuck out of my head!"

Apparently so.

"I think the fish is talking to us," said Julian.

"I am no fish!" said the voice that wasn't really a voice. "I am an aboleth, a denizen of the underworld."

Tim's eyes were tearing up as he coughed. "You're a denizen of a shithole. Seriously, how do you live in that?"

"I was betrayed by my own kind. When we consume a creature, we gain their memories. I know many terrible secrets. The other aboleths feared my growing power and imprisoned me here, where I've wallowed for years in my own waste."

"It didn't look, or smell, like this a minute ago."

"My powers of illusion are strong, and your minds are weak."

"Why didn't they just kill you?" asked Julian.

"The temptation to consume me, inheriting my knowledge, would be too great. But one day my skum shall find an underground river or lake, and I shall escape into the outside world and be free to exact my revenge."

"Is that why they're digging all those tunnels?"

"You are correct, elf."

Well, not technically, since I killed them all.

Bal'Horzahg turned to Cooper. "You did what?"

"Shit. Did I say that out loud?"

Tim and Julian glared at Cooper.

"He can read our minds, asshole," said Tim. "What the fuck were you thinking?"

Cooper frowned. "It's probably obvious now, in context."

"No matter," thought Bal'Horzahg. "You shall make suitable replacements."

"Fuck that," said Tim. "We're getting the fuck out of here." He turned around and started walking.

"Stop!" thought Bal'Horzahg.

Much to Cooper's surprise, Tim did as he was told. He faced the aboleth and got down on his knees. "I serve only you, mighty Bal'Horzahg."

"Shit," said Cooper.

"Very good," thought Bal'Horzahg. "The little one's mind is weak."

"Whoa," said Tim. "I blacked out there for a second. What happened?"

"Once I've turned you all to skum, you shall dig more tunnels until you find me a way out of this pit."

"I've got a better idea," said Julian. "Why don't we go get a wagon, and we can travel overland and drop you off in a lake or something?"

"Outside of water, my skin would dry out and I would either die or be severely weakened. Perhaps I would survive, but my spawn would surely not."

Julian peered past the aboleth. "You've got kids?" He'd found his in for Diplomacy.

"Not yet," thought Bal'Horzahg.

"Oh."

Cooper nodded for Julian to keep that line of question going.

Julian shrugged. "Is there a Mrs. Bal'Horzahg down there with you?"

"We aboleth are hermaphroditic."

"Your blood doesn't clot properly?" asked Cooper.

Julian shot him a quick glare. "That's hemophilia."

Cooper scratched his ass thoughtfully. "He's into kids?"

"Dude!" said Tim. "Shut up!"

"It means we have both male and female sex organs," explained Bal'Horzahg.

Good. Then you can go fuck yourself.

"You shall pay for your insolence!"

"Sorry!" said Cooper, Julian, and Tim simultaneously.

Cooper looked at Tim. "Were you thinking, 'He could go...'"

"Low hanging fruit," said Julian. "It just popped into my head."

"He left himself wide open for it," said Tim. "I couldn't help —"

"SILENCE!" Bal'Horzahg was thinking in his outside voice now. "How dare you insult me! I, who have devoured the king of the merpeople?"

"Oooh," said Julian. "That's very impressive. He must have had some interesting memories."

"Silly elf. You try to win me over with flattery. Are you not aware that your deepest thoughts and motives are as plain to me as this toxic sewage in which I dwell?" Bal'Horzahg raised one of his tentacles out of the dark brown sludge and held it out toward Julian. "Come, touch me and let your transformation begin."

"I willingly obey," said Julian, reaching his hand out and stepping forward.

Cooper wondered if he should interfere, or whether Julian had a trick up his sleeve. "Uh... Julian?"

Julian took another step forward. "I want to be skum."

Cooper looked at Tim, who stood there watching with no sign of emotion, then back at Julian. "Are you sure? Because it kind of seems like it sucks."

As Julian was about to touch the tentacle, Bal'Horzahg began drifting to the right, like he was teasing Julian into stepping into the putrid water.

"Wait... happening to... what..." Bal'Horzahg's thoughts were fragmented and panicky. Cooper couldn't keep up with them. Suddenly, the giant fish plunged beneath the liquid filth. Cooper thought he could see a small whirlpool forming in the middle of it.

"Hey," said Julian. "What happened? Where's Bal'Horzahg?"

Cooper didn't know if it was Julian, Tim, Bal'Horzahg, or all three of them, but somebody had to be fucking with him.

"That asshole is still lingering in his mind," said Tim, digging his finger deep into his ear. "Motherfucker really gets up in there."

Cooper put his hands on Julian's shoulders. "He was about to turn you into skum. Did you want that?"

"I did," said Julian. He rubbed his temples. "Now I've got kind of mixed feelings about it."

"Let's get the fuck out of here."

"No," said Julian. "We should wait and talk it out more with Bal'Horzahg."

"We could do that," said Cooper. "Or..." He punched Julian in the face, threw him over his shoulder, and looked down at Tim.

"Hey, man," said Tim. "I'm cool."

Cooper scooped up Tim and started to run.

"Stop!" said Tim.

"No!" Cooper kept running. "Don't make me punch you too. I don't want to be alone down here."

"I think I saw something back there."

"Was it a harpoon?"

"No."

"Then I don't give a fuck."

Tim squirmed under Cooper's arm. "I spotted a pattern of rocks on the wall. They looked like purposely arranged handholds. It might have been a way out."

Cooper continued bounding down the stairs. "I don't know why that slimy asshole went all Das Boot on us, but if he comes back, and we're all standing around jerking off at some fucking rocks, he's going to dig into our brains and turn us into skum."

"What's the alternative?" asked Tim. "How the hell else are we going to get out of — JESUS CHRIST!"

Cooper stopped at the mouth of the tunnel. A stream of liquid shit had flowed up from one of the lesser tunnels and into the pool enough to darken a good quarter of it, but had since subsided.

Near the wet and chunky brown path, wandering around like a zombie, was some kind of mud-monster. It was dripping and moaning, its short fat arms stretched out in front of it.

"Mwaaaaah! Whaaaaa!" the mud-monster groaned.

Cooper dropped Julian and Tim at his sides.

"Ow," said Tim.

"I'll take care of this." Cooper charged at the creature, mentally reclassifying it as a shit-monster when its smell hit him. "Fuck the demon ass you squirted out of!"

"No, Cooper!" cried Tim. "It's —" Whatever else he said was lost in the crash of Cooper and the shit-monster colliding and splattering into the dirt.

Cooper had no weapons, so he straddled the shit-beast and punched it repeatedly.

"Cooper!" cried his foe, shielding its shit-face with its shit-arms. "Stop!"

It knows my name.

Cooper throttled its shit-throat with both hands. "Get the fuck out of my head!"

"Idiot!" said Tim, suddenly on Cooper's back. "That's Dave!"

Cooper stopped slamming the creature's head into the dirt, but kept his hands firmly around its neck. "Bal'Horzahg turned Dave into a shit-monster?"

"He's not a shit-monster," said Tim. "He's just Dave, covered in shit."

Cooper released Dave and stood up. "That's disgusting. What the hell is wrong with you?"

Dave weakly raised his middle shit-finger up at Cooper.

"Honestly, Dave," said Tim. "Where have you been? And why are you covered in shit?"

Dave wiped a thick coating of shit from his face with both hands. He was no less brown, but the non-bearded parts of his face were now recognizable. "I heal me." He groaned and sighed as the magic sorted out his bumps and bruises. "They locked me in a cell."

"We guessed that much," said Tim. "They locked us all in cells. The rest of us escaped pretty easily."

"I escaped too, but it wasn't easy."

"What the fuck did you do?" asked Cooper. "Crawl through a whale's asshole?"

"I couldn't open the gate, so I Shawshanked my way through the wall. I started tunneling upward, hoping to reach the surface. Instead, I hit the bottom of some sort of shit reservoir. When it broke, the pressure blasted me right through the gate. It was up to my waist in no time. It rose up the tunnel faster than I could climb. I honestly thought I was going to drown in liquid shit." He looked at the mouth of the tunnel he'd come from. "I guess it stopped."

"Bal'Horzahg," said Tim. "He plugged the hole."

"You mean he's actually fucking himself?" asked Cooper.

Dave squinted at him. "What?"

"No," said Tim. "He'll die without moisture. He swam down to plug the hole that Dave made."

"So he's plugging Dave's hole?"

"Technically, I... Shut up, Cooper."

"How does it feel, Dave?"

"Shut up, Cooper," said Dave. "Who the hell is Bal'Horzahg?"

"He's an aboleth."

The whites of Dave's eyes widened against his shit-caked skin. "You guys met an aboleth? How are you still alive?"

Cooper snorted. "You opened your hole in the nick of time."

Tim glared up at Cooper. "Would you knock that shit off?" He looked back at Dave. "But yeah, that's true. You saved us, buddy. We owe you." Tim was speaking conspicuously less prickish than he normally did.

Dave shrugged. "It was my pleasure."

"Good," said Tim. "Because we need you to do it again."

"What?"

Tim licked his lips. "Listen, Dave. There's a pattern of discolored rocks on the wall right near the aboleth's pool. They look like handholds. It's my guess that was how the skum went in and out when the need arose."

"And?"

"And we need somebody to go up there and lower a rope through the pool trap while the aboleth is distracted."

"Why me?"

"Because it knows that's our only hope of escape," said Julian, rubbing his swollen black eye. "It'll die if it doesn't transform at least one of us into its slave, so that we can repair the leak and bring it food."

"What happened to you?" asked Dave.

"Cooper punched me in the face."

Dave glared at Cooper. "Dude, what the hell is wrong with you?"

"I —"

"Hang on," Dave continued. "I still don't see why I'm the one who has to go. Tim's sneakier. Cooper's faster and a better climber."

"But you're more expendable," said Cooper.

"Screw you guys. I'm not —"

"You're wiser," said Tim.

Dave rolled his eyes and scoffed. "Leave the flattery to Julian. You suck at it."

"No flattery," said Tim. "Just game mechanics. Your Willpower saving throw is modified by your Wisdom bonus. Julian and I failed, and Cooper almost certainly would have as well. You're the only one of us who stands a chance at resisting Bal'Horzahg's telepathic commands."

Dave looked from Tim to Cooper, then Julian, who both nodded their agreement with Tim's assessment. "Goddammit. Where's your rope."

"I don't know," said Tim. "They took all my shit."

Dave rubbed his shitty hands together. "Well I guess we'd better go and find that first. Without a rope, the plan kind of falls apart, right?"

"I've got a rope in my bag you can use," said Julian. "Right outside the pool trap."

Dave lowered his head. "Goddammit." He raised a finger to Julian. "Swap me a horse for a heal?"

Julian backed away from Dave's shit-covered finger. "I'll be okay. Horse is on the house." He pointed to the ground next to Dave. "Horse!" A horse appeared, a slightly lighter shade of brown than what Dave was covered in.

Cooper helped Dave's fat, naked, shit-slathered ass onto the horse, in spite of its protesting whinnies.

"Fuck you, horse," said Dave. "This is no picnic for me either."

"Good luck, Dave," said Tim.

"Godspeed," said Julian.

"Follow the plot," said Cooper. "Do his taxes and steal his shoes."

Dave scooped some shit out of his beard and flung it at Cooper. "I don't know if you're being stupid or just an asshole, but I —"

"Go horse!" said Julian.

The horse jolted forward. Dave only barely managed to hang on. Before long, they were both out of sight. A few more minutes and they couldn't even hear the horse's hooves, except for Julian, probably.

Cooper, Tim, and Julian sat on the edge of the newly murky pool, idly watching Ravenus, who was still pecking away diligently into the back of the dead skum's head.

"JESUS CHRIST!" Dave's voice finally echoed down the tunnel. As he said it, a torrent of shit-water gushed out from the tunnel in which Dave had been imprisoned and flowed into the center pool.

Julian started to stand up, but Tim caught him.

"We can't help him," said Tim. "This is pass or fail. If he fails, he'll be transformed before we ever get there. If he passes, we're only needlessly risking our own lives by following."

Thirty minutes or more passed. The shit river stopped flowing again, and Ravenus was making good progress on the skum corpse.

"Do you think this is a good sign or a bad sign?" asked Julian.

"Hard to say," said Cooper. "Dave's slow as shit. Whether he's coming back to rescue us or kill us, he'd take a while."

"He might not be doing either," said Tim. "Bal'Horzahg might just be biding his time, keeping Dave there in the hopes that we get desperate enough to investigate."

Julian frowned. "So the collective evidence is pointing toward 'Bad Sign'."

"Not necessarily," said Tim. "It's also possible that Dave is just —"

SLURP. BLURP. The sound came from the ceiling.

"The pool trap!" said Julian. "It's opening!"

The gelatinous circle in the ceiling rippled as the sphincter-like opening at the center puckered, then slowly opened, squeezing out Dave like a bearded newborn babe. His body was pasty white again, having been cleansed of shit. It glistened with a fresh coating of lube. With a wet, slurpy release, he broke free from the ceiling and plummeted toward the water below, stopping just short of crashing into Ravenus.

"Ow!" cried Dave. "Son of a bitch, that hurts!"

One end of a rope was tied around his ankle.

"What took you so goddamn long?" asked Cooper.

"Fuck you!" said Dave.

"And why didn't you just throw the rope in?" asked Tim.

"Do you honestly think I didn't try that? I threw the fucking rope in. It didn't work. I tied it to a log. Still didn't work. The trap wouldn't spring until I was in it. I thought I had enough rope to make it to the water, but I was wrong. So can you please hurry the fuck up? I'm in a lot of pain right now."

Cooper, being the best climber, as well as the only one strong enough to pull anyone else through the hole from the other side, was selected to climb to the surface first. The rope was slippery with a generous coating of lube-water, making for a greater Difficulty Class on Cooper's Climb checks.

With each failed attempt, Cooper got a little bit higher up the rope, scraping more and more of the slime off. Of course, that meant that he repeatedly landed a little bit harder on Dave with each successive failure. He honestly wasn't trying to hit Dave in the nuts every time he came down, but what could he do?

On the seventh or eighth try, Cooper finally broke the surface of the upper pool, and was breathing fresh forest air.

Tim climbed through next, followed by Julian and Ravenus.

After giving their arms a rest, and with the help of another of Julian's summoned magical horses, they successfully pulled Dave's fat ass to freedom.

The End

B.Oar Guests
ROBERT BEVAN

B.OAR GUESTS

(Original Publication Date: June 24,2016)

"This place gives me the creeps," said Julian. The living room of this house was at least as big as the dining area of the Whore's Head Inn, and a great deal cleaner. But there was more to his unease than a fancy sofa and a rug more valuable than him and his friends combined should account for. "There's something familiar about it, but I'm absolutely positive I've never been here before."

Ravenus dug his talons into Julian's right shoulder. "I share your concerns, sir." It was an unnecessary statement. Being Julian's familiar, he and Julian shared all their feelings, whether they wanted to or not, via their Empathic Link. He was only talking to break the uneasy silence of the room. "Also, I can't shake the feeling that we're being watched."

Though Julian felt the same way, he hadn't wanted to bring it up until he was sure that the flutters of motion he kept perceiving just beyond his periphery were more than paranoia.

"It's just the flicker of the fire playing tricks on your eyes," said Dave.

It would have been a reasonable explanation in a reasonable world, but Julian had seen a lot of weird shit since entering the world of Caverns and Creatures. Tiny gremlins peeking out from behind vases or mischievous spirits warping light as they darted about the room were perhaps less likely candidates than shadows cast by the firelight, but certainly not outside the realm of possibilities. Dave could dismiss Julian's feelings all he wanted, but neither he nor Tim had moved more than ten feet away from Cooper, and it certainly wasn't because of the warmth of the fire.

"I'm sweating my balls off," said Cooper. Though his half-orc form was mostly silhouetted against the flames, Julian could make out streaks of sweat running through the filth down his bare chest. "Why do I have to stay so close to the —"

A fart ripped out of Cooper's ass like a god was squeezing a roll of bubble wrap. The fireplace roared as the light in the room grew to near blinding intensity. It only lasted a second, the fire having consumed all but a trace of fart.

"That's why," said Tim. "This is a classy place, and we don't need you fucking this up for us by stinking up the whole goddamn house."

Dave's head jerked to the right. His eyes darted back and forth like he was trying to get a lock on something he was sure he'd seen.

"What's the matter, Dave?" asked Julian.

"Fine, you've got me. I'm starting to sober up now, and there's definitely something weird about this place. Maybe we should just go."

"Are you out of your fucking minds?" asked Tim. "The hottest piece of ass in Cardinia just asked us back to her place to meet her friends."

"And then disappeared for half an hour. Where are all these friends? I don't see any friends."

Tim shrugged. "They're probably all getting ready for us. Rubbing scented oils on each other, having a pillow fight, whatever the fuck girls do to get horned up."

"I don't hear any pillow fights," said Cooper. "What if there are no friends? What if she wants to take all four of us at once, or for us to do things to each other while she plays with her cooch?"

"Plays with her..." Tim unstoppered his flask and gulped back a swig of stonepiss. "Where the hell is that even coming from?"

"Dude, this shit happens. Rich people get bored with normal hookups. They have to keep upping the stakes to get aroused. All

I'm saying is that maybe we should talk about some ground rules before she has us all spanking and dick-slapping each other."

Julian expected Tim to continue berating Cooper for his wild speculations, but Tim stared off into the distance, biting his lower lip.

Even Julian had to admit that what Cooper was saying made more sense than an extraordinarily good-looking woman randomly inviting the four of them over for some wild sex party with her and her seemingly non-existent friends. "I could use a drink."

Tim offered his flask.

"No thanks," said Julian. "I can't handle straight stonepiss like you can."

Wheels squeaked as a small trolley rolled out from behind a luxurious blue sofa. On top sat a powder blue porcelain tea set, complete with cups, saucers, a sugar bowl, and a large teapot. It rolled right up to Julian, then a little further as he took a step back.

"Don't worry," said Tim, who actually looked relieved. "This is one of those toys that rich people have to impress their guests. Whenever someone says they're thirsty, the trolley rolls up to them and offers some tea. Simple Contingency and Telekinesis spells. You'll learn those when you become a less-shitty sorcerer."

Julian laughed nervously. It was kind of charming. "So what do I do?"

"Guys, stop!" said Dave. "I know what this place is! We have to get out of here right now!"

"First, you ignore Dave." Tim removed the lid from the teapot and emptied his flask into it. "Next you spike the drink." He delicately picked up a teacup by the handle. "Then you take a cup." He frowned, holding the cup close to his eye. "Hmm... there's a chip in this one." He shrugged. "Doesn't matter. Finally, you —"

"What's your name?" said the cup, wide eyes and a happy smile appearing on its side.

"JESUS!" cried Tim, flinging the cup to the floor, where it

shattered into a billion porcelain shards.

"Sacré Bleu!" said a voice from behind Julian. "He has killed Crack Baby!"

Julian looked back at Cooper. The candlestick on the fireplace mantel, standing behind a decorative fringe of silk roses and vines, had ignited all three of its wicks... and also sprouted a face.

"You hotheaded fool!" said the clock next to the candlestick. "Do you have wax in your ears? We were specifically told not to reveal ourselves until instructed to do so."

"Shut up, Monsieur Clockwise, you heartless timepiece! Ze halfling has killed Crack Baby!"

"It was an accident," said Tim. "I didn't expect it to... Hang on... Did you say its name was Crack Baby?"

The candlestick raised its candle arms. "It is a... how you say... nick name? He is a child, with a crack on his head." It frowned. "He was, anyway."

Mr. Clockwise bowed his head. "His mother suffered a similar accident years ago."

"Hmph!" said the candlestick, folding his arms indignantly. "Zis time was clearly an accident. Ze case with Madame Potter, I still have my doubts."

"You can't prove anything, Waxoff!" the teapot slurred through its mouth-spout. "If you'd kept your filthy wick to yourself *hiccup* she might still be with us today."

Waxoff raised his chin. "I never touched her."

"You son of a bitch! I can still taste the wax on her spout!"

The teacups surrounding Mr. Potter rattled in their saucers, but chose not to reveal their faces.

"Oh dear, oh dear!" said Mr. Clockwise. "Did someone spill wine in Mr. Potter?"

"Heh heh heh..." Mr. Potter's laugh was not at all pleasant. "Not this time, Clockblocker. This was the good stuff."

Waxoff slapped himself in the forehead. "Little halfling, what have you done?"

The hands on Mr. Clockwise's face spun in opposite directions.

"Oh dear, oh dear, oh dear. This is not good."

"What's going on?" asked Tim.

"Monsieur Potter has zis problem, you see," said Waxoff. "He cannot handle ze alcohol."

"I'll show you what I can handle, you limp-wicked son of a *hiccup*. Come over here, and I'll kick your waxy ass."

"No," said Tim. "I mean in a more general sense. What the fuck is going on here?"

"It's Mordred," said Dave. "I don't know how we didn't catch on as soon as we met her in the tavern. Her tits were threatening to burst out of that yellow dress. She wouldn't stop rattling on about how much she loves books. Her name is Bella."

"Shit!" said Cooper. "It all makes sense. Mordred is Bella!" He scratched his ass in thought. "Now I'm conflicted. Does this make it gay?"

Dave shook his head. "No, Cooper. Mordred just ripped off another story and dropped it into his fantasy world." He stroked his beard. "I wonder if Mr. Potter's alcoholism was his doing, or if it happened after we showed up."

"Oh dear, oh dear," said Mr. Clockwise. "If the master sees this, we'll all be doomed!"

"Take it easy, Tick Tock," said Tim. "He should sober up if I pour all the booze out of him. Hell, I was planning to do that anyway."

"I'd like to see you try it, half-man!" Mr. Potter's cheeks swelled up as he took a deep, bubbly breath through his spout, then aimed it, tight-lipped, right at Tim.

Tim stopped mid-step. "You wouldn't."

The corners of the spout-mouth turned upward in a sinister grin.

A key turned in the lock of the door on the far side of the room.

"She's come back!" said Waxoff. He looked down at his base, which was obscured by fake vines and roses. "French Tickler! Hurry and hide zis mess!"

A wooden handle poked up wide-eyed from behind the silk greenery, then raised a feather to wipe the side of her mouth.

"Oh dear!" cried French Tickler, revealing herself to be a living feather duster as she hopped over the roses and fluttered to the floor.

Ravenus ruffled his feathers, and Julian felt a stirring in his loins.

"Dude," whispered Julian. "She's a cleaning tool."

"What have you done?" cried French Tickler, scurrying across the floor as fast as her feathers would carry her.

Ravenus hopped down from Julian's shoulder and met her at the porcelain shards. "Good day, ma'am," he said with a bow.

"What are you doing, stupid bird!" said French Tickler. "Get out of ze way, or make yourself useful and lift ze rug. If ze master learns of zis, both of our feathers will be plucked for sure!"

Ravenus stared blankly at her, clearly dumbfounded. To a casual observer, it may have been mistaken for love at first sight, but Julian knew better. His familiar could only understand the Elven language, which was English with a terrible British accent, rather than a terrible French one.

Julian cleared his throat, then fake-coughed the words, "Lift the rug."

"Ah, very good!" Ravenus used his beak to pick up the side of the rug. French Tickler swept the remains of Crack Baby under it, finishing just as the door swung open.

"Bella!" shouted every piece of animated houseware in unison.

Bella scanned the room sternly, her hands balled in fists on the hips of her now unmistakably recognizable yellow dress, then grinned wide.

"You scamps! You weren't supposed to introduce yourselves until I got back!"

"What can I say, Mademoiselle?" said Waxoff. "Monsieur Clockwise has a... how you say, fat mouth?"

Mr. Clockwise's hands shot up to noon. "It's big mouth, and no

I don't! You spoke before I did."

Bella rolled her eyes as she glided across the floor. "These two, always bickering." She took Waxoff down from the mantel and caressed his center candle with one finger. "Don't get too overheated, Waxoff. I may need you later, in the library."

Tim looked smugly at Julian, his eyebrows raised.

Julian had had his doubts before, but he now surmised that Tim was correct. The way she said 'library' was dripping with innuendo. Though he found it odd that someone rich enough to own all of these magically-animated knickknacks would be using a candle instead of a more conventional living sex toy.

"So," said Tim. "Please tell us more about your friends."

Bella beamed down at him. "Of course! Have you met everyone? This is Waxoff, that's Clockwise, and French Tickler..."

Tim's expression grew dimmer with each name. These were not the Girls Gone Wild that he had assured them of.

"Um...," said Cooper. "Do you have any friends who are vacuum cleaners?"

Bella paused. "I beg your pardon?"

"Never mind."

"Okay." Bella smiled brightly as she stepped toward the trolley. Julian, his friends, and every anthropomorphic utensil in the room winced as the rug crunched under her foot. Fortunately, she was the only one who seemed not to notice. "And these are the teacup kids. Oh my, where is Crack Baby?"

"He's gone to meet his whore of a moth—"

Tim plugged a finger into Mr. Potter's spout. "He's, uh... We're playing Hide-and-Seek. He's hiding."

Bella looked sternly down at the shitfaced teapot. "Mr. Potter."

Tim looked up at Julian.

They couldn't keep this up while Bella was standing right there interrogating him directly. Julian shrugged and jerked his head to the side. Tim removed his finger.

"Yes, m'lady?"

Bella put her hands on her hips. "Why have you not yet served our guests?" She picked up Mr. Potter and poured his contents into his children's heads.

Faces gradually sprouted onto the sides of the cups, but they lacked Crack Baby's adorable cheer. These faces were cross-eyed, tight-lipped, and puffy-cheeked, like they were all about to throw up. One by one, they began to waddle off of their saucers in random directions.

"I hope it's still warm enough," said Bella. "Mr. Potter needs a lesson in manners."

"I beg your forgiveness, Miss." Mr. Potter's voice was the very definition of sobriety. "I was out of sorts. I promise I'll never —" His eyes widened, looking down at the trolley. "No!"

"Shit!" said Tim, as the teacup nearest him stepped off the side. He managed to catch it before it hit the floor, then hurriedly passed it off to Dave as a second cup teetered on the edge.

Julian picked up the remaining two cups to avoid further incident, and passed one of them to Cooper.

The combination of Cooper's stench and it's likely first experience with alcohol was too much for the little guy to take. Hot boozy tea poured out of the side of the cup all over Cooper's chest and down to his loincloth.

"Son of a bitch!" cried Cooper as the infant teacup's vomit soaked through to scald his dick. "This is why I never hold babies."

Bella rushed over to take the teacup from Cooper's hand. "Oh my! Are you okay?"

"I may need a minute before we head off to the library, but I think I'll — Oh, you were talking to him."

"I'm much better now," said the teacup, which Bella hugged firmly in her ample cleavage.

Dave and Tim necked back their own tea, Dave presumably to avoid being vomited on, and Tim presumably just for the booze. Julian tried to gulp his own, but could only manage sips. The combination of hot tea and stonepiss was just about as palatable as he'd expected it to be.

"Do you have any food here?" asked Dave. "Or something else to drink?"

Bella placed Mr. Potter back down on the trolley a little harder than was strictly necessary and narrowed her eyes at Dave. "I'll see if I can find something in the kitchen." She stomped toward the same door she'd just come from, giving Crack Baby's remains a good crunch on the way.

Why that would be giving Julian an erection, he didn't even want to contemplate. Unless it was something... "Ravenus!" He scanned the floor just in time to catch Ravenus's and French Tickler's tailfeathers disappearing under the blue sofa. He supposed that was marginally less disturbing as he double-layered the sides of his serape to hide the growing bulge in his crotch area.

"What crawled up her ass?" asked Tim when the door finally slammed shut.

Julian made eye contact with everyone to try to keep their eyes above his waistline. "I think she might have taken offense to Dave's request. It was like saying her hospitality hasn't been good enough."

Dave's face looked like he was having a hard time taking a dump. "Can I talk to you guys..." He glanced at Waxoff and Mr. Clockwise. "...in private?"

As discreetly as they could, Julian, Dave, Cooper, and Tim placed their cups back onto the trolley, then shuffled a few steps away from the confirmed living objects in the room and huddled together.

"Dibs on the feather duster," said Cooper.

Julian laughed. "Good luck with that. I think someone's already beaten you to the punch."

Everyone's gaze lowered to Julian's crotch. His efforts to conceal the bulge only brought more attention to it.

"You sick fuck!" said Cooper. "You shoved her down your pants?"

"What? No! I... it's Ravenus."

Cooper scratched his head. "You shoved Ravenus down your pants?"

"Julian! Cooper!" said Dave. "Shut the fuck up. I didn't bring you over here to call dibs. And seriously, you picked the feather duster before Bella?"

Cooper and Tim's eyes widened. "Dibs on Bella!" they said in one voice.

Dave closed his eyes and lowered his head.

"What did you bring us over here for?" asked Julian.

"I have a really bad feeling about this."

Cooper put a hand on Dave's shoulder. "Is this your first time?"

"No!"

"First time with a woman?"

"Shut up, Cooper!" Dave shook Cooper's hand off his shoulder. "It's not the woman I'm worried about. Mr. Clockwise mentioned a master, and he looked like he was about to shit his gears. Is it not painfully obvious to anyone but me who this master is?"

"We don't know that Mordred ripped off the entire movie," said Julian. "Maybe Bella's the master."

"I don't think so. She's a little unhinged, maybe, but she hardly seems terrifying."

"If there's a..." Tim glanced back to make sure they were still alone, then lowered his voice. "If there's a beast running around this place, then why the hell would Bella be running around in the middle of the night picking up random dudes in a tavern?"

"Maybe he likes to watch," said Cooper.

Tim grimaced. "I don't know if I'm comfortable doing it while there's a giant wildebeest man whacking off in the corner."

Cooper bit his lip and nodded slowly. "I think I can manage."

"But what if he wants to do more than watch?"

"Assholes!" said Dave. "Shut the fuck up! It wasn't in the middle of the night. It was mid-morning. We were still drinking from the night before."

A feeling of dread came over Julian, mixing awkwardly with

Ravenus's arousal. He hoped he wasn't screwing up his familiar's mojo. "Where are you going with this, Dave?"

"Maybe she was just in for some breakfast. We chatted her up and pretended to be interested in all her talk about books. But her tits were all up in our faces, so we took everything she said about her passion for books as innuendo."

Tim squeezed his head between his palms like he was trying to produce thoughts like orange juice. "Hang on. So you're saying there's not going to be an orgy?"

"I'm saying there's a giant monster around here with a bad temper and insecurity issues. What do you think he's going to think when he finds four drunk assholes drinking his booze, in his living room, chillin' with his hot-ass girl? You think he's going to buy that 'We just wanted to check out her book collection' bullshit? Cooper can't even fucking read!"

"Dude," said Cooper. "Don't tell her that. You know, just in case you're wrong."

The key turned in the lock. Julian, Dave, Cooper, and Tim sprang back to their former location like the rest of the floor was made of lava.

When the door swung open, Bella glided in holding a smaller tray with four crystal shot glasses on it, and a small matching decanter. Neither the decanter nor the glasses appeared to be alive, and all of them contained some kind of dark blue liquid.

"Use your Diplomacy," Dave whispered to Julian. "Tell her politely that something's come up, and we need to leave right away."

"I hope you gentlemen will find this suitable," Bella said contemptibly to Dave. "It's a blueberry wine, made with berries I picked myself from the garden outside."

Dave smiled weakly and looked to Julian.

"We, um..." said Julian. "We have to go now. My grandmother died."

"Oh my!" said Bella. She pursed her lips in thought. "Just now?"

"Yes."

"But how did you learn of this news?"

Shit. "She and I were very close. We have, or rather had, an Empathic Link."

Bella frowned, her gaze falling to his junk. "We express our grief in different ways."

Julian feigned a distress-induced stomach cramp, letting his serape fall loosely over his erection. Dammit, Ravenus! How long does it take to fuck a feather duster?

Bella set the tray down on the other side of the drink trolley. Mr. Potter stared longingly at the dark blue liquid.

"You mustn't leave without first sampling the wine," said Bella. "I'd been saving it for my seventeenth birthday, but now I've already poured it."

Tim and Cooper coughed.

"My," said Cooper. "You've blossomed early."

Tim stepped forward. "I think I'll have that drink now." He, Julian, Dave, and Cooper took their glasses.

Julian raised his glass to Bella. "Happy birthday." Dave, Cooper, and Tim mumbled something along the same lines. It was clear that all four of them were in agreement that it was definitely time to leave. They tilted their heads back and dumped the contents of their glasses down their throats.

Julian found the taste surprisingly bitter for blueberry wine, and it had a consistency just a little thinner than honey. His vision started to blur as his mind grew foggy. He turned his head, but the network was laggy. His vision followed a second later, and with some concentration, he was able to focus on a stunning, healthy-bosomed woman in a yellow dress.

"You're pretty. What's your name?"

A stunning, healthy-bosomed woman in a yellow dress smiled at something on the floor near him. He turned his head to follow her gaze, and his vision dragged along like the other end of a heavy accordion. A little boy lay face down on the floor with an empty shot glass in his hand.

"You shouldn't be drinking, little boy."

A stout, bearded midget fell on top of the boy, and some kind of monster swayed like he might fall next.

Julian looked down at his own crotch. "Why am I so... goddamn horny right now?" His vision darkened as he felt his body falling backward. He didn't feel himself hit the floor.

*

"Hello?" a voice echoed from some distance away. Cooper's voice.

Julian opened his eyes, but it did him no good. He was engulfed in complete darkness. The floor he lay on was rough damp stone. It felt slimy on his fingertips.

"Hello?" Cooper said again. "Come on, man. Talk to me!"

Shit.

"Are you alive or not?"

Shit shit.

"I swear to God, if you don't speak to me, I'm going to take a dump in your head."

What?

"Cooper?" Julian called out.

"Julian?"

"Who are you talking to?"

"The bucket in my cell."

"Oh." That raised a number of questions in Julian's mind, but the most prominent was, "Why?"

"Common courtesy," said Cooper. "I don't want to shit in it if it's magically alive, do I?"

That made more sense than Julian was anticipating. "You're a good man, Cooper."

Though Julian knew in his mind and in his heart what the following sounds and smells were, he tried to convince himself that it was just a forty-year-old can of spray cheese. If that bucket was alive, it must have a hell of a Willpower Save.

"Jesus Christ!" shouted Tim from Julian's left. "What the fuck is that?"

"I think that blueberry wine was laced with something," said Cooper. "It's giving me the runs."

"Where are you? Specifically, I mean. And more general, where the hell are —" CLANG "Son of a bitch!"

"We're in some kind of dungeon," said Cooper. "Our cell doors are locked."

"Thanks, Cooper," said Tim. "I just found that out... with my face."

Someone was still unaccounted for. Julian took a moment to clear the cobwebs out of his mind.

"Ravenus!" said Julian when he was able to focus. "Has anyone seen Ravenus?"

"No," said Dave from the cell adjacent to Julian's. "But I'm fine. Thanks for asking."

Shit. "I was going to say you next."

"No you weren't. Shut up."

"Come on, man," said Julian. "He's my familiar, and you're..."

"I'm what?"

Julian frowned. "I... I don't actually know how to finish that sentence."

Slow clapping from Dave's cell echoed annoyingly through the dark dungeon. "Well done, Captain Diplomacy. I'd say that's what a Natural 1 sounds like."

"Uh-uh," said Tim. "That was a piss poor Diplomacy roll to be sure, but a better example of a Natural 1 is when you talk about your goddamn dead grandmother while sporting a raging hard-on."

"That wasn't my fault!" said Julian. "It was Ravenus."

Cooper snorted. "I guess that explains why he was worried more about the bird than you, Dave."

Tim, Dave, and Cooper shared a laugh.

Julian pointed middle fingers in the directions Cooper's and Dave's voices were coming from, as they were the only ones who could see in the dark. "You know what? Fuck all of you."

Dave stopped laughing. "How are we going to get out of here? Tim, can you pick the lock on your cell door?"

"I don't think so," said Tim. "Not in the dark with nothing to use but my dick."

"Okay," said Dave. "How about you, Cooper?"

"I don't think my dick will even fit in the hole."

"No, stupid! I meant can you break through the door with your Barbarian Rage?"

"I can give it a shot." Cooper breathed in and out a few times. "I'm really angry!"

A series of grunts and groans started in low, then rose to a crescendo joined by the clanging of steel bars, and finally petered out with a long wet fart... and possibly some shit.

Cooper took a few more breaths. "Um... no."

"Shit!" said Dave. "That leaves you, Julian. Do you have any spells memorized that can get us out of here?"

Julian shrugged. "I have Mount."

"Of course you do." Dave sighed. "Well, give it a try, I guess."

Julian stood up and waved his arms around to make sure he had enough room in the cell to summon a horse. Satisfied, he pointed his hand at the floor.

"Horse!"

Displaced air shifted around him. His summoned horse whinnied nervously. Being called into existence would be disconcerting enough without being in total darkness as well.

Julian groped the air until he found the horse's mane, and stroked it gently. "Easy, girl... or boy." He couldn't tell if it was male or female in the dark without groping around for its junk.

The horse calmed its trembling and whinnying as a stream of pungent urine loudly splattered the floor under it.

"That's okay, buddy," said Julian, continuing to stroke its mane. "You feel better now?"

"Julian!" said Tim. "How about a little less bonding and a little more door kicking?"

"Alright! Give me a second." Julian discovered that his cell wasn't quite as big as he thought. It took some maneuvering to get the horse completely turned around. "Okay, friend. Let's see what you've got. Give us a good kick."

The horse leaned down and kicked its rear legs back. There was a loud clang of hoof against steel.

"Nice job!"

"Not nice enough," said Cooper. "The door didn't budge. They're strong as fuck."

Dave sighed. "I figured that would be the case after Cooper couldn't break it."

"Well shit," said Tim. "Now what do we do?"

"Now we wait," said Dave.

"Wait for what?"

"Yeah," said Cooper. "That plan sucks ass."

Dave cleared his throat. "If you'd let me explain." When everyone remained quiet, he continued. "I've been thinking about this. We've obviously come in somewhere in the middle of the movie. Bella has already succumbed to Stockholm Syndrome, which is why the Beast allows her to come and go as she pleases. But we know we haven't gotten to the end yet, because all the servants are still furniture and shit."

"So what?" said Tim.

"Yeah, seriously," said Cooper. "I mean, I'm sorry your childhood was so shitty that it earned you an encyclopedic knowledge of a little girl movie, but how the fuck is that supposed to get us out of these cells?"

"I'm just saying that maybe we can exploit our knowledge —"

"Your knowledge."

"Fine, asshole," said Dave. "My knowledge of the story to our advantage."

Julian guided his horse back around to face the cell door. "I'm not even convinced that we're 'in' the movie. I mean sure, there are similarities, but we don't know for sure that Mordred ripped off the entire script."

"It's all we've got to work with," said Dave. "And if I'm right, then I think our best chance of escaping is when that dickhead... What's his name, Garçon? Anyway, when he and the villagers come to raid the house."

"Sorry," said Julian. "It's been a while since I've seen the film, but didn't the villagers get their asses kicked?"

"Yes. But we are outside variables. Tim has already killed one of the Beast's servants."

Julian sighed. The little flicker of hope Dave had given him was snuffed out. "You really think taking out Crack Baby is going to turn the tide of battle?"

"Hey shitheads," said Tim. "For the record, that was an accident, and I kinda feel bad about it. So could you maybe shut the fuck up?"

"I'm talking about the butterfly effect," said Dave.

"That shitty Ashton Kutcher movie?" said Cooper. "Shit, I was way off. I thought we were talking about... Hold up, I don't remember any talking teacups in The Butterfly Effect."

"Not the movie, idiot. The scientific principle that tiny variables can lead to enormous differences in —"

A door creaked open to Julian's left, beyond Dave and Tim's cells, letting in the faintest flickering light. The light grew stronger as Waxoff shuffled into view, followed by the squeaky-wheeled drink trolley. Mr. Potter sat on top, but his children were absent.

"Jackoff!" said Cooper. "What the fuck, man? Let us out of here."

Julian cleared his throat. "His name is Waxoff."

"Whatever. I'm not good with names."

Waxoff raised his candle arms and his hand-flames flared up like torches. "Silence!" When his flames died back down to normal, he continued in a calm tone. "Ze prisoners will present their soup buckets."

"Fuck," said Cooper. "That's a soup bucket?"

Julian knew it was pointless, but felt he had to make a token effort at Diplomacy. "Why are we locked up? Why are you doing

this?"

While Mr. Potter vomited soup into the buckets Tim and Dave held out to him, Waxoff shuffled to Julian's cell and narrowed his eyes at the horse.

"What is zis dumb animal doing in here?"

Don't volunteer any information. Keep them guessing. "How should I know?" said Julian. "I just woke up."

Waxoff raised his eyebrows and smiled at Julian. "Ha ha! Ze joke is on your, monsieur! I was talking to ze horse!"

"Wow," said Cooper. "I haven't heard a joke that shitty since... um... Dave, when's the last time you made a joke?"

"Soup bucket!" snapped Mr. Potter. The trolley had now rolled in front of Julian and Cooper's cells.

"Fuck off," said Cooper. "I'm not hungry.

Tim and Dave paused their slurping to laugh. Poor Cooper. But Julian had to admit, it was kind of funny.

Mr. Potter turned to face Julian. "And you?"

It occurred to Julian that he might make a show of solidarity with Cooper by joining him in a hunger strike, but neither Mr. Potter nor Waxoff seemed the slightest bit put off by Cooper's refusal to eat. Anyway, he would need the energy.

He looked around his cell, now illuminated by Waxoff's flames. He found his bucket under his horse, filled to the rim with horse piss.

"Shit," said Julian. Back to the hunger strike. He straightened and folded his arms. "I'm not hungry either!"

Waxoff shrugged. "Suit yourself." He continued past Julian and Cooper's cells, and the trolley followed.

As the light from Waxoff's candles moved further down the hall, another prisoner held his bucket out from the cell next to Cooper's. His face was obscured by long, matted hair, but Julian figured him for a human from the look of his large filthy hands.

When the other prisoner had been served his paltry ration of soup, Waxoff led Mr. Potter's trolley back to the dungeon entrance.

Julian waited a full minute, once again engulfed in darkness, before addressing the mysterious stranger.

"Excuse me," Julian called out. "I know you're there. I saw your hands. Who are you?"

"Why don't you ask the dwarf?" said the stranger. His voice was deep, but rough, like it hadn't been used in a while.

Julian turned his head the other way, staring into pitch-black darkness in the other direction. "Dave? Friend of yours?"

"I have no idea who he is," said Dave. "I didn't even see his hands."

"I am the one you spoke of," said the stranger. "My name is Garçon."

"Shit!" said Dave. "If you're here, then —"

"That is correct. The battle you spoke of is not in the future, but in the past. Nearly one month ago, by my calculation. A terrible catastrophe. My hubris brought many a good man to an early and grisly death."

"But you managed to survive," said Tim, his tone suggesting just a hint of accusation.

Julian tried to glare at him, but then remembered that neither one of them could see.

"'Tis true, child," said Garçon. I deserved not the mercy of the gods, and was certain I had instead suffered their wrath. For I was bitten by the one you call the Beast. Then I was thrown off the rooftop and impaled upon an iron spike. My departure for the deep Abyss seemed imminent. But in their mercy, the gods saw fit to spare me. I woke up in this cell, my wounds all healed, but I'm a hollow shell of the man I once was."

"I know how you feel," said Cooper. He sounded uncharacteristically sincere.

"Do you, friend?"

"Sure. I feel like I just shat my entire insides out."

Tim clapped his hands once. "Well, if feelings time is over, how about we brainstorm a way to get out of these cells?"

"It's hopeless," said Garçon. "I flexed against these bars with all of my considerable might, but to no avail. Make yourselves comfortable, friends, for all hope is lost."

Julian shook his cell door. "Quiet, Garçon! We still have a chance. We have a man on the outside, don't forget."

Garçon grunted. "And this man on the outside, he is big and strong enough to face the Beast and all of its minions alone? Enough to lay siege to this whole accursed house single-handed-ly?"

"Well, he's technically more of a bird than a man. But he's already in the house."

"You said he was outside."

"I meant he's outside of the dungeon."

"No, I'm not," said Ravenus. "I'm right here, sir."

"Ravenus!" said Julian. "What are you... Have you been here the whole time?"

"No, sir. I've only just arrived."

"How did you get in here?"

"I hitched a ride under the drink trolley."

Julian had pinpointed his familiar's voice as coming from atop the horse's rear, and tried to face that direction as he spoke.

"Listen, buddy. I've got kind of a dangerous mission I have to send you on. Do you think you're up for it?"

"Anything for you, sir!"

"I wouldn't ask this of you if all of our lives weren't on the line, but I need you to search the house and find a key to these cell doors."

"I thought you might say that, sir. And so I've already taken the liberty."

The bars of Tim's cell clanged, as though he'd jumped on them like a spider monkey. "Are you fucking with us, bird?" he asked in a British accent.

Ravenus started to gag and retch.

"Ravenus? Are you alright?" Julian was mildly concerned, but didn't sense any distress from his familiar.

Something splattered on the floor, like pudding dropped from a height.

"Dude, stop it. You're starting to freak me out."

Something else dropped on the floor, but this something clinked.

"You swallowed it?" asked Julian.

"Yes, sir. In case I was discovered."

"Way to go, Ravenus!" said Dave. "When did he become a badass?"

"What the fuck is going on?" asked Cooper, who couldn't understand the Elven tongue. "All I saw was a bird squawk until he threw up. No one ever gets all excited when I do that."

Julian poked the puddle of bird vomit on the floor until his finger touched something metallic. He picked up the key and wiped it on his serape.

"How did you find this so fast?"

"The lady showed me where it was," said Ravenus.

"Bella?"

"No, sir, the other one."

"French Tickler? She betrayed her own people to help you?"

"I don't mean to boast, sir. But I have a very persuasive cloaca."

There was no point in waiting around in the dark anymore. Julian held the key up in front of his face. "Light."

The dungeon lit up immediately, bright light radiating from the black key.

Dave and Cooper shielded their eyes.

"Mercy of the gods!" cried Garçon, his face pressed against the bars of his cell. "You've done it!"

Julian unlocked his own cell, his friends' cells, and finally Garçon's cell.

The past month had not been kind to the old villain. Garçon's torn shirt hung loose on his withered frame. His unshaven jaw was still strong, but his dark hooded eyes were dull with defeat.

The five of them stood, along with a bird and a horse, in the corridor between the cells.

"So..." said Dave. "Now what?"

"Now we get the fuck out of here," said Tim. "Garçon, do you know where we are in relation to the front entrance? Or maybe just a first floor window? I'd like to avoid as much living furniture as possible."

Garçon scratched at his long stubble. "If I had to guess, I'd say we're below the kitchen."

"Where's the library?" asked Julian.

Cooper squinted and rubbed his chin. "I think it's two doors down from who gives a shit. Why the fuck do we need to go to the —" His eyes focused past Julian. "Dude, are you okay?"

Julian turned around. Garçon was sweating profusely. His hands were trembling.

"It's j-j-just as I f-f-f-feared," said Garçon. "I am afflicted with the same curse as that wretched beast."

"How did that happen?" asked Cooper. "Did you also tell an old lady to fuck off?"

Everyone looked at Cooper.

"What? So I saw the movie. Fuck you guys."

Garçon's skin began to sprout coarse black hairs. The two biggest toes on each bare foot, and the three smallest ones, melded together to form two large pointed toes. He wailed in agony as his knees locked straight, then began to bend backwards. The wails turned to squeals as his face elongated, sprouting tusks from the bottom of his mouth, his nostrils morphing into a pig snout.

"Cooper," shouted Tim from conspicuously farther back than he had been. "Push him back into the cell."

"Fuck that," said Cooper. "He's got shingles or some shit."

Julian backed away from Garçon. "We should get out of here."

"Let's go!" Tim and Dave were at the end of the corridor, holding the thick wooden door open. Julian led his horse toward the stairs beyond the open door. Cooper followed behind them.

At the top of the stairs there was another thick wooden door, but when this one was opened, the other side was disguised as a plain section of wall, indistinguishable from any other section of wall in the kitchen.

"Secret door," said Julian. "Cool."

"Yeah, real cool," said Tim. "Please get this horse out of here."

Julian led the horse through the secret doorway into a kitchen big enough to accommodate a medium-volume restaurant. The soup smell in here was much more potent than it had been in the dungeon, where it'd had to compete with half-orc shit and horse-piss. It was coming from a black, three-legged cast iron cooking pot, big enough to boil Tim whole, in a large hearth. Julian's stomach rumbled.

Once Cooper was inside, he slammed the door behind him and leaned all his weight against the disguised door.

"The intruders have escaped the dungeon!" announced a steel serving set. A pair of angry eyes had appeared on its domed cover, and it spoke through lips formed from cover and tray.

The cooking pot likewise revealed its true nature, taking what appeared to be a defensive position behind a wooden washtub as fast as its three short legs would carry it.

"We are not your enemies!" said Julian. "We only want to get —" A steel cleaver bit into the pantry door next to Julian's head. The handle was dripping water. Julian looked in the direction it had flown from and saw the cooking pot pulling its handles out of the washtub. One handle held a bread knife, and the other a rolling pin.

"Hit the deck!" Cried Julian.

The horse started whinnying and screaming. This was a little too much excitement so soon after it had come into existence.

Cooper slid down the wall to a sitting position on the floor. A homicidal cauldron was enough to deal with without adding a Garçon monster into the mix.

Julian, Tim, and Dave ducked behind the cupboards that stood between them and the pot hurling handleful after handleful of cutlery. Knives got stuck in the cupboards above. Spoons bounced off onto he floor. Forks did a bit of the former and a lot of the latter.

The horse's screaming stopped. Julian looked back just in time to see a dozen bloodied knives and two forks fall simultaneously to the floor from where the horse had been standing just a moment ago.

"Goddammit!" said Julian. "Is two hours really too much to ask?"

THUNK THUNK

The section of wall Cooper was leaning against challenged the power of the friction between his ass and the floor. He should have wiped.

CRASH SMASH

Dishes were exploding on the cupboards above them. Had Mr. Cooking Pot run out of knives?

"We have to make our move now," said Tim, staring down at the broken porcelain shards accumulating on the floor. "I don't have any shoes. I don't want to have to John McClane my way out of here."

There was a good twenty feet of open space between the end of the counter and the door out of the kitchen. Julian remembered how Bella had a weird habit of locking the door every time she left the living room. If the master of the house had her following some kind of weird containment protocol, there was a good chance the kitchen door would be locked.

"Guys!" shouted Cooper. "Dude seriously wants in the kitchen. I don't know how much longer I can hold him back."

Dave shrugged. "It looks like he's out of knives. He can't very well kill us with dishes, can he?"

Julian licked his lips. "Grab a fork. We might need you to pick that lock."

"One step ahead of you." Tim produced a fork from his pocket.

"All right," said Julian. He looked at Dave. "We need to cover Tim."

"With what?"

"With whatever." Julian peeked over the counter top, bracing himself to be hit in the face with a flying dish. He found the serving set and grabbed it by the handle atop its domed cover.

"Unhand me at once, you brute!" said the serving set.

Julian ducked back down and held the set out to Dave. "Take the tray."

"Once the master hears of this, you will be AAAH AH AAAAH!"

"We'll be what?" said Dave, holding the steel tray.

"I think we just ripped his jaws apart," said Julian. "He can't form consonants now."

"AH AAAAAH AAAAAAH AAAH!"

Julian looked back at Cooper. "Hold him just a little bit longer." He nodded at Dave and Tim. "Let's go."

Julian and Dave used the cover and tray of the serving set as shields while escorting Tim to the door leading out of the kitchen.

The iron pot flung dishes like Frisbees. The serving tray raised cries of vowels every time it caught one.

While Tim worked on the door, Julian and Dave crouched beside him, hiding as well as they could behind their makeshift shields. Finally the lock clicked open.

The cooking pot stopped throwing dishes. "Hey!" It threw down its dishes and ran out from behind the washtub.

"Come on, Cooper!" shouted Dave.

Cooper sprang to his feet and ran across the kitchen. Behind him, the door swung open to reveal the bipedal pig-monster Garçon had become.

The pot reached Julian and Dave just before Cooper did, and they swiped at it with their pieces of the serving set. The pot fought back with its little handle arms. As far as fights go, it was a pretty piss-poor effort from both sides.

Cooper ended the fight abruptly by grabbing the pot by the rim and pulling it backwards. It crashed onto the floor, spilling gallons and gallons of hot delicious soup all over Garçon's projected path.

"SQUEEEE!" cried Garçon as his hooves slipped out from under him. He landed with a splatter in the chunky brown liquid.

The cooking pot's arms weren't long enough to push itself back upright, but they were long enough to grab one of Garçon's legs.

"Let's go," said Tim.

While Garçon wrestled a cast iron pot, Julian, Tim, Dave, and Cooper hurried through the door and found themselves in the great foyer, where tapestries of what Julian assumed were likenesses of the prince in his pre-beast days hung on the side of a grand curved staircase.

"There's the front door!" said Dave. "Let's get the hell out of this place."

Julian looked up the staircase. "We have to get Bella."

"Fuck that," said Cooper.

"Dude," said Tim. "She's sixteen."

"No. I meant fuck the idea of going to get her."

Tim nodded. "Oh, right. I'm with you there."

"Come on, guys," said Julian. "She's a prisoner here the same as we were."

Dave shrugged. "She seems happy enough here to me."

Julian glared at him. "You're the one who brought up Stockholm Syndrome, dickhead." He glared down at Tim, then up at Cooper. "You all leave if you want. Ravenus and I aren't going to allow a little girl to grow up as some pervert-monster's sex puppet."

Ravenus poked his head out from under Julian's serape. "Well spoken, sir." He gave the others a glare as well.

Cooper frowned. "It sounds kind of shitty when you put it that way. Fine, I'm in."

Dave looked at Tim, then back at Julian. "We don't actually know that we're in the story. That was a guess. This could be a completely original..." He looked at his feet. "Okay, fine."

"Goddammit," said Tim. "Lead the way, Prince Charming."

Julian ran up the stairs as fast as he could. At the top he found a long hallway lined with doors leading who knew where. "She's probably in the library. Let's start from the right and hope we find her before we find the Beast."

"No," said Dave. He pointed at the double doors at the left end of the hallway. "It's over there."

"How do you know?" asked Julian.

Dave looked at his feet again and put his hands behind his back. "I recognize the doors."

Cooper snorted. Tim chuckled.

"Come on," said Julian. He ran toward the doors Dave had indicated and pulled gently on the handles. They swung open easily and silently.

Bella was reclined on a purple chaise lounge, reading a book, in the most enormous privately owned library Julian had ever seen. The large window on the far wall displayed a beautiful full moon rising over the countryside. Waxoff stood on a nearby end table, supplementing the moon's light while reading over her shoulder.

Julian cleared his throat. "Bella?"

Waxoff looked up and yelped, but Bella calmly finished the paragraph she was on and placed a bookmark between the pages before looking up from her book.

"You've escaped," said Bella. "Well done."

"We've come to rescue you," said Julian.

Bella clapped her hands. "How wonderful! Just like in a storybook. Who are you rescuing me from? Brigands? Pirates?"

"We're here to rescue you from the Beast," said Dave.

"The Beast?" Bella's smile faltered. "What beast?"

"Take your pick," said Tim. "We let Garçon out of his cell too before we found out he was a wereboar."

Julian looked at Tim. "Is that really a thing?"

"But if we have to get specific," Tim continued, "the Beast we were referring to is the one who —" His eyes watered as he waved his hand in front of his face. "Jesus Christ, Cooper. Was that you?"

Cooper took a step back. "Sorry. I haven't had anything to eat but fucking poison. My insides are all messed up. I think I just need one good solid fart to sort me out."

Dave coughed. "That one wasn't good enough? It smells like a dumpster behind a cheese factory."

Cooper's fart must have started wide and low, then risen with the subtle drafts of the hosue. Julian smelled it right about the same time Bella grabbed Waxoff and waved him in front of her face. Waxoff, in turn, was waving his fire hands in front of his own nose.

When Bella was finally able to speak, she said, "Did you say Garçon turned?"

"Yes," said Tim, his voice like a toad with throat cancer.

"Interesting. I was keeping him alive to see if that would happen." She looked at Julian. "You say he escaped as well, but he's not with you. Did you..."

"No," said Julian. "He's downstairs in the kitchen, fighting a cast iron pot."

"Big Blackie?"

"Whoa!" said Dave. "Was that what he was called before he turned into a pot?"

"Hang on." Julian stared hard at the pretty, large-bosomed girl in the yellow dress. "Are you saying you're the master of this house?"

Bella batted her eyelashes at Julian. "Why of course! Who were you expecting?"

"I don't understand," said Dave. "Who did Garçon fight a month ago?"

"That was the old master. He was no good at all." Bella placed Waxoff back on the table. "He imprisoned my father and passed his curse on to me."

Cooper scratched his left armpit. "You changed? Were you, like, a dude before?"

"And then had the gall to try to make me love him. He's no different than Garçon, or any of the rest of you." Her tone suggested that she was no longer in a playful mood.

Tim glanced back at the double doors. "So, the old master. Did you..."

Bella smiled at Tim. "Garçon did most of the work. I just finished him off."

"I don't remember that happening in the movie, Dave. Maybe it was in the sequel?"

Dave swallowed hard. "I don't know. That went direct to video."

"I can see why," said Cooper. "That shit got dark."

Dave and Tim looked to Julian expectantly. Cooper continued to scratch his armpit.

"Okay," said Julian, not really sure how to follow it. "You've clearly got some man issues." That already sounded wrong. "It's understandable, given how much you've been through. But we're not interested in your..." Nope. That won't work either. "Think back to when you met us in the tavern. You thought we were decent guys, right? Why else would you have invited us here?"

Bella shrugged. "A girl's got to eat." Coarse black hairs sprouted out of the top of her breasts as her dress began to tear at the seams.

By the time Julian looked up, her face had completely transformed into that of a wild boar. The fact that it took that much motivation for him to look away from her breasts made Julian concede that she might have had a point about men.

"Run!" screamed Dave, waddling back toward the double doors.

The four of them made it out into the hallway before Bella's transformation was complete, but Garçon was limping up the staircase, bloody drool dripping from his massive tusks.

"Shit!" said Tim. "Cooper, keep those doors closed. They're just wereboars. We might be able to take them one at a time."

"Take them with what?" cried Dave. "We didn't bring any weapons!"

Julian pulled back the part of his serape that Ravenus was tucked under. "You can't help us. Fly somewhere safe."

"Very good, sir." Ravenus pushed off of Julian's chest and dove over the railing.

Julian genuinely wanted his familiar to be safe, but he was surprised at just how little coaxing it took for Ravenus to ditch him like that.

When he looked back, Tim had emptied the contents of his pockets out onto the floor, and was spreading out a bunch of silverware he had apparently stolen from the kitchen.

"Arm yourselves," said Tim, holding on to two dinner knives.

Dave picked up a knife. "Fucking dinnerware? This isn't even pointy. What are we supposed to do? Smother him with a layer of mayonnaise?"

Julian grabbed a fork and a knife, but gave Tim a disapproving glare.

"What?"

"We weren't in enough trouble as it was? You had to go and steal their cutlery too?"

"Everyone knows you can only hurt a lycanthrope with silver weapons. I was thinking ahead, taking a precautionary measure."

Julian scoffed. "So how do you explain the spoons?"

"Fuck you. How's that for an explanation?" Tim had a point. There would be time for arguing later.

Julian stood up and brandished a knife and fork as if he were threatening an aggressive pork chop instead of the snarling monstrosity that was grunting and snorting as it hooved its way up the stairs. "Garçon! Don't do this, man. Stay back!"

"It's no use," said Dave, his sweaty hands also wielding a knife and fork. "This is his first time turning. He probably doesn't even know who he is. He's confused, angry, and hungry."

Tim held up the two knives he'd kept for himself and stood next to Julian. "Cooper, grab something to fight with. Our only hope is to take out Garçon before Bella gets out here. Everyone get ready to rush him on three."

Ravenus let out a battle caw that filled the cavernous foyer and hallway. He soared over the railing just as Garçon was getting to the top of the stairs, and he wasn't alone. French Tickler, his feather duster lover, was clutched in his talons.

"Ravenus, no!" cried Julian as Ravenus flew directly at Garçon.

From the last stair, Garçon made a wild swipe, which Ravenus narrowly avoided, and French Tickler sprayed a cloud of dust from her feathers into his face.

Garçon squealed and screamed, blindly flailing his arms, as he lost his balance and tumbled backwards down the staircase.

"Goddamn," said Cooper. "Bitch needs some Vagisil, or fucking Pine-Sol, or —"

The library doors swung open, flattening Cooper against the wall. A fully transformed Bella stood in the doorway, flaring her piggy nostrils. Her red-eyed gaze fell to Julian's knife and fork, and she snorted.

Julian knew a crotchful of dust wasn't going to save them this time.

A sound somewhere between a groan and a squeal rose from the bottom of the staircase. Bella looked over the railing and snarled down at Garçon. Before anyone had the chance to make a paltry attempt at stabbing her, she shoved Dave and Julian out of her way and bounded down the staircase, taking the stairs four at a time.

"Even better," said Tim. "Let those two duke it out, and we'll have an easier time with the winner. Back in the library."

Julian didn't know why Tim wanted to go back into the library. It seemed like they should keep an eye on the fight so that they'd know what they were up against when the victor came after them. If he was being honest, he was still concerned about Bella as well. He didn't want her to be ripped apart by Garçon, but he also didn't like the idea of having to stab a sixteen-year-old girl to death. He followed everyone into the library, unsure of whom he was rooting for in the wereboar battle below.

When Tim pulled the doors closed behind them, Dave spoke up.

"Why are we in the library? You wouldn't rather watch the fight?"

Tim shook his head. "We need every advantage we can get.

I can get my Sneak-Attack bonus in if we're flanking whichever one of those assholes walks through the door. So I'm thinking I'll stand on this side, and Cooper can stand on the other side. Julian can stand over by the sofa and fire a Magic Missile. As soon one of them steps through the door, we give it everything we've got."

"Where should I stand?" asked Dave.

"A few steps back from the door. You can be bait."

"Why do I have to be bait? Julian can summon a horse to be bait."

"Dude! We're fighting with fucking forks and shit. We need Julian's Magic Missiles."

Tim crouched next to the left side of the doorway, gripping his two knives and ready to pounce.

Cooper stood on the other side, using a fork to scratch his ass.

Julian swapped his knife for Dave's fork since he would be fighting from a distance... in the beginning anyway.

Dave muttered some half-sarcastic gratitude, and Julian considered whether he wanted to sit on the sofa or stand behind it. He ultimately decided that it wasn't going to offer him that much protection from one of those beasts outside, and his feet could really use a rest. He could cast a Magic Missile sitting down as easily as he could standing up, after all.

"Oh my god," said Cooper. "Here it comes."

Tim cautiously leaned toward the door. "I don't hear anything."

Cooper grinned. "No, I was talking about —"

"Coopcr!" cricd Dave. "Behind you!"

Julian looked at Cooper's rear and found Waxoff sneaking out from behind a purple ottoman, one of his flame hands pointed at Cooper's ass. Waxoff took a deep breath and prepared to pull his flame-thrower move when Cooper let rip the most epic shit-speckled fart Julian had ever witnessed.

The initial spray turned Waxoff brown just nanoseconds before the flame ignited, shooting out a plume of fire, like the breath of a dragon, out of Cooper's asshole.

It lasted at least ten seconds, maybe fifteen. Waxoff melted into a puddle of shit-tainted wax down the sides of a very much un-animated brass candle holder. The bookcase behind him had caught on fire, the dry pages of the old tomes crackling and passing the flames outward and upward.

When it was done, Cooper stood up straight. "I feel so much better now."

Julian, Tim, and Dave just stared in silent awe.

"The fuck's wrong with you guys?" said Cooper, evidently not yet aware that he'd set the library on fire. "Why don't you grow the fuck —"

Garçon flew through the double doors, smashing one in half and knocking the other off its hinges, and straight into Dave. From the state of him, struggling to get back up on his hooves, Julian guessed that he had not entered the library of his own volition.

Davehurriedlyrolledawayfromtheexhausted-but-no-less-terrifyng monster and stood back up.

Bella stomped into the library, her bloodthirsty gaze fixed on Garçon The bloodied yellow scraps hanging from her body were now unrecognizable as having once been a dress.

In all the excitement, nobody remembered to attack either of the wereboar. Julian didn't even know which one he was supposed to prioritize. Garçon looked like he might actually be only a couple of Magic Missiles away from dropping dead, but Bella was clearly the more dangerous of the two... at least until she turned back into a naked woman. No, girl.

"My books!" cried Bella. She ran to the bookshelves, her illegally stunning breasts bouncing with each step.

Julian shielded his eyes and made a run for the exit. "I'm not looking! I'm not looking! I'm not —" He ran into Garçon, sending them both to the floor. "Excuse me." He got back up and started running again, more concerned about not looking at Bella than by not being ripped apart by a wearboar.

When he made it to the double doors, he found that Tim and

Dave were also shielding their eyes. Only Cooper was unabashedly gawking at her.

"No fucking way she's sixteen."

"Cooper!" said Julian. "Stop staring!"

"It's cool. She turned back into a pig."

Julian looked. Bella had indeed changed back into a wereboar to deal with another attack from Garçon. She kept him at bay with one kicking hoof while simultaneously throwing as many books as she could save away from the spreading fire.

"Let's go!" whispered Tim.

The four of them crept quietly through the doorway. Even Cooper and Dave's heavy footsteps were drowned out by the roar of the fire. When they got to the bottom of the stairs, Ravenus and French Tickler were waiting by the front door.

"Well well, sir," said Ravenus. "I've got a tingly feeling in the cloaca. What have you been getting up to?"

"Nothing!" said Julian. "You're just aroused by your lady-friend here."

"It's not me, sir. I'm all spent. Need some time to replenish the troops, if you catch my meaning."

Dave grimaced. "Looks like someone's got the hots for a sixteen-year-old pig-woman." It was easy to judge, being the only one wearing boner-concealing armor.

"Ha!" said French Tickler. "Have no fear, Monsieur Elf. Mademoiselle Bella is twenty-three."

Cooper pumped his fist. "I called that shit."

"How do you know how old she is?" Dave challenged the feather duster.

"I was ze one who told her to lie about her age. I thought it might keep her safe from... How you say... ze predator?"

"Shit!" said Cooper. "Is he here, too? How many movies did Mordred rip off at once?"

Julian looked at Ravenus and French Tickler. They did make a cute, if unconventional, couple. He hated to break two lovers apart. And really, how much of a burden could a feather duster be?

"Why don't you come with us?"

Ravenus looked at him with wide eyes. Julian's heart skipped a beat.

French Tickler smiled. "I cannot, monsieur. My place is here, next to my husband, Waxoff."

Julian and Tim exchanged troubled glances.

"We have a complicated relationship, but he is ze love of my life." French Tickler raised a feather to the side of Ravenus's beak. "But you will always have a place here." She placed the tip of the feather on the base of her handle."

"Awesome," said Tim. "Good luck with that. We really need to be going now."

*

When they had ridden Julian's magical horses far enough away from the house, they slowed down to a trot.

"Are you okay?" Julian asked Ravenus, who was perched on his shoulder.

"Of course I am, sir. Why wouldn't I be?"

"I meant about your lady friend. All that stuff she said back there."

"She couldn't speak Elven, sir. I have no idea what she was on about."

"Oh. It's just that I sensed you getting a little panicky back there when we were parting ways."

"Of course I was, sir. Excuse me for saying so, but I thought you'd gone mad when you invited her to tag along."

"I just thought —"

"That would have thrown off our whole dynamic, wouldn't it?"

Julian shrugged. "I don't know if it would have been that —"

"And can you imagine me being seen in public with her? Me, a raven, and her, a... I don't even know what she is!"

"Alright, already. I got it. I'll run it by you first next time."

Ravenus ruffled his feathers. "I'm in the prime of my life, sir. Far too young to be getting tied down."

The End

Wight Trash
ROBERT BEVAN

WIGHT TRASH

(Original Publication Date: July 15, 2016)

The tattooed bare-chested half-orc behind the rough wooden desk continued writing on a piece of parchment as Tim, Julian, Dave, and Cooper entered the shipping container-sized office.

"Excuse me," said Tim. "Is this the Cardinian Trash Dump?"

The half-orc continued writing, not even sparing them a glance. "It is."

Tim wasn't expecting much in the way of pleasantries from a garbage man, but some basic acknowledgment would have been nice. He looked at Julian, who had a better temperament to deal with this sort of bullshit.

"Is that really what it's called?" asked Julian. "Trash Dump?"

"What's wrong with that?" said Tim. "It's a place where the city dumps its trash."

"I don't know. Those words just don't sound good together. I feel like it should be abbreviated, or the words should be combined into something catchier, or —"

"Maybe you can pitch some ideas at the next town hall meeting. For now..." Tim slowly and deliberately moved his gaze toward the city employee behind the desk, who was still ignoring the four of them to the best of his ability.

Julian cleared his throat. "We're here about the job."

"Waste retrieval or perimeter control?"

Julian looked to his friends for guidance on how to answer the question, but they had nothing but shrugs to offer.

"We understood this was a mercenary position."

The half-orc stopped writing. "Oh, that job." He scanned

them each in turn. He nodded approvingly at Dave, the only one of them decked out in proper armor, but squinted at his leopard-furred forearm. For Julian, draped in a filthy serape, he gave a small snort. He only looked at Cooper long enough to wince and move on. Though they were both half-orcs, Cooper's severely low Charisma score often made for jarring first impressions. When his eyes fell on Tim, a wide toothy grin spread across his face.

It was always the same wherever he went. Tim thought that in a world where halflings are a common race, people wouldn't treat them like the ten-year-old kids they resembled. He was continuously let down in that regard.

"Yeah, that fucking job," said Tim. "So what is it? You need us to rough up some dudes behind on their payments? Go out and collect protection money? Sabotage a rival agency's trash collection cart?"

"Hold on," said Julian. "I don't want to do anything like that."

The half-orc behind the desk looked confused. "Rival agency? Sanitation is controlled by the Cardinian city government. It's a public service."

"Oh," said Tim. "Then what's the problem?"

"No one knows how it started, but this place has become overrun with wights."

"That doesn't sound so bad," said Cooper. "Hell, where we come from, that's a sign of a good neighborhood."

The half-orc squinted at Cooper like he was trying to look directly at the sun. "And where do you come from?"

"Gulfport, Mississippi."

It was too early in the day for this shit. Tim needed a drink. He mustered up what patience he could and looked up at Cooper's stupid face. "He's talking about the undead."

"What, like zombies?"

"Yes, Cooper. Like zombies." Tim turned back to the half-orc behind the desk. "Not a problem, sir. We've dealt with the undead before. We can kill a few wights."

"Whoa!" said Julian. "Wait just a second, Tim, and think about what you're saying. Zombie or not, what sense does it make to discriminate based on race? I mean, would you honestly feel better having your face gnawed off by a Central American or Sub-Saharan African zombie?"

"Goddammit!" said Tim. "Wight. W-I-G-H-T. Okay?"

Cooper hung his big half-orc head and frowned. "Not cool, man. You know I can't spell."

Julian folded his arms. "That's okay. Neither can Tim."

"These are no mindless zombies," said the half-orc. "Wights are far more powerful and dangerous. You would do well to fear and respect them if you wish to survive."

Dave stepped forward. "Sir, I understand that you may have had some unfortunate run-ins with whites in the past. But is it as bad as you're making it out to be? I mean, look at yourself. You don't appear to be missing too many meals, you've got a nice government job, you —"

"For the love of fuck!" cried Tim. "Would all of you please just shut the fuck up for two goddamn minutes?" He turned back to the half-orc. "Please excuse my friends, sir. They're... um... What's the polite word for retarded?"

"Your mother?" suggested Cooper.

Tim ignored him, keeping his attention focused on business. "It's been a while since I looked at the Monster Manual. Can you explain to my friends exactly what a wight is?"

The half-orc nodded solemnly. "In days gone by, the term 'wight' simply meant 'man'."

"Like, before the Civil War?" asked Cooper.

Tim squeezed the handle of his crossbow and glared at Cooper, then turned back to the half-orc behind the desk. "How about just giving us a brief rundown on the differences between zombies and wights?"

"A zombie will simply tear you limb from limb until you die. A wight will turn you into one of their own, which is why we have a problem."

"Cultural assimilation," Julian whispered.

"Okay, that's it." Tim turned around and held up his crossbow, but didn't point it at anyone just yet. "I swear to god. The next person who speaks is getting shot in the face."

"You gentlemen seem well qualified for the task," said the half-orc. "My name's Mung. It's a pleasure to meet you." From behind his desk, he produced a large square of folded burlap cloth. "This is for the heads."

"You want us to put their heads in a bag?" asked Julian.

"Proof of kill. You collect five silver pieces per head upon your return."

Cooper snorted. "We're getting paid loose change for head. Finally we can know what it feels like to be Dave's mom."

Tim and Julian shared a chuckle. Even Mung joined in.

Dave turned red in the face. "Your mother's so —"

The office door swung open, sparing Dave the embarrassment of an almost certain terrible retort.

Two human men stood in the doorway. One wore armor that looked like it was composed of pieces fished out of this very junkyard. His thick brown mustache poked out of both sides of the mask of his cylindrical helmet. He looked like the Tin Man in an underfunded middle school production of The Wizard of Oz, except he wielded a war hammer in one hand and a bargain-basement coaster of a holy symbol in the other.

His companion wore a simple leather tunic, though it was perhaps a size too small. His broad muscly body threatened the stitching at the seams. The only possession he carried on his person was a long wooden spear with a steel head full of barbed serrations.

The armored man took a step into the already crowded office. He smelled like canned meat. "I, Morgan Flynn, Cleric of Dionys, Defender of Truth, Harbinger of Justice, and my companion, Balroth Stonefist, answer the city's call to arms!"

"I'm confused," said Cooper. "Did you just introduce, like, six guys? Or —"

"Silence, cretin!"

Mung cleared his throat. "Will you all be working together, or would you prefer to act as two separate parties?"

"We do the gods' work!" said Morgan. "We did not come here to babysit women and children."

That was all Tim could stand. "Who the fuck are you calling women and —"

"Enough!" said Mung, slamming a fist on his desk. "I have work to do. Common sense dictates that you would be wiser to work together, but —"

When Tim glared over at Morgan, Morgan was making a thumbs-up gesture over his crotch, with his thumb pointed toward Tim. It was a bizarre and unfamiliar gesture to Tim, but one that he could only interpret as disrespectful.

Tim pointed at Morgan. "I will end you, motherfucker! I will piss on your fucking corpse!"

"Ahem," said Mung. His fake throat-clearing was not excessively loud, but he had a certain presence that made him difficult to ignore. "As I was saying. If pride and petty squabbles mean more to you than survival, so be it." He tossed another folded square of burlap to Morgan's silent henchman. "But I suggest you all direct your hostility toward the wights."

Julian shook his head. "That sort of thinking doesn't lead to progress."

Mung slid open a large door opposite the entrance, revealing a five-foot by ten-foot cage of thick steel bars. Beyond the cage was a stadium-sized walled enclosure which Tim found to be cleaner than he'd expected for a place meant to contain all of the garbage of a city the size of Cardinia. There were piles of refuse scattered here and there on the barren ground, but not nearly as much as Tim thought there should be. The air didn't smell too bad either, aside from Cooper's contributions. Maybe Cardinians were big into recycling.

"Do not open the gate on the far side until after I've closed this gate." Mung pulled up the near gate by a horizontal bar attached to it. Smoothly, the gate slid open, revealing the sharp points on the bottom ends of the vertical bars, which would be buried a good six inches when the gate closed. "Everybody in."

Cooper was the first to walk into the cage, followed by Dave, then Julian. Tim took his group's rear, but was followed into the increasingly crowded cage by Morgan Flynn and Balroth Stonefist. Balroth's spear was too long to fit in the cage, so he had to poke the top of it through the bars of the roof.

They were all stuffed in so tightly when Mung pulled the gate back down that it was difficult to move. If wights were to reach through the bars and attack them right now, they'd truly be fucked.

Tim put his small halfling stature and his rogue stealthiness to good use by tying Morgan's boot laces together.

"What are you waiting for?" said Morgan. "Open the gate already!"

"I can't figure out how the latch works," said Cooper.

Dave grunted, and his ass was suddenly in Tim's face. "Let me try. Unnnnngggg... shit. I can't reach it from this angle."

Tim ducked down and squirmed his way through a forest of legs until he reached the gate on the far side. "Do I have to do everything for you guys?"

"What the hell is that?" cried Julian.

Tim poked his head between Julian's legs and looked outside the cage. A monster far more grotesque than his vague recollection of the Monster Manual illustration had prepared him for scuttled toward the cage. The pointy-toothed grinning freakshow appeared to have once been human, judging by the scraps of rotted clothing hanging from its twisted limbs. Yellow-grey skin stretched tight around its face, topped by a filthy crop of Don King-style hair.

"Shit," said Tim. "It's a wight."

"Good luck, gentlemen," said Mung as he slid the office door closed behind the gate.

Dave and Cooper were frantically arguing at the gate on the other side. Tim crawled over to see what the holdup was.

"Pull up on the handle!"

"I'm trying! It's stuck."

"Then try pushing down."

"It won't budge."

Tim squeezed himself upright against the gate bars until his head met something hard and inflexible. "Ow. Fuck, that hurt." He re-positioned himself with the side of his face pressed against Dave's ass, which appeared to be everywhere at once, to get a better look at what he'd hit his head on. It was the gate handle. "You dumb bastards. You're on the side with the hinges!" He reached out and gave the handle a tug, spilling himself, Dave, and Cooper outside of the cage.

Morgan pressed his back against the opposite side of the cage as the wight reached both hands ind its long pointed tongue through the bars. Morgan fumbled with his holy symbol while Balroth struggled to get his spear in fighting position.

"Know the power of Dionys and flee, foul creature!"

Tim didn't know if Morgan had rolled a piss-poor turning check, or if he was just a shitty cleric, but the wight now appeared to be grabbing at the holy symbol, managing to graze it with one finger.

"How dare you defile this... this... bwaaaaahhh!" Morgan grabbed the wight's wrist with one hand, pressed it back against the bars, and smashed the elbow with his hammer.

Balroth, by this time, had maneuvered the base of his spear shaft through the bars on the side of the cage opposite the wight and pulled the head in through the roof bars. He plunged the head deep into the wight's chest. The wight screamed as it stumbled backward, leaving behind what Tim guessed were tendrils of lung hanging from the barbed spearhead.

It's scream turned to a gurgle as brown blood spilled out of its mouth, covering its chin and mingling with the blood flowing out of its chest wound. Showing more intelligence than a zombie, it chose not to re-engage the people in the cage, but rather focused its wild eyes, burning with icy blue hatred, on Tim.

Tim shivered as the creature's gaze met his own. It only had time to take a single step in his direction before Tim pulled the trigger of his crossbow. His hands were shaky, and he barely managed to hit the creature in the upper part of its already-damaged arm.

The wight stopped screaming and snarling, and collapsed like a sack of moldy fruit. It must have been down to its last Hit Point.

Tim grinned at Morgan. "Guess that's a kill for us."

"Back away, halfling!" said Balroth, shifting the gore-coated spearhead two inches in Tim's direction, but he was unable to point it directly at him because of the bars.

"So Fabio can talk after all." Tim pulled his bolt out of the dead creature's arm. It barely even had any blood on it. He doubted he had ever seen so superficial a wound. He looked back up at Balroth. "This is our kill. If you want the head, you can come and take it from us."

Balroth was trembling with anger, which impeded his efforts to remove his spear from between the cage bars. "I shall take all of your heads in the service of Dionys!"

"Calm yourself, Balroth," said Morgan. "Let the fools have their ill-gotten victory. I've a feeling we'll be collecting their heads before long." He sneered at Tim. "You and your friends would do well to stay out of our way."

Tim placed his bolt over his crotch and wiggled it at Morgan and Balroth as they exited the cage and walked away in search of more undead prey.

"What a dick," said Cooper.

Ravenus peeked out from under Julian's serape. "What is that wonderful smell? Has someone prepared breakfast?"

Now that undeath was no longer binding the wight's body together, the poor bastard really started to reek.

"Well well," said Tim. "Look who finally decided to wake up."

Ravenus looked at him blankly.

Tim knew the bird couldn't understand anyone but Julian unless they spoke with a British accent, but Tim was only concerned

with Julian understanding him. "He's getting fat."

Julian stroked Ravenus's feathers. "I know."

"If you keep letting him sleep until he smells food, he's going to be too fat to fly."

Ravenus cleared his throat. "I'm terribly sorry to interrupt. But does anyone else want the eyes?"

Tim shook his head. "They're all yours."

"No," said Julian. "We need its head in-tact." He turned his head away from his familiar. "And you need some exercise."

Even Tim's callous heart was saddened to see Julian denying his familiar its favorite thing in the world. "I'm not saying you have to start starving him right out of the gate. Let him eat the eyes. I think the wight's head will still be plenty recognizable as such."

Julian looked down at the horrifying remains of the dead creature at their feet. "But what if he gets White Disease or whatever? I don't want him turning into a seagull."

"Don't worry," said Tim. "Everything you just said is... I don't even have the words for how stupid it was."

"Okay, Ravenus," said Julian. "Make it quick."

The wight's eyes had shriveled down to raisins by the time Ravenus finally got to eat them. Tim looked away and was relieved that they didn't make that horrible slurping sound. They probably just snapped right off the rapidly decaying optic nerves.

"Not much of a meal," said Ravenus. "But I rather enjoyed the texture. More chewy than usual, but lacking that satisfying juicy burst."

Dave looked back at the wight, winced, and turned away again.

That was good enough for Tim. He didn't look back. "Cooper, can you chop that thing's head off and kick it into the bag?"

"Sure thing."

THWONG

That might have been a chop, but it sounded too far away, and more like the release of a large amount of tension than an axe chopping through a neck.

"The fuck was —"

Dave collapsed under a pile of garbage-studded excrement about the size of a small car, which had just fallen straight out of the sky.

"Dave!" cried Tim. "Are you okay?" The shit-pile landed with a splatter, so parts of Dave were visible through the top, meaning it wasn't yet necessary for Tim to go digging for him.

Dave struggled to roll himself over and rise to a sitting position. "I think so." He spit some shit out of his mouth. "What just happened?"

Cooper looked up at the sky. "I think God just took a dump on you."

Tim laughed.

Julian cupped his hands over his mouth and lowered his voice. "Do you believe in me now, Dave?"

"Everything's a big joke to you guys," said Dave, wiping shit out of his beard. "Look at me. I almost get killed by a flying ball of shit. Do you wonder how that might have happened? No. Try to think of ways we might avoid getting killed by flying shitballs in the future? Of course not. Your first instinct is always to laugh at Dave. Ha ha ha, Dave's covered in shit again. Ha ha ha, Dave got kicked by a horse again. Ha ha ha, Dave—" His eyes widened as a blob of transparent jelly slopped over his mouth and nose.

"Ha ha ha," said Cooper. "Dave's coughing up splooge again."

Tim's eyes adjusted. The jelly blob was attached to a jelly arm, which was pulling Dave backward into some giant wall of jelly. The splattered shit on the ground dissolved into the slowly-approaching wall.

As Tim stepped back, he got a view of the whole thing. It was at least ten feet tall, and just as wide. A perfect cube of living digestive slime, with Dave's unconscious or dead body suspended in the middle of it.

"Gelatinous cube!" cried Tim. He had no idea these things were so big.

"That's really what it's called?" asked Julian. "Who's in charge

of naming stuff in this game?"

"Would you shut up and — FUCK!" Tim tumbled out of the way as a pseudopod shot out of the cube at him. He caught it with one hand as it slowly retracted, drew a dagger with his other hand, and sliced off the appendage. Even as it melted into lifeless jelly, Tim felt the pins and needles of numbness in his palm and fingers. At least Dave probably wasn't feeling any pain.

"FUCK YOU, JIZZBOX!" said Cooper, tearing into the cube with his axe.

The gelatinous cube shot four pseudopods at Cooper's face, chest, leg, and crotch.

"Flgbbghffgb!" said Cooper as his whole body was pulled into the cube. Poor Cooper must have made his Saving Throw vs. paralysis, because he continued to struggle once inside.

The cube stopped advancing. It waved pseudopods lazily at Tim and Julian, but didn't lash out like before.

"Cooper!" said Julian, cautiously jabbing at the cube with his quarterstaff. "What do we do?"

"You're a sorcerer, fuckwit!" said Tim. "Use magic!"

Julian held his staff in the air with one hand and thrust his other hand toward the cube. "Magic Missile!"

Two bolts of energy flew out of Julian's palm, causing two sections of the cube to burst like giant zits. The cube reformed into its proper shape almost immediately, but Tim thought it looked smaller than before. And it was definitely slower. Maybe Cooper was too gross to digest... or too big.

"Julian!" said Tim. "Summon a horse!"

"You want to just ditch them?" Julian sounded shocked.

"No. Just summon the biggest goddamn horse you can! Hurry up!"

Julian pointed at the ground. "Horse!" A majestic black steed, clearly bred for the battlefield, appeared next to him. "Now what?"

"Feed it to the cube."

"What?"

A pseudopod wrapped around Tim's leg and started dragging him in. "Do it!" he cried, dodging another blob of slime aimed at his face.

"Horse, go that way!" Julian commanded. The horse followed its master's orders, charging directly into the cube, where it was completely engulfed in a matter of seconds. It had apparently also made its Saving Throw, as it joined Cooper in thrashing around inside the cube.

Tim cut himself free, but he could feel a burning sensation on his leg where his skin had made contact with the slime. Dave and Cooper didn't have much time.

"Great," said Julian. "It ate my horse. Now what?"

"It's using most of its power to digest," said Tim. "Hit it with everything you've got." He hacked at it with his dagger, meeting little resistance.

"Flbbm... rgggbly... ubgggbbly!" said Cooper from within the cube. Tim didn't have to understand him to know he was saying, "I'm really angry!" He had invoked his Barbarian Rage.

The gelatinous cube trembled as Cooper's muscles grew inside it. Large cloudy bubbles formed in the jelly near his ass. He swung his axe around is if through water, and an entire upper corner of the cube slid off, melting into a puddle on the ground.

Cooper vomited slime as his head broke free from the surface. After a deep breath, he shouted, "FREEEEDOOOOOM!"

He tore at what remained of the cube with his claws and axe, not looking in the least bit concerned that he was still being digested from the waist down.

"Get Dave!" shouted Tim.

There was something like understanding in Cooper's wild red eyes. His erratic gaze darted back and forth until it locked onto Dave, still floating helplessly in the clear goo. "GET DAVE!" He raised his axe over his head with both hands.

"No!" said Tim. "Rescue Dave!"

"OH!" Cooper scooped up three pseudopods that had latched onto his chest and ripped them out of the cube. He plunged his

other arm into the slime until he reached Dave. "Unnnnnnnngg-ggggggg!" Dave came out like a newborn calf, only more bloody, slimy, and generally disgusting.

Having done what was asked of him, Cooper got back to the rage-fueled task of beating the shit out of his enemy. He didn't even bother with his axe. He just dove into what was left of the cube headfirst and used his bare hands to tear it apart from the inside.

SHLOP SHLOP SHLOP

Julian beat the shrinking cube with his staff until it finally lost its quasi-solid form and melted into a spreading pool of lifeless ooze.

His horse was bald and bleeding in places, but dammit it was still standing. Tim smiled at Julian. Good for — Oh shit, Dave!

Dave lay on his back, covered in slime. His skin was patchy and blistering with second-degree acid burns. The leopard fur on his forearm had completely dissolved, revealing a grey band of arm-skin beneath. He didn't appear to be breathing.

Tim wiped as much slime off Dave's breastplate as he could before putting his ear to it.

"Jesus Christ," said Cooper, having come out of his rage. He, too, was covered from head to toe in slime. "I feel like Dave's mom at the end of a shift."

Julian bonked Cooper on the head with his quarterstaff. "Dude. Not a good time."

"Oh, shit. Sorry. Is he all right?"

Tim pressed his ear harder against the breastplate, straining to hear a heartbeat. "If you two would shut the fuck up for a second, I'll let you —" There it was. It was faint, but it was definitely there. "He's alive! He's going to pull —"

BLEEGGGGGGHHHHHH

Tim caught a gushing faceful of Dave's slime vomit.

"AAAAAAAAAHHHHHH!" cried Dave. "IT HURTS! IT HURTS! OH MY GOD IT HURTS!"

Tim spit out slime and chunks of whatever Dave had last eaten. "Heal yourself, stupid."

Dave slapped both palms on top of his head. "I heal me!" He sighed ecstatically as his burns faded. When it was done he sat up and frowned at the fresh leopard fur which had grown back on his forearm. "Damn. I was hoping I'd finally gotten rid of that."

Cooper pointed a finger at Dave. "I could use some of that too."

Dave touched Cooper's finger. "I heal thee."

Cooper let out a fart of relief as Dave's healing magic coursed through him.

Julian cleared his throat and glanced at his partially digested magical horse.

"Forget about it," said Dave. "We've been through this."

"He saved your life. Look at him. He's suffering."

THWONG

There was that sound again. What the hell was that?

"Cooper saved my life," said Dave. "And if your stupid horse is suffering so much, just put it out of its —"

"Look out!" cried Tim, having spotted the flying glob of refuse hurtling out of the sky toward them.

"SHIT!" cried Dave, Julian, and Cooper as they dove out of the way.

When Tim heard the splat, he reasoned it was safe to look. All that was left of Julian's Mount spell was a horse-sized interruption in the new pile of filth splattered on the ground.

Tim looked up at the sky, tracing the trajectory of the shitpile. "They're catapulting the garbage over the walls. Probably so they don't have to deal with the wights."

"This is bullshit," said Julian. "We signed up to fight Whitey."

"Wights."

"Nobody told us anything about having to dodge flying piles of shit or avoid being eaten by gelatinous lubes."

"Cubes."

"Whatever. This sucks."

"It's actually kind of smart when you think about it," said Tim. "The gelatinous cubes eat the garbage. It's a perfect waste disposal system."

Julian kicked a blob of soiled jelly. "They could have at least warned us. Shown us a training video or something."

"That's actually pretty clever too," said Dave. "What kind of person do you think signs up for this kind of high-risk shit-pay job?"

"Violent sociopaths with nothing to lose?" asked Tim.

"Exactly. People who contribute absolutely nothing to society. In other words, —"

"Us," said Cooper.

Dave shrugged. "I was talking about PCs in general, but yeah."

"PCs?" asked Julian. "You mean, as opposed to Macs?"

"Jesus, Julian," said Tim. "How long have you been in this game. Player Characters, like all of us, as opposed to NPCs, like the bakers and farmers and shit who have families here and a vested interest in maintaining an orderly society."

"I thought they didn't realize they were in a game."

"They don't. We're not PCs to them. We're just narcissistic assholes who society would be better off without."

Julian frowned. "I thought we were supposed to be heroes."

Tim gave Julian a sad smile. "When's the last time any of us did anything heroic?"

"So they want us to die?"

"They don't care whether we die or not," said Dave. "It's win-win for them. If we kill more than four wights before we turn into wights ourselves, there's a net decrease in the total number of wights, and the city doesn't have to pay us anything."

"And there's four more fuckwits off the streets," added Tim. "Shit. I hate it when Dave's right about something."

Julian tugged on his long elf ears. "What about Morgan and Balroth? Are they PCs too?"

"I don't think so. They're probably just run-of-the-mill assholes."

"So what do we do now?"

"We do our job, and hope they pay us instead of shoot us when we're done." Tim looked westward at the sun beginning to sink in the sky. "We'd better take out as many as we can before it gets dark." He looked down at their only kill so far. Its head was still connected. "Dammit, Cooper. Would you please chop this thing's head off so we can get moving."

"Screw you, dude," said Cooper. "I got distracted."

Tim turned away and listened for the chop. When it came, it was immediately followed by a loud squawk.

"Ravenus!" said Julian.

When Tim looked at the dead wight again, its head was separated from the body, but the rotted clothes over the torso were convulsing like the creature had just snorted a line of powdered rocket fuel.

Ravenus backed out from under the clothes and glared up at Cooper, insofar as a bird is able to glare. "What the devil do you think you're doing? You scared the willies out of me!"

Cooper didn't understand the Elven language, but he must have been able to glean enough from the context. "I didn't see you, asshole. What the fuck were you hiding under there for?"

Julian put his hands on his hips. "Have you been eating this whole time?"

Ravenus lowered his head. "I'm sorry, sir. The underarm skin was thin and crispy, not unlike those 'nachos' you so enjoy."

"Great. Now I'll never be able to eat nachos again."

THWONG

"Shit!" cried Tim. He looked up and quickly spotted a third ball of shit-garbage sailing in their direction. "Run!"

Dave, Cooper, Julian, and Ravenus scattered like cockroaches when the light comes on. Tim, already having an eye on the trajectory, merely jogged backwards a safe distance until the catapult's payload landed squarely on the dead wight. The severed head still lay next to the body, only visible now as a conspicuous lump of shit.

"Fuck," said Tim.

Cooper walked back and frowned down at the head. "This is

more shit than head now. I'm not sure it's worth five silver pieces to carry it around all day."

Julian smiled at him. "You're thinking about it wrong. What's it worth to you to be able to hand that guy who sent us in here a big ball of shit and demand that he pay us for it?"

Cooper nodded. "That makes it worth it." He opened the burlap sack and kicked the head inside.

Tim walked over close to Julian. "Now that's how you use the Diplomacy skill."

Over the next couple of hours, they managed to add five more wight heads to their collection. Tim tried to think up ways to slaughter them more safely and efficiently, but nothing he thought of seemed like it would work better than ganging up on them one at a time and straight-up beating the shit out of them until they stopped moving.

When the sun got low on the horizon, Tim looked in the sack and frowned. "Thirty silver pieces isn't much for a day's work."

"It's not so bad," said Julian. "That's the going rate for betraying saviors."

"Aren't you supposed to be Jewish?"

"I read."

Tim looked back at the cage where they'd entered. Still no sign of Morgan and Balroth. "If we want to keep fighting, we'll need to light up a torch. I can't see in the dark like the rest of you."

"There's some light over there," said Dave.

Tim looked in the direction Dave had indicated. In the daylight, it had looked like nothing but more featureless barren ground. But now that it had grown dark enough, Tim could make out the faint glow of firelight coming from what looked like a wide pit. "What the hell is that?"

Dave shrugged. "Maybe it's where they burn the trash."

"They don't burn the trash," said Julian. "They let the slime cubes eat it."

"Then maybe it's where they used to burn the trash before

someone thought up the gelatinous cube idea." He stroked his freshly gelled beard. "But then, why would it still be burning?"

"Probably a magic, eternally-burning fire," said Julian. "I don't imagine that's too difficult a spell."

Tim scanned his surroundings, searching for any flicker of torch or lantern light, but finding none. "Those two assholes are probably over there. They're both human, and can't see in the dark any better than I can."

Cooper narrowed his eyes at Tim. "You look like you've got a terrible idea brewing."

Tim nodded and grinned. "Oh, I do."

"Are you thinking of pushing those guys into the fire pit?" asked Julian.

"What? No. Why would you even... Okay, now I'm thinking of that. But that's just harmless fantasy. My original plan is much more practical and much less murdery."

Dave sighed. "Okay. Let's hear it."

"I'm going to lift their sack."

Cooper scratched his armpit thoughtfully. "You want to check out their taint?"

Tim winced. "What? Ew. No. I meant I'm going to pinch their wight heads."

Cooper grimaced. "That's even worse. What are you, a fucking dermatologist?"

"Goddammit, Cooper! I'm going to steal the bag in which they keep the severed heads of the wights they've killed. Is that fucking clear enough for you?"

"Would it have killed you to say that the first time?"

"They're not going to just hand over their sack," said Dave. "If we try to take it, they're definitely going to put up a fight."

"I didn't say we're going to steal it," said Tim. "I said I'm going to steal it. By the time they realize it's missing, I'll be long gone."

"And what are we supposed to do?"

"Just stay conspicuous. Light up four torches so that, from a distance, it looks like we're all together. I'll sneak off alone and

snatch the bag while they're fighting a wight."

"That sounds risky," said Julian. "What if you get swallowed by a Jell-O monster? We won't even be able to hear you call for help."

"I'll take Ravenus with me."

Julian bit his lower lip. It was clear that his concern for the bird was far greater than his concern for Tim. "Okay." He pulled back one side of his serape, and Ravenus flew up to perch atop his quarterstaff. "You're going to go with Tim on a little mission, okay?"

"Very good, sir," said Ravenus. "I'm happy to serve however I may."

"You stay in the air. If he gets into trouble, you come back and tell us. Do not try to help him on your own. Do you understand?"

"Absolutely, sir."

Tim folded his arms. "Your concern is touching. Can we go now?"

Julian looked up at Ravenus, then down at Tim. "Be careful."

Ravenus flew down and tried to land on Tim's shoulder, but there wasn't enough room. The goddamn bird seemed almost as big as him up close. He finally gave up and landed on the ground.

Tim spoke in a British accent so the bird could understand him. "I'm going to sneak from trash pile to trash pile." He pointed to a nearby pile. "I'll move in a clockwise pattern around the circumference of the fire pit. You take to the sky. If you see those two guys we met earlier, come and find me."

"Right-O!" said Ravenus. He flapped his way up into the darkening sky.

Tim focused on Stealth as he dashed toward his first objective. It felt good to be doing something rogue-ish. There was a long list of things he and his friends were terrible at, and 'covert operations' was at the top of it. Any situation requiring even a modicum of subtlety would be ruined with a trumpeting fart, or a screaming horse, or Dave's fat ass falling down some stairs.

But this was what Tim's character was built for. High Dexterity. Maxed out ranks in Stealth. He was but a whisper in the breeze. A flickering shadow in —

"Fuck!" he managed to say before his face hit the dirt. Looking back to see what he'd tripped on, he found a giant bone sticking out of the dirt. Who knows what kind of prehistoric monstrosity it had once belonged to. "I'm glad you're dead, asshole."

Fortunately, he had planted his face right next to the garbage pile he'd been heading toward. Mostly scrap metal and smaller animal bones, it looked as though a gelatinous cube had sucked it dry of all organic matter some time ago.

Tim peered into the fading light to find his next objective. The fire from the pit was faintly reflected in metal scraps from two trash piles at the edge of his view. Either one would do. Just to be on the safe side, he squinted, trying to detect any sign of a gelatinous cube in his path, be it a particularly flat path of dirt, a trail of slime, a shimmer in the —

"Looking for me, sir?"

"Jesus!" Tim looked up and found Ravenus perched on a bent iron bar. "What the hell are you doing here? You're supposed to be scouting for those two assholes."

"I've found them, sir," said Ravenus. "They're hiding just beyond that rubbish heap over there." He nodded in the direction Tim had been just about to run to.

"Shit. Which one?"

"The one on the right, sir."

Maybe that was a lucky break. If Tim was able to reach the pile on the left without being detected, the close proximity would give him an advantage when it came time to make his move. "Good work, Ravenus."

Tim scanned his intended path one more time for dinosaur bones, or rocks, or holes, or anything else that might trip him up. It looked clear.

After a deep breath, he bolted out from behind his cover, barely touching the ground as he ran on his toes. He slowed down as he reached his target, not completely trusting that Ravenus

knew his right from his left.

"But what are they doing?" Morgan's voice came from the far side of the right-side garbage pile.

Tim ducked behind the left-side pile and concentrated on their conversation while he scanned for danger.

"It looks like they're just standing there," said Balroth. "Why is the half-orc holding two torches. Can half-orcs not see perfectly well in the dark?"

Morgan laughed like a snarling cat. "He's probably too stupid to realize that. I wonder where the little one's run off to."

Right here, motherfucker.

"His companions likely grew weary of his big mouth and murdered him."

Dude, I'm literally right here, asshole.

"As stupid and impulsive as he is, I would guess he's gotten himself lost," said Morgan. "The others are holding up torches because halflings can't see in the dark. Should we acquire his head, I may keep it in a jar."

That sick twisted fuck. Tim glanced down at his crossbow and toyed with the idea of shooting them each in the junk and running like a motherfucker, but he doubted he'd get very far. Then he spotted what he'd been looking for all along. Near a trash pile at the outer edge of his vision, a wight trudged aimlessly away from the fire pit.

Tim searched the garbage pile next to him for something to throw. He needed something small enough to grip in one hand, but with a bit of weight to it. He settled on the skull of what was either a child or a halfling, feeling a little bad that he couldn't tell the difference. But he couldn't have asked for a better projectile. With a thumb through one of the eye-holes, it was as if it were made to be thrown.

"Alas, poor Yorick," Tim whispered as he hurled the skull halfway between the wight and the two assholes. "Get thee to a nunnery!"

The wight stopped dead in its tracks and looked in the direction of the sound.

"What's that?" said Morgan.

The wight let out a howl like a velociraptor who'd just stepped on a Lego.

"It's one of them!" said Balroth.

"Behold the power of Dionys, wretched creature!"

The wight hissed, its eyes filled with terror. It turned and fled into the darkness.

Balroth sighed. "Must you do that every time?"

"I didn't hear you complaining when the wight dropped dead instantly."

"That happened once."

"Quit your moaning," said Morgan. "We're doing the gods' work. Now hurry up. It's getting away."

As soon as Tim heard their footsteps, he hurried the other way around his garbage pile and darted to the one they had been hiding behind. Just as he'd hoped, their burlap sack-o-heads was just sitting there unattended. He estimated it to have at least twice the number of heads that he and his friends had collected.

"Well done, gentlemen," murmured Tim. "And thank you."

The bag was heavier than he'd expected, forcing Tim to drag it on the ground. Unable to rely upon Stealth, he had to instead rely upon the wight keeping Morgan and Balroth busy for a while.

"Ravenus!" Tim grunted as he dragged.

"Right here, sir." Ravenus was flying in tight circles over Tim's head. He flew down and landed on the bag.

"Go tell Cooper to get over here and help me. And tell the others to put out their torches and start moving counter-clockwise around the fire pit. We'll catch up to them."

"I'm afraid Cooper and I don't communicate very well."

"Then tell Julian to tell Cooper, dipshit. This isn't that complicated."

Ravenus ruffled his feathers. "I don't appreciate being talked to that way."

Tim sighed. "I'm really sorry. Okay?"

"Okay. Apology accepted."

"Great. Now get your fat ass in the air and go."

Ravenus dug his talons deep into the burlap. "I... have... a... cloaca!"

"Jesus Christ, Ravenus. Would you please get your fat-ass cloaca in the air and go?"

"Hmph!" said Ravenus, flapping off into the darkness.

Tim felt sweat running down both sides of his face as he dragged the sack. He was exhausted, but running on spite. "Stupid fucking bird thinks I'm going to apologize for —" A moist glob of something landed on his head. "The fuck?"

"My cloaca sends its regards, sir." Ravenus's voice was headed in the direction of his friends.

"Why you son of a..." Tim dropped the bag and aimed his crossbow at the night sky. He couldn't see Ravenus, but he pulled the trigger anyway.

"OW!" cried Cooper's faint voice a couple of seconds later.

Oops. Natural 1. Tim grabbed the lip of the bag again and started dragging.

A few minutes later, his friends' torches all went out. It was full dark now. If any wights or gelatinous cubes attacked him, he wouldn't know it until they were right on top of him. Knowing this, Tim was more comfortable in the dark than fearful of it. There were only two creatures out there who would actively be seeking him when they discovered their missing bag, and neither of them could see in the dark any better than he could.

"Tim!" Cooper called out.

Tim looked toward the fire pit and found Cooper's silhouette facing him. He dropped the bag and placed a finger over his mouth as severely as he could.

Tiny lights shone from his left. Lamp lights. Shit.

"Goddammit, Cooper!"

Cooper jogged toward Tim, and Tim dragged the bag to close as much of the distance between them as possible.

"Damn," said Cooper when he reached Tim. "They've got a

shit-ton of heads."

"They'll have two more if we don't high-tail it out of here. Pick me up and let's go."

Cooper held the sack of heads over his right shoulder and Tim under his left arm. The ride was turbulent and the stench nearly unbearable, not entirely unlike traveling by bus.

"Over here!" said Dave after what seemed like an eternity of nauseous bouncing.

Cooper dropped Tim and the bag.

"Nice haul," said Julian. "They must have a good system worked out. There's half of them as there are of us, and it looks like they have at least twice as many heads. Mung was right. We should have worked together. We might have cleaned this whole place up and learned one or two things about strategy in the meantime."

"Mung can eat my ass," said Tim. He peered back in the direction they had just come from. The lamp lights were farther away than they'd been before, but not as far as they should be at the rate Cooper was running. Morgan and Balroth were slower, but still headed in their direction. "We have to move the heads from their bag to ours, then throw their bag in the fire."

Cooper snorted, looking down at one of the heads which had rolled out of the bag. "Someone drew a dick on that one."

Tim looked at the head. There did indeed appear to be a phallus on its forehead, though it was burned into the taut, decayed skin rather than drawn on. "That's weird. Who would burn a dick into someone's forehead? I mean, besides us?"

"That's the symbol of Dionys," said Dave. "I noticed the same image on Morgan's holy symbol."

"Damn it!" said Tim. "They're marking their bounties in case someone tries to steal them."

Cooper frowned. "What a couple of assholes."

"Can you rub it off?" asked Julian.

"No. It's too deep, probably seared right into the skull." Tim lifted the lip of the bag to peek in at the rest of the heads. "They're

all like that."

Julian squinted out at the approaching lamp lights. "What are we going to do? Give them back?"

"Fuck that," said Tim. He kicked the one head back into the bag and looked up at Cooper. "Chuck it into the fire pit and we'll pretend we never saw it."

Julian and Dave both appeared to have objections on the tips of their tongues, but neither of them spoke any aloud.

Cooper grabbed the top of the sack, swung it around his head once, and hurled it deep into the middle of the fire pit.

"OOMF!" cried a voice from the bottom of the pit.

Julian looked at the rest of them. "Did you guys just hear —"

"Yeah, I fucking heard it," said Tim. "Who the hell is down there?"

Dave stood on the edge of the fire pit. "Tim, give me your rope."

Tim's curiosity was piqued enough for him to grant Dave's request without question. He pulled the rope out of his backpack and handed it over.

Dave held the coil in one hand while he fed the rope, one loop at a time, into the pit.

"Are you trying to rescue him?" asked Cooper.

"No," said Dave, continuing to feed the rope down. "I have a theory. I suspect that Julian was right about this being a magical fire, but I think it's all magic and no fire."

"Jesus, Dave," said Tim. "You're managing to make both magic and fire boring as shit. Just get to the point, will you?"

"It's simple. If the rope doesn't burn, then the fire is merely an ill— SHIT!"

Before anyone had time to react, the coil tightened around Dave's hand, and he was pulled into the pit, disappearing into the flames. The sound of his armor crashing into dirt came a second and a half later. His voice rose above the flames. "Ow."

"Holy shit!" said Julian. "Dave's on fire! What do we do?"

"Take it easy," said Tim. "He's fine. People on fire don't say

'Ow' or 'Oomf'. That's what he was just trying to tell us. The fire is an illusion."

"Well something just yanked him into the pit."

Tim nodded. "That's true." He looked down into the pit. "Dave? You okay?"

"Stay back, foul beast!" said Dave. "The power of... uh... my holy symbol compels you!"

"I guess probably not then." Tim let himself hang from the edge of the pit and carefully slid down the steep, but not completely vertical wall. Sliding into the fire, he was relieved at the feeling of not being burned alive.

Now that the illusion was successfully challenged, Tim found he could see through the fire just fine. He could still see that it was there, but now it looked more like just a semi-transparent representation of fire. Other things — real things — were plainly visible, such as Dave holding out his holy symbol, and the wight crouched down and cowering before it at the base of the wall.

"You turned the undead," said Tim. "Way to go."

"Thanks," said Dave. "Now what do we do with it?"

Tim called up to Cooper and Julian, who he was surprised he could see almost clearly standing at the edge of the pit. "It's safe, guys. Come on down."

Julian slid down the side, not quite so gracefully as Tim had, with Ravenus flapping down behind him.

"Cannonball!" shouted Cooper, grabbing his knees as he jumped into the pit.

The wight's bones crunched under Cooper's considerable weight. Blood and guts splattered out like a popped meat balloon.

Tim shook his head. "I guess that answers the wight question."

"Are you okay, Cooper?" asked Julian.

Cooper stood up and looked at the dead pile of bones, dust and suddenly rotting meat beneath him. "Lucky he was there to break my fall. In retrospect, that was kind of a dumb thing to do."

"Just chop its head off and put it in the..." Tim looked at Cooper, then at Julian. "Did you guys leave the bag up there?"

Julian looked up at the edge of the pit, then back down at Tim. "We were in a hurry. We thought Dave was —"

"You there!" said a voice like a man's whose balls had just been slammed in a car door.

Tim turned around. He'd been so preoccupied with their immediate situation that he hadn't yet scoped out the rest of this pit. Standing next to an altar in the middle of the pit was a bald man with a black, pointed goatee. On his left arm he wore a small round shield, adorned with a red skeletal hand against a black background.

The shield immediately struck Tim as out of place, as it was the only form of physical armor he wore. His black and red robes appeared to have been hastily designed to match is shield by an inexperienced apprentice tailor. Where the shield's hand was menacing and kind of badass, the hands on the robes looked like they had been painted on the same way a child draws their first Thanksgiving turkey.

"Dude," said Dave. "It's the guy from Manos: The Hands of Fate!"

"Silence, dwarf!" said the mysterious trash pit dweller, spreading the arms of his robes out dramatically, causing pages of the large book on his altar to turn. "Speak not of my hands!"

Tim wouldn't have noticed if the guy hadn't brought it up, but he did have tiny, delicate hands. Out of the corner of his eye, Tim also noticed Julian whispering something to Ravenus, once again tucked under his serape.

"I'm sorry, sir," said Dave. He lifted up his own left arm. "I've got this weird leopard fur thing going on, so don't feel —"

"I said silence!" said the strange man, pounding his little fist on the table. He looked down behind the altar. "No, not you. I'm sorry. Did Daddy scare you? Come on up here." He crouched down behind the altar.

"Go! Now!" whispered Julian. Ravenus sprang out of his chest like a black feathered xenomorph and flew out into the night.

When the man rose from behind the altar, he placed a black

cat on top of it. The side of the cat's fur also bore a crudely painted red hand. Tim felt bad for it.

"Now," said the man, gesturing down at the spilled sack of heads by his feet. "Who is responsible for this?"

"Not us!" said Tim. "We found those like that." He wondered if he had to make a Bluff check on telling the truth if the truth sounded like complete horseshit. Better just to move the dialogue along. "So... Who the fuck are you, anyway?"

"I am Grand Wizard Dominus Traldar! Commander of wights!"

Julian cringed. "Grand Wizard? Really?"

"What?" asked the Grand Wizard. "What's wrong with that?"

"It just carries sort of unpleasant connotations where we're from."

"More unpleasant than necromancy?"

Julian looked at Tim, who just shrugged. "I don't know. That's a tough one. Let's just call it different unpleasant."

The Grand Wizard stroked his pet's fur. "Perhaps you will not find it so unpleasant once you have joined my army."

Tim wondered if their best bet wasn't to just jump him right there and then. If he was a powerful spellcaster, then he might be able to disintegrate them all before they got anywhere near him. If, on the other hand, he was more like Julian, whose greatest magical feat was the ability to summon a horse, they could just beat the shit out him and be on their way. Unfortunately, the majority of the grey area between those two extremes would likely see one or all of Tim's group dead.

"That's a cute cat," said Julian. "What's his name?" Was he stalling for time, or was he oblivious to the potential danger they were in and genuinely interested in this guy's pet cat? With Julian, it could go either way.

"His name is Mr. Whiskers." The Grand Wizard scratched under Mr. Whiskers's chin. Tim felt bad that the cat had more to be ashamed of than the shitty red hand painted on his fur.

"How original!" said Julian, unconvincingly. To be fair though, the Difficulty Class on that Bluff check would have been pretty fucking high. "Do you, uh... like music?"

It was now painfully clear that Julian was stalling for time, and failing miserably. Tim picked up the slack.

"What is it you plan to do with us?" Tim demanded, already knowing full well what he intended to do with them. His comment about them joining his wight army didn't leave a lot of room for interpretation.

"Have no fear, tiny halfling. It will only hurt for a second. Once my wights drain your soul from your body, you'll feel no more. But you'll be more powerful than you ever were in life." The Grand Wizard's eyes widened. "You'll have wight power."

"Oh come on," said Julian. "Again, there are so many different ways you could have phrased that."

The Grand Wizard put his non-shield hand on his hip. "I'm not sure you're appreciating the gravity of the situation you're in. Under the circumstances, your constant nitpicking of my choice of vocabulary is —"

CRASH

VWOOOOOOOOOSH

"HORSE!"

Unmistakably real fire burst out from the book atop the altar like time lapse video of a blossoming flower... which was made out of fire. Also, a horse materialized behind the Grand Wizard.

Mr. Whiskers jumped off the altar.

A look of horror came over the Grand Wizard's face as he started toward his burning spellbook. "NOOO — Oomf!"

Julian's startled horse kicked the Grand Wizard, sending him flying through the air to land in a heap at Tim's feet.

"Hold him!" cried Tim. "Make sure he can't move his —"

A fiercely adorable meow rang out, followed shortly after by Dave's muffled screams. Mr. Whiskers had attached himself to Dave's face.

Tim determined that Dave was competent enough to handle a house cat all by himself. He needed to focus on the shield.

Cooper pounced on the wizard, putting them in a 69 position.

He gripped the wizard's ankles with his hands and pinned the arms down with his knees.

Tim grabbed the shield and tried to pull it off the wizards' arm. "And don't let him speak!"

"Get off of me this instant, you filthy —"

The Grand Wizard's words, and Mr. Whiskers's feline screams were overpowered by a thunderous wet fart.

Tim wasn't at an angle from which he could see the wizard's face, but judging by the expression on Julian's, Cooper's fart was more than a fart. "Did he just...?"

"Yeah," said Julian. "He's probably going to want to wash that off before his next Klan meeting." Ravenus landed on Julian's shoulder, and Julian looked relieved for the distraction. "Everything go okay, buddy?"

"Couldn't have gone better, sir," said Ravenus. "They didn't even know I was there."

"You saved our butts. Do you want some eyes?"

Ravenus looked down at the Grand Wizard, who was gagging and weeping. "They've got shit all over them, sir."

"I was talking about the heads in the bag. They have the chewy kind you like."

Tim wasn't having any luck trying to pull the shield loose, so he felt around for the buckles.

Mr. Whiskers's caterwauling came to an abrupt end.

"Dude," said Cooper. "You killed the cat?"

"No," said Dave. "I didn't kill it. I just knocked it out."

"What kind of monster are you?"

"Look at my fucking face?"

Tim finally got the shield loose. He turned around to look at Dave. Dave's face was riddled with parallel sets of bleeding claw marks in every direction. He looked like he'd been attacked by a whole gaggle of cats. Still, they were superficial wounds compared to what a lot of creatures in the C&C world could dish out.

"Don't be such a baby. I think a Zero Level Heal spell should take care of that." Tim knew he didn't have to tell a cleric when

or how to use his own healing magic. Dave had only neglected to do it so far so that he could show off how much he'd sacrificed for the good of the team. As if they were going to give him a fucking Purple Heart for punching out a cat.

"My shield!" cried the Grand Wizard. His nose must have still been clogged with shit, because he sounded like he had a cold. "You must give it back! I need it to control the wights!"

"I know, asshole. That's why I took it away."

"But you don't understand. I was keeping them at bay until after we'd talked. In retrospect, that seems unwise."

"I hear you, buddy," said Cooper.

"I was lonely." The wizard looked at Tim with pleading shit-caked eyes. "They'll be coming for all of us now. Dozens of them! You must return my shield!"

"Fuck no," said Tim. "If we need it, we'll use it ourselves."

The Grand Wizard shook his head. "The shield will only serve one master per day. I've already used it today. It's powerless in your hands."

"Well you're a Grand Wizard. You can just Fireball them or some shit."

"I've depleted my magical energy for the day."

"You used up all your spells? Doing what?"

The wizard frowned. "Entertaining myself, mostly. It was getting late, and I wasn't expecting visitors."

"Can't you just jerk off like a normal person?" Tim focused on his Sense Motive skill, and judged the wizard to be telling the truth, with regard to the danger they were all in as well as with his lack of spells. "Get off of him, Cooper."

Cooper let one last fart squeak out before standing up.

The Grand Wizard sprang to his feet and rushed to the altar. The fire had died down, leaving behind the broken twisted remains of an oil lamp. The spellbook had been completely consumed.

"My book!" said the Grand Wizard between sobs. "All that time and money, wasted!"

"I'm sorry," said Julian. "You didn't leave me any choice." He placed Mr. Whiskers's still-unconscious body on the altar in front of the wizard.

"How did you do that, anyway?" asked Tim.

"The same way you did. I sent Ravenus to go swipe a lamp from those guys. I figured the guy with the spear would need to put down his lamp while he was fighting. How'd you know about the shield?"

Tim laughed. "That was simple. What the fuck else is this gangly asshole going to use a shield for? He's no necromancer. He's just a shitty illusionist who got in over his head playing with evil power he's too stupid to under—"

"NYEEEEEEGGGGHHHH!" cried Julian's magical horse, which had wandered away from the fire. Undead hands gripped it by the throat. The horse's large brown eyes were wide with terror. The wight's cold blue eyes shone with sadistic glee.

"Shit!" said Tim. "They're here." He passed the shield to Julian. "Keep this away from him, but don't put it on. It might be evil." He fired his crossbow, hitting the horse, which vanished from the wight's grip.

Julian glared at Tim. "Evil, huh?"

"I was aiming for the wight, asshole."

Julian aimed his open palm at the wight.

"Don't," said Tim. "We can handle them as long as they're coming one at a time. Save your spells for when we need them."

The wight ran at them, its slobbering tongue wagging out of its mouth.

Cooper rushed up to meet it first, swinging his greataxe upward into the creature's undead junk. "Fuck you!" The axe tore up into the wights crotch, easily through the pelvic bone, up into its intestinal area.

It didn't seem fazed as it wrapped its dead hands around Cooper's neck.

Cooper croaked, "Fuuuuuuuuuck!"

Dave waddled up and swung his mace as hard as he could into

the wight's back. "Hiyah!"

The wight let go of Cooper's neck, slid down his chest, and collapsed into a pile of gore at his feet.

Cooper massaged his neck. "Hiyah? What the fuck was that? Toddler karate?"

"Screw you, Cooper. I just saved your ass. The least you could do is show a little —"

"Hey guys?" said Julian. "Where's the Grand Wizard?"

Tim looked back at the altar. Both the Grand Wizard and Mr. Whiskers had disappeared. He scanned the surrounding area. Nothing but illusionary fire as far as he could see. The fire was transparent, but not completely so. At a distance, it had the same effect as a light fog, and Tim noticed that he couldn't see the edge of the pit. What he could see, however, were wights stepping out of the fire-fog from every direction.

"He probably turned invisible," said Tim. He waved his dagger in wide arcs all around him, but sliced nothing but air. Julian, Cooper, and Dave waved their quarterstaff, axe, and mace around likewise, like blind murderers. Their efforts revealed nothing while a dozen wights closed in.

"We'll give you the shield," Tim called out. "Keep the wights back and we'll work something out."

"No," said Julian. "I have a spell for this."

"If you summon another goddamn horse, I'll —"

"Glitterdust!" Julian threw his hands in the air like a birthday party magician.

The air around them was suddenly thick with sparkling glitter. Tim could feel it in his ears and nose. It stung his eyes, nearly to the point that he couldn't —

"What the fuck?" said Cooper. "I can't see anything!"

Tim blinked until he could see Cooper stumbling around, covered from head to toe in glitter, like a drunk Vegas hooker. "Well don't worry. You look fucking fabulous."

"I forgot about that part of the spell," said Julian, who was tapping the ground in front of him with the bottom of his quarterstaff. "Can anyone see? Where's the Grand Wizard?"

Tim looked around for a human-shaped mass of sparkles, but only saw Dave kneeling next to the altar. "He's not here. He's fucking gone."

"That's impossible," said Julian. "There's nowhere he could have —"

"Look at this!" said Dave, still seemingly mesmerized by the altar. "The stone slab on this side of the altar isn't catching any glitter."

Tim cocked his crossbow and peered through the glitter storm for wights. "What are we doing now? Reinforcing gay stereotypes? Who gives a shit about the interior décor of a goddamn garbage pit? If you haven't noticed, we're outnumbered at least three to one, and two of us are fucking blind."

"I don't think it's real," said Dave. He pushed on the wall, and his leopard-furred forearm disappeared into the stone. "It's a secret door!"

No time to think. Tim would take what he could get. He grabbed Julian by the arm and led him to the altar. "Come this way, Cooper! Follow my voice."

As soon as Dave's last boot disappeared into the stone, Tim guided Juilan's head in, then went back for Cooper.

Cooper banged his head twice on the top of the altar, but managed to duck under the lip on his third try.

Tim didn't like the idea of following Cooper's ass so closely with his own face, but he liked the idea of being mauled by a horde of sparkling wights even less. He slipped into the secret passage and breathed a sigh of relief when the wights didn't follow.

A wooden stairwell led down to an earthen tunnel, supported by rough wooden beams, like an old mine tunnel. At the bottom of the stairs, a glittery Cooper shimmered in the faint glow of a small Light stone hanging from the ceiling by a short length of twine.

"Are you okay?"

Cooper groaned. "I've been better."

"Where's everyone else?"

"How the fuck should I know? I'm blind."

"Keep your voice down. I'm going to go ahead. Follow along at a distance." Tim followed the tunnel, keeping as quiet as he could. If Dave and Julian weren't making any noise there might be a reason for that. Tim briefly considered that the reason could be that they were already dead, but that wasn't a useful line of reasoning.

It didn't take long for him to reach the end of the Light stone's radiance, and once again he found himself groping around in the dark.

With one hand sliding along the tunnel wall, and the other stabbing the air in front of him with his dagger, Tim continued along until he saw a speck of light far off in the distance.

With a goal in sight, he quickened his pace, stopping only once, when his arms got tired, to switch guiding and stabbing hands.

When he finally made it to where the light at the other end of the tunnel was visible, he saw Julian standing at the bottom of a rusty iron ladder. His serape sparkled like a sequined ball gown. He was gazing vaguely in Tim's direction, but obviously still blind.

At the top of the ladder, Dave was poking his head through a hatch, the wooden cover of which was resting atop his helmet.

"Psst," said Tim.

Julian looked suddenly alert, looking more specifically in Tim's direction, but way over his head. He pressed his finger firmly over his lips, then beckoned Tim over. He waited a few seconds, then whispered. "We're under Mung's office. He's in there chatting with the Grand Wizard."

Tim nodded. "I knew it. Those two assholes are in cahoots."

"Slow down. We don't even know that there's a conspiracy here. Dave's 'luring PCs to their deaths' theory sounded a little far-fetched to me."

"Maybe it's not that," said Tim. "Maybe those two guys are acting on their own, looting the bodies of fallen mercenaries and selling their shit, you know?"

"No, I don't know. There's absolutely no evidence to support that."

"Did you see any wights carrying weapons?"

"No."

"Did you see any weapons lying around on the ground?"

"No, but that doesn't mean —"

Tim cleared his throat. "I rest my case."

Julian frowned. "Did it ever occur to you that you and Dave are merely projecting your own callous disregard for others onto innocent people?"

Tim balled up his little fists. "We should have killed the wizard while we had the chance."

"Of course, now that option's off the table," said Julian. "I mean, seeing as how we don't know how far up this conspiracy goes."

Tim scratched behind his ear. "Hmm... That's true. We don't want to get mixed up in..." A realization dawned on him. "Goddammit, Julian. You and your fucking Diplomacy skill."

The sides of Julian's sparkly mouth twitched upward slightly. "I assure you, I have no idea what you're talking about."

"I've got a better idea anyway. We'll hide out here in the tunnel until morning when we can use the shield, then go back out into the garbage pit, climb out over a wall, and sell this thing for a fuckton of money."

Julian nodded. "We're taking away their white power and making some coin on the side. I think I can live with —"

WRAAAAWROOOOOW

"FUCK!" cried Dave as he fell off the ladder and landed hard on his back. Four deep parallel cuts oozed blood and glitter from his left cheek. With some effort, he placed a finger on his uninjured cheek and croaked out his incantation. "I... heal... me."

"What'd I miss?" asked Cooper, who had finally caught up to

them.

"Mr. Whiskers just kicked Dave's ass again," said Tim.

Cooper snorted. "Awesome."

The hatch opened. "Who's down there?" asked Mung.

Tim frowned. "Also, we're fucked."

To Tim's surprise, the hatch closed again.

Julian pulled back his serape, which had protected Ravenus from the worst of the Glitterdust spell. "Fly back out the way we came in," he whispered. "There's a fake stone or something."

"But sir, I can't leave you to —"

"If we get arrested, I'm going to need you on the outside."

Ravenus hung his head. "Very well, sir." He flew off down the tunnel and vanished into the darkness.

The hatch opened again. "Come on," said Mung. "Get up here right now, and no harm will come to you."

Tim would have felt better if he hadn't brought up harm in the first place. "How do we know we can trust —"

A sound like a phone book being slowly ripped in half, accompanied by a rapidly expanding cloud of sparkles erupted from behind Cooper.

"Fuck it. We're coming up." Tim started up the ladder. When he surfaced at ground level, he found that the hatch opened up under Mung's desk.

"What happened to you?" asked Mung. "Were you involved in some kind of pixie orgy?"

"Sure," said Tim. He didn't want to put up with any bullshit any longer than he had to. "Listen, let's cut to the —" He noticed that Mr. Whiskers and the Grand Wizard weren't there. The room was completely empty but for Mung's desk, and the half-full burlap sack sitting on top of it. "Are you here alone?"

Mung shrugged. "Typical government understaffing. Why pay three men when you can pay one man to do three men's jobs? You know how it is."

"Bullshit!" said Dave, huffing and puffing as he climbed out of the hatch. "I heard you talking to —"

Tim pressed his heel down firmly on Dave's sausage fingers.

"Yaaaaaaah!" cried Dave.

Tim eased up on Dave's fingers. "My friend here thought he heard more than one voice coming from up here."

Mung frowned. "I'm auditioning for a play. I was practicing my lines."

"You see, Dave? He was practicing his lines." Mung wouldn't have told such a bald-faced lie unless he was really dumb, he thought they were really dumb, or he was laying down some heavy subtext that they were supposed to pick up on. Tim suspected a little from column B and a little from column C.

The subtext in this case: Don't start no shit, won't be no shit. If they could make it through the front door without making mention of the Grand Wizard or the little racket he and Mung were running, they would be allowed to live.

"Right!" said Dave, nodding vigorously. "Practicing his lines." He looked at Mung. "Well done, sir. You sure had me convinced."

"Are you guys insane?" Julian was crawling out of the hatch, blinking rapidly. His vision must have been returning. "What about your face, Dave? Mr. Whiskers scratched the shit out of you."

"My face is fine, Julian!" Dave licked his palm and rubbed the dry, glittery blood off his cheek. "See?"

"Oh... um... okay." Julian didn't get the subtext as quickly as Dave, but at least he recognized that he should shut the hell up.

Cooper came out of the hatch like he was riding a volcanic eruption and banged his head on the bottom of the desk. "Ow! Goddammit!"

The bag atop the desk spilled over. Wight heads rolled out. One of the heads was covered in shit and missing its eyeballs.

"Those are our heads!" said Tim.

"I'm afraid not," said Mung. "Those heads were turned in by the two gentlemen who arrived with you."

"Those thieving, lowlife sons of —"

Julian nudged him with the shield. "It's okay. Let's let the man get back to his theater practice."

Tim nodded. "Right. Thanks for everything. Sorry we didn't kill any wights. You win some, you lose some."

"Not so fast," said Mung. "I see you've got a new shield there, elf."

Julian shrugged. "It's a piece of junk. I found it in one of the scrap piles. I thought I might paint a picture on it or something. You know." He gave Mung a wide friendly grin, which Tim thought to be a bit much.

"This wasn't a treasure hunt. That's city property."

Julian looked at Tim. Everyone in the room knew what that goddamn shield was. Mung was spouting that city property bullshit to keep within the subtext. Tim nodded for Julian to hand it over. What a fucking waste of a day.

A noise came from the other side of the door that led out to the trash dump. It was something like a muffled scream or howl, followed by a thud. Tim pretended not to hear it.

"What the fuck was that?" asked Cooper.

"Nothing," said Mung. He started herding them to the front door with his wide half-orc arms. "Thank you for coming. Feel free to come back anytime." He slammed the door shut behind them.

"What a fucking asshole," said Tim.

Julian smiled down at him. "Cheer up. I'll buy you a drink."

"What the fuck are you so giddy about all of a sudden?"

Julian pursed his lips. "That's a good question. I don't actually know."

Tim started walking toward Cardinia's West Gate. "It's your Empathic Link to that stupid bird, isn't it? He's probably off somewhere fucking a goose or something."

Julian called out toward the sky. "Ravenus?"

"Right here, sir!" Ravenus's voice was equally chipper and annoying. He flapped down and landed on top of Julian's quarterstaff.

"What are you in such a good mood about. Just happy to see

us alive?"

"Well there is that of course, sir. But there's more."

Julian nodded. "Go on."

"That man in the black and red robes, the one with the cat."

"The Grand Wizard, yes?"

"That's the one, sir. He was in that safety cage, surrounded by wights who looked like they had personal grievances with him."

"They must remember who controlled them," said Dave.

"Well good for him," said Julian. "I hope he's learned a lesson."

"Oh he has indeed, sir," said Ravenus. "You see, I pulled up the latch and opened the gate."

The giddiness of Julian's facial expression vanished like a slaughtered magical horse. "Oh my god. We need to get out of here right now."

"Maybe we should hang out in the woods for a while," suggested Dave. "In case they put out an APB for four glittery idiots and a bird."

Tim was in dire need of a drink, but couldn't argue Dave's reasoning.

While they waited in the forest for the last remnants of the Glitterdust spell to wear off, Tim spotted an adorable, wide-eyed nocturnal monkey climbing up the trunk of a nearby tree. One of those kinds that looked perpetually surprised. Beautiful creature. He aimed his crossbow and pulled the trigger.

With naught but a tiny chirp, the monkey fell out of the tree and hit the ground, dead as a post.

Tim picked up the monkey carcass by the bolt sticking out of its neck and held it up toward the branch Ravenus was perched in. He cleared his throat for a British accent. "Cheers, bloke. Jolly good work today."

The End

Probing The Annis

ROBERT BEVAN

PROBING THE ANNIS

(Original Publication Date: August 16, 2016)

"How big is this forest?" asked Julian. "How have we not randomly stumbled upon a road in three days?"

Tim sighed. "We would have been home a long time ago if it wasn't for Dave's shortcut."

"You were the one who wanted to take a shortcut," said Dave. "I told you I didn't have any ranks in the Survival skill."

"It's a Wisdom based skill. You're supposed to have this incredible fucking Wisdom score."

"And I said it would be wiser to stay on the goddamn road!"

"Everyone calm down," said Cooper, not usually the voice of reason among the four of them. "So Dave fucked up. It's not the end of the world."

Dave shook his meaty dwarven fist at Cooper. "I didn't fuck up! I said we should —"

"Everybody shut up!" said Julian. He was suddenly overcome with panic. As there was nothing particularly panic-worthy in his immediate surroundings, he assumed the feeling must be coming from his familiar. He gestured for everyone to crouch down and stay quiet. He whispered, "I think something, or someone, just scared the shit out of Ravenus."

"How hard is that?" asked Dave. "He's just a bird."

Cooper snorted. "About as hard as I got looking at your mom's Pornhub videos."

"Fuck you, Cooper."

"Dude, I was agreeing with you. I didn't get hard at all. Hell, I was afraid I'd never get hard again after that shit with the donkey."

Tim threw a pine cone at Cooper's face. "Knock it off. You're being even more of an asshole than usual."

"I'm fucking hungry, man," said Cooper. "Ragging on Dave's mom is the only sustenance I've got."

"Ow!" said Dave, his head jerking forward as Ravenus bounced off the top of it and landed on the ground in the middle of the group. He looked at Cooper. "Have you ever tried raven?"

"Apologies," said Ravenus, flipping himself over and getting up on his large black feet. He shook the dirt off his back feathers, then looked up at Julian. "I saw something in the forest, sir."

Julian's heart was beating hard. "What was it?"

"Two large women."

Tim and Dave frowned in confusion at each other.

"Will you please calm down?" said Julian. "You're going to make my heart explode. I don't think two large women warrants this kind of response."

"That's what the bird is so freaked out over?" said Cooper, the only one of them who couldn't understand Ravenus's speech. "He'd shit himself if he ever set foot in a Walmart."

A grim thought occurred to Julian. "What if we've stumbled upon some kind of special Mordred fantasy zone?"

"Are you fucking serious?" asked Tim. "This whole goddamn world is a Mordred fantasy zone. How are you only now coming to terms with this?"

"That's not the kind of fantasy I was talking about." Julian paused to collect his thoughts. "He created all these game characters, right? And he could possess the body of anyone he created? Maybe he also made himself a variety of pleasure stops out in remote places where he didn't think anyone would ever travel. He inhabits the body of some burly woodsman and pays his women a visit from time to time between gaming sessions."

Tim, Dave, and Cooper gazed thoughtfully into the distance, no doubt imagining that was exactly what they would do if given similar power.

Tim was the first to snap out of his imaginary harem trance. "You think Mordred's a chubby chaser?"

Julian shrugged. "He's a big guy. Maybe he likes a —" He shook his head clear of jiggly naked women. "Who cares what his tastes in women are?"

Tim, Dave, and Cooper shared an exchange of glances, then slowly raised their hands. Even Ravenus raised a wing.

Julian looked down at Ravenus. "Why?"

"Ravens are curious by nature, sir."

"They might have food," said Dave. "How else do they stay so fat out here in the woods?"

"And booze," added Tim enthusiastically.

Cooper stuck a finger two knuckles deep into his ear, perhaps trying to scratch his brain. "He might have them programmed to be perpetually horny."

Julian frowned at Cooper. "You really want to sink to Mordred's level?"

Cooper looked down at his crotch. "Dude, give me some credit. I can probably sink an inch or two deeper."

"Jesus Christ," said Tim. "Just stab me in the fucking ears. I don't need the image of your scabby dick sinking into anyone in my head."

"You know, guys," said Julian. "That fantasy zone theory was just that. A theory. I'm probably way off base with it." He looked down at Ravenus. "What were the two ladies doing when you saw them? Were they kissing each other? Or licking? Or spanking? Or putting their fingers in each others' —"

"Fucking enough already!" said Tim. "Let the bird talk."

Ravenus looked back and forth between Tim and Julian a couple of times, then answered. "None of that, sir, as far as I could tell. One of them was tied to a tree, and the other was lighting a fire under a large iron tub."

Tim grinned at Julian. "Sounds like your theory just got confirmed."

"What?" said Julian. "How does that sound even remotely like a sexual fantasy?"

"Aw shit." Cooper rubbed his hands together. "What did the bird say? Midgets? Ping pong balls? Jell-O?"

"He saw something that sounded a lot more like cannibalism than porn, at least to a sane person."

Dave cleared his throat. "Then maybe we should check it out just the same. We can't very well leave an innocent large woman to die, can we?"

That was just like Dave, masking his true motivations to make himself look like a hero.

"Fine," said Julian. "Let's go sneak a peek at the big girls, and then get back to finding our way back to Cardinia."

Ravenus dutifully led them to the clearing in the woods, but Julian could still feel the unease in his familiar's mind. "It's just beyond those trees, sir."

"Stop," said Tim as Cooper started forward. "Let's be smart about this." He looked up at the branches of a nearby tree. "We'll scout the scene before rushing in there. Cooper, give me a boost up to that first branch, would you?"

Cooper grabbed Tim by the torso and tossed him onto the branch, where he landed as sure-footedly as a bird.

Julian pulled a coil of rope out of his bag. "Tie this to the branch. I'm coming up."

"Why?"

"I want to see what Ravenus is so freaked out about."

Tim rolled his eyes. "Fine."

Julian had a feeling he would comply. It was an excuse to have a drink while Julian climbed up the rope. Sure enough, as soon as Tim's knot was secure, his flask was out before Julian started climbing.

The branches above the first branch were closer to each other than the first branch was to the ground, allowing both Tim and Julian to ascend with ease.

Tim was smaller than Julian, had a higher Dexterity score, and a bonus to his Jump skill, which allowed him to climb the tree much faster than Julian. But he stopped suddenly. The look on his face matched the dread Julian felt through his Empathic Link with Ravenus.

"Holy shit!" Tim spoke softly enough such that Julian wouldn't have heard him without his elf ears. There was something more nefarious afoot than two big girls making out in a tub of Rocky Road.

The first thing Julian saw as he reached Tim was a very tall woman, at least eight feet, standing with her back against a thick pine tree, her hands tied to the trunk above her head. She was obviously a giantess of some sort. Not particularly heavyset, by giant standards. Ravenus must have been referring to her height. Her face appeared pained and distressed as she struggled to free her bound wrists.

Two women, rather than one, were manning the cauldron Ravenus had mentioned. They were hunch-backed, but looked to be just as tall as their captive if they were able to stand upright. With their misshapen backs to him, they didn't look all that frightening. Maybe they weren't in the running for Homecoming Queen, but —

Julian gasped.

When they turned, he could see their faces and hands. They had deep blue wrinkly skin, long pointed noses, and fingernails like blackened dagger blades.

"Ravenus!" Julian whispered.

"Right here, sir." He was perched on the branch just above Julian's head.

"You said there were only two."

"One of them must have been inside at the time."

Julian looked at the clearing again. There was some kind of artificial earthen mound, covered in hanging vines. He supposed that it might serve as the old crones' home.

"Why didn't you think to mention that one of the women you saw had wrinkly blue skin?"

"If you don't mind me saying so, sir, the subject of skin color has more than once set the four of you off in heated and confusing discussion."

Julian nodded. "It can be a bit of a hot-button topic where we come from. Still, you might have mentioned how horrific-looking she is."

"I didn't want to be rude, sir. And I don't feel I have an adequate appreciation for your elven standards of beauty."

"I say we get the fuck out of here," said Tim.

Julian glared at him. "We can't just leave that poor giant woman there to be murdered and eaten."

Tim looked down at Dave and Cooper. "We'll put it to a vote."

Julian felt the struggle between doing what was right and his own cowardice fighting for dominance inside him. He knew in his heart that agreeing to a vote would just be justifying cowardice. Dave would side with Tim. The best he could hope for was a stalemate, unless they let Ravenus break the tie. Doubtful.

"Agreed."

They climbed down the tree and described what they'd seen to Dave and Cooper.

"It sounds like a trap," said Dave.

"What?" Julian had to hand it to Dave. He always came up with creative excuses to tuck tail and run.

"You said all three of them are approximately the same height. That doesn't seem a little odd to you?"

"Not really," said Julian. "Most of us were within a couple of inches of each other before we turned into..." he waved his hands between the four of them. "... all this shit."

"And what are the odds that we arrived here just in time to rescue this woman from being eaten? How long does it take to ready a cauldron?"

"Depending on what they're cooking, it could take quite a while."

"So let's say it takes hours," said Dave. "That amounts to nothing on a long enough timeline. Of all the times we could have stumbled onto this clearing, how small a window is it to arrive here between the time she was captured and the time she was killed? That doesn't seem just a little bit convenient to you?"

Tim shrugged and took a swig from his flask. "That could just be game mechanics."

Dave glared at Tim, obviously not appreciating the crack in their solidarity. "What are you talking about?"

"We might need to activate a trigger to initiate certain events. Remember the RPGs on the NES?"

"NES?" asked Julian, proud of himself for at least remembering what RPG meant.

Tim sighed. "Nintendo Entertainment System. Jesus, didn't you have a childhood? What the fuck did you do all summer?"

"I went to the pool, rode my bike, played outside with my friends."

Cooper put his hand on Julian's shoulder. "You poor, poor bastard."

Julian looked at Tim. "You were saying something about a trigger?"

"Let's say you walk into a village, and there's a woman there with a sick baby. You move your character over to face the mother and press the A button. She tells you her whole spiel about her kid, and you keep hitting the A button because who gives a fuck, you just want to know what she needs. You with me so far?"

Dave and Cooper nodded.

"I guess," Julian lied.

"Depending on the choices you've made in the game, or how shitty you are at playing it, there could be discrepancies of months of game-time for when you even reach that village. Every time you sleep at an inn to replenish your Hit Points, that's another whole day gone by."

This didn't match Julian's experience with RPGs. "You could replenish all your Hit Points by spending one night in an inn?"

"It was a simpler time. May I continue?"

"Sure."

"Now let's say I'm playing the game at my house, and Dave's playing the game at his house. It could take Dave six months to find the same mother and child that I find within a couple of weeks, because he sucks."

"Fuck you," said Dave. "I preferred platform games."

Tim had likely purposefully antagonized Dave just so that he could pause for a drink. When he was done, he continued. "In real life, that fucking kid would have been a worm-ridden corpse by the time Dave showed up. But in the game, he's just as sick when Dave shows up as he is when I show up. It's a side quest which isn't triggered until you actually talk to the mother. She sends you out to go collect some bullshit herbs. You bring them back, the kid gets better, and the mother is so grateful that she gives you the Heartstone Gem that you need to continue along in the game."

Julian tugged on his long ears. "So... How does that apply to our current situation?"

"Who knows? Maybe not at all. I don't know all the technical details of how this game works. But if it works anything like the example I just explained, those two old women might stir that pot forever unless we step in to rescue their captive." Tim took a swig from his flask.

Julian frowned at Tim's flask. "How do you still have anything left in there after three whole days?"

Tim shrugged. "I'm small."

Dave rubbed his hands together. "If Tim's theory is correct, no one gets eaten or murdered if we just mind our own business and go on our way."

"It's just a theory," said Julian. "And not a very convincing one. You were all convinced about my fantasy zone theory a few minutes ago."

"I'm still not unconvinced," said Cooper. "How gross did those old blue bitches look?"

It was time to break out the Diplomacy. Julian folded his arms. "Are you guys really going to tell me you're so afraid of a couple of old ladies that you'd let an innocent person die rather than face them?"

Tim, Dave, and Cooper glanced knowingly at each other, and Julian felt even more like an outsider.

"You saw those fingernails," said Tim. "How frail do you think those two old ladies are to be able to get so old living in this monster-infested forest? Even if we were to try some sort of ill-advised rescue mission, it wouldn't involve marching in there and facing them head on. We'd have to slip in unnoticed somehow."

"You're sneaky," said Julian.

"Yeah, and I'm three fucking feet tall. That woman's wrists are tied ten feet up on that tree. How the hell am I supposed to get up there unnoticed? Climb up her tits?"

"I'm sure she'd be understanding."

"Why don't you send Ravenus?"

Julian shook his head. "It's too dangerous to send him in there alone."

Tim stoppered his flask. "You were ready to send me in there alone."

"Ravenus is a bird," said Dave. "He wouldn't look out of place landing on a branch."

"As long as he keeps his fucking mouth shut," said Cooper.

Julian had managed to talk himself into a corner with his own Diplomacy skill. The others were right. Objectively speaking, sending Ravenus in there alone posed the least amount of risk to everyone. It was either that, or let the giant woman die.

"We'll have to distract the old ladies."

Dave frowned. He'd clearly been hoping Julian would choose to ditch the giant. "Do you have any ideas?"

"We could set a forest fire," suggested Cooper.

Julian licked his lips. "I've got something a little more subtle in mind."

Tim shook his head. "You're going to summon a goddamn horse, aren't you?"

"No," said Julian. "I mean, I'm not just going to summon a

horse." He pointed at the ground. "Horse."

A brown horse appeared next to him, saddled and ready to ride.

Julian removed his right boot. "I'm going to create a story." He fixed the boot into the right stirrup so that the top of it dragged along beside the horse.

"Horse and Boot," said Cooper. "A timeless classic."

"Very funny."

"I'm kinda with Cooper here," said Tim. "I don't really get what this story is supposed to be."

"That's exactly the point. I let the horse wander into the clearing, drawing the old ladies' attention to it. While they're pondering what events may have led up to this, Ravenus should have plenty of time to claw through the ropes binding the giant woman."

"I'd say that's the dumbest idea I've ever heard," said Dave. "But you've had dumber, and they've worked."

Julian looked at Ravenus. "You'll be taking most of the risk. What do you think about my idea?"

"Positively brilliant, sir. I'm honored to be a part of it."

Tim took hold of the rope still hanging from the tree branch. "I, for one, would like to see this brilliant plan play out." He started climbing.

"I'm with you," said Cooper. He was tall enough to jump up and grab the first branch without the rope.

Julian struggled up after him, and Dave needed to be pulled up. But soon enough, they were all in the tree, Cooper and Dave cringing at their first view of the wrinkled blue women.

Once Ravenus had taken his place on a branch of a tree near the edge of the clearing, Julian whispered down to his magical horse. "Go!"

The horse walked casually toward the clearing. Julian lost sight of it through the trees for a full minute. Thinking it had wandered off course, he felt a sense of relief at the thought of having to call off the mission. They'd have to think of another plan. Hopefully one that didn't involve Ravenus going in alone.

His anxiety was doubled when the horse suddenly reappeared exactly where it was supposed to be, much too close to the clearing for him to do anything about it.

As he'd expected, the two crones looked curiously at it when it came into the clearing. They hobbled slowly toward it with the support of the same sticks they'd been using to stir the cauldron.

Julian nodded at Ravenus, who then made his move.

The giant woman grinned as Ravenus landed on the branch her arms were tied to. Just as he started clawing his way through, she grabbed him.

SQUAAWWWK!

"Ravenus!" Julian cried.

An equine scream rang out. When Julian looked at his horse, the old women had sunk their nails into its flesh. They both grinned in Julian's direction as the horse vanished into a whiff of magical energy.

"Shit!" said Dave as he fell backward off his branch.

Julian was no less unnerved by their horrible faces, but he'd been hugging the trunk. He looked for Ravenus again. The giant woman held his wings against his body. Her hands were turning blue and growing long black fingernails. Her back hunched over as her hair darkened and her skin turned wrinkly and blue.

Tim and Cooper were on the ground by the time the transformation was complete. Julian looked down at them.

"It was a trap. The giant is one of them."

"I called that shit," said Dave. His face was bruised and bleeding. He'd apparently hit a few branches on the way down. Julian was sure he should feel good about that, but Ravenus's confinement and terror were overriding any of his own feelings.

When Julian looked again, the old woman holding Ravenus squatted on the ground. A cloud of green vapor began seeping out from under her ragged, filthy skirt. It soon obscured both of them from view, and Julian felt a new sensation.

His stomach turned as he breathed short shallow breaths.

There was no point in trying to contain it. Lunch was coming back up. Still clinging to the trunk of the tree, he doubled over and vomit spewed from his throat like an exploding can of equal parts peas and botulism.

"Goddammit," said Dave, just after the splat.

Julian actually felt a little bit of relief fighting through Ravenus's terror. He hoped that his puking on Dave was giving his familiar at least a little comfort.

Getting down from the tree proved challenging, as Julian's stomach felt like it was spinning in a random orbit around his body. When he made it to the lowest branch, he let himself drop to the ground. It might have hurt if his nausea hadn't been distracting him. He picked himself up and began stumbling toward the green smoke, now seeping out of the clearing between the trees.

"Julian!" said Tim. "Stop, wait!"

Julian paused only long enough to throw up one more time and give the finger to whomever wasn't coming with him.

Once he was engulfed in the green fog, he was completely blind and even more nauseous. He felt his way from tree to tree, his eyes stinging, and his insides threatening to abandon his body entirely. It was as though he were trapped inside a bag of old rotten eggs.

He choked and gagged as he made his way farther into the clearing. He wanted to call out Ravenus's name, but he was having enough trouble simply breathing. A particularly heavy fit of coughing sent blood rushing to his head until the green fog faded into black.

Julian didn't think he could have been out for more than a second, but when he came to, the air was clear. He could breathe and see. But he couldn't move.

If Tim, Cooper, and Dave were any indication as to why he couldn't move, it was because he, like them, was bound from the shoulders down in a tight coil of rope. They were sitting up against a stack of firewood. Julian was facing them. From the ache in his back, he guessed he was leaning against the stump of the tree which had provided said firewood.

Julian looked down to confirm that he was, indeed, completely swaddled in rope. The four of them sat helpless in hemp cocoons. Even Ravenus hung upside down from a branch, coiled down to his neck in twine. To make matters worse, Julian could feel the rope against the skin of his right foot. His boot was still missing.

"You followed me," said Julian. "Whatever happens, I want you to know I appreciate that."

Dave frowned through his vomit-crusted beard. "That really makes it worth it."

"Where are the old ladies?"

Cooper looked past Julian. "They all went into the side of the mound. They've been in there a while."

Tim was the only one of them who had a high enough Dexterity score, and enough ranks in the Escape Artist and Rope Use skills to have a prayer of getting out of his bindings, but he was also the only one who was still asleep.

"Dave," said Julian. "See if you can wake up Tim."

Dave, being a dwarf, wasn't especially lithe to begin with. With his body coiled in rope as tightly as it was, it was a wonder he could manage to squirm at all. But with all their lives on the line, he shifted his broad torso around until he was facing Tim. "Tim," he whispered. "Tim! Tim!"

Tim's only response was a chunky tendril of drool.

"Tim!" Dave repeated, leaning over to nudge him with his head. "Tim!" He leaned too far, falling over and planting his face in Tim's lap.

Cooper snorted. Dave and Tim looked like a fat maggot going down on a skinny maggot.

Undignified as they may have looked, Dave had at least succeeded in waking Tim up.

"Dave?" said Tim. His eyes widened like Dave's head was made out of bees. "Dave! What the fuck, man?" And with that, all hope of a quiet escape was lost.

To Tim's credit, he had just woken up, and Dave's peculiar and untimely decision to grunt and thrust his face against Tim's crotch only added to the ambiguity of the situation.

Dave discontinued his head thrusting and sighed. "Sorry, man. My nose itched like a sonofabitch."

"I see our guests have awakened," croaked a haggish voice from behind Julian. Tim and Cooper looked scared shitless. Dave glanced up, then quickly shoved his face back into Tim's crotch.

Julian fell backward trying to get a better view. Three giant blue women stared down at him. Up close, they were even bigger and more horrible. Their faces were a mass of sagging, wart-riddled wrinkles. Their filthy black hair was so infested with roaches and centipedes that it moved like stormy seas atop their heads. They grinned down at Julian and his helpless friends through chipped yellow teeth. But their eyes were worse than anything. Orbs of bulging red capillaries surrounding solid black irises. Maybe not the worst thing. It was a toss-up between the eyes, the hair, and the skin. All of it was the worst thing.

"Are you hags?" asked Tim.

Julian turned his head to glare at him.

Tim stuck his tongue out at Julian. It was a poor substitute for the middle finger he no-doubt would have offered instead if he could move his arms. "That's what they're called in the Monster Manual."

"Aye," said the woman in the middle. "We are Annis."

Cooper tried to hold his breath, but giggles and snot bubbled out through his nose.

"She said Annis," said Dave. "It's a type of hag."

This conversation was only going to lead to bad places if Julian didn't intervene. He flipped his head over and blurted out the first thing he could think of. "My name's Julian. What's yours?"

"My name is Annie."

Diplomacy was working well so far. In spite of the balance of power weighing heavily in the hags' favor, she was willing to engage in a civil conversation.

"It's a pleasure to meet you, Annie the Annis."

Julian may as well have called her Biggus Dickus for how his friends reacted. He should have expected laughter from Cooper and Tim. For being a decade older than he was, they were about as mature as Tim looked. But Dave was a humorless fun-sponge at the best of times. He turned his head back to Dave and attempted a 'What the fuck is wrong with you?' look with his eyes.

"I'm sorry," said Dave. "We knew a girl in high school who had a... similar nickname."

Julian turned back to the annis. "Listen. Maybe I can't make much of a case for why they don't deserve to die. But Ravenus and I are good people."

"No one need die this day," said Annie. "Death is but one of your options."

"Oh," said Julian. "Options are nice. What's Option B?"

Annie grinned at her two silent companions, then at Julian. "One of you must give me your seed."

All residual chuckles from his friends stopped abruptly.

Julian held on to a flicker of doubtful hope that she might have mistaken them for wandering farmers. "I think we might have, like, half of an apple. You're welcome to whatever seeds you can —"

"The seed of your loins!" said Annie. "I wish to bear a child before I'm too old to do so."

"Surely, you've got plenty of time," Julian lied. Her face looked like Yoda's scrotum.

"Excuse me," said Tim. "Sorry to interrupt. We're really flattered and all. But is there, by any chance, an Option C?" It wasn't a polite question, but considering that Options A and B involved death and arguably worse, Julian supposed there was little point in trying too hard not to offend.

"Excuse us," said Annie. She and her companions stepped away and huddled together. Julian caught pieces of their conversation.

"We can't. We'll lose them all."

"They came for the bird once. They'll come back for it again."

"If the others were smart, they'd knock the elf unconscious and escape."

"I don't think the others are smart."

"What if they're killed by girallons? Then we all have to share one bird."

"We'll give them the eye."

"Hmm..."

That last suggestion seemed to satisfy the three of them, leading Julian to suspect that 'the eye' was more than just a stern look and a warning to not be killed by girallons, whatever the hell they were.

The three hags approached Julian and his friends.

"There is a third option," said Annie.

Tim, Cooper, and Dave exhaled.

"What is it?" asked Julian, more cautious than relieved.

"You must travel deep into the forest and find the Amulet of Mighty Fists. It was worn by a monk whom we have reason to believe perished in this very forest not long ago."

"Awesome!" said Dave. "We'll take Option C."

"Whoa," said Julian. "Hold on just a minute. Let's not rush into anything."

"I assure you I've taken all the time I need to think this through."

"Just shut up for a second." Julian flipped his head toward the hags. "Would it be possible for my friends and I to discuss this amongst ourselves?"

Annie nodded. "Very well." She twitched her long fingernails, and one of her companions produced a dagger from beneath her rags.

"That's my dagger," said Tim, as if petty theft was currently his biggest concern.

The annis with the dagger sliced the rope near Julian's ankles, giving his feet some room to wiggle. She did likewise with Tim, Cooper, and Dave.

They could have hurried the process along by cutting the ropes near their hands as well, but chose not to. It was either some kind of psychological game they were playing at, or they just found it entertaining to watch their captives wiggle, squirm, and roll in the dirt.

Tim was the first one free of his bindings, which accelerated the process as he helped to free up Cooper and the two of them went on to assist Dave and Julian. Ravenus still hung upside down from the tree branch. He was awake, but remained quiet.

Julian knew better than to request his familiar be allowed to join in the conversation. His seed wouldn't be of any use to the annis, and he would be their hostage if Julian and his friends chose Option C.

They huddled on the other side of the tree from where the annis remained.

"What are girallons?" asked Julian.

"They're like gorillas," said Dave. "But with two extra arms."

"That's it?"

"Pretty much."

"That's so stupid. You can't just throw a couple of extra limbs onto an existing animal and call it a monster."

Tim cleared his throat. "Were you going somewhere with this? Why are we talking about girallons?"

"The annis said there were girallons in the woods."

"I didn't hear them say that," said Cooper.

Julian pointed to the pointed tip of his left ear.

Cooper nodded. "Sweet."

Julian looked at Dave. "Are we strong enough to fight them?"

"Who?"

"Jesus Christ, Dave! Pay attention. The girallons."

"You could have been talking about the annis."

"I know we can't fight them. They incapacitated all of us with an old lady fart."

Dave stroked his beard. "I don't know. I don't remember what the Challenge Rating is for a girallon."

"It doesn't matter," said Tim. "Even if we could take down a few of them, there's no telling how long we'd have to wander around in the woods on a wild goose chase for a magical item which may or may not even exist. Option C, in all likelihood, amounts to the same as Option A."

Cooer pulled his finger out of his nose. "I forgot. What was Option A?"

"Death."

"Shit. That's no good."

"The only option still on the table isn't much better," said Tim. "One of us is going to have to probe that annis."

Everyone took a moment to cringe and shudder before Dave asked the obvious question.

"How do we choose who does it?"

"I vote Dave," said Cooper. "His first time should be memorable."

Dave gave him the finger. "Tough shit, Cooper. We can't vote now, because you just tainted the process."

Tim rubbed his chin. "Interesting. How do you figure?"

"By declaring his own vote early, he ensured that both you and Julian would also vote for me. Not because you're an asshole like Cooper, but because you want to save your own asses, and that would guarantee you an automatic majority."

Tim sighed. "Dave killed democracy. Any other ideas?"

The obvious answer was Julian, seeing as how it was his familiar who was keeping them all from just running away. He wondered why no one had brought that fact up.

Cooper was a loyal friend, and was probably still hoping Dave would have to do it. Dave had a high Wisdom score, and was possibly weighing the long-term repercussions of throwing Julian under the bus. But Tim's motivation for keeping quiet was still a mystery. Perhaps it had something to do with why he was squatting down and playing with grass.

Tim stood to his full three-foot height. "We'll draw straws." He cupped his hands together and made the tips of four blades of grass sprout from between his thumb and index finger. He raised his arms and offered Dave the first choice.

Dave licked his lips and wiped his right hand over the leopard fur on his left arm, either to remove sweat or for some new luck ritual. He placed his fingers on one blade of grass, then switched to a different one, keeping his eyes on Tim's. Tim raised his eyebrows and gave him a weak smile. Dave grunted, then pulled one of the blades he hadn't yet touched. Without knowing the length of the straws, it was impossible to tell if Dave was holding the short straw, or one of the long ones.

Next was Julian's turn. He didn't trust Tim any more than Dave did, knowing Tim had a high Intelligence score, a bunch of ranks in the Sleight of Hand skill, and a sense of ethical responsibility as small as his little halfling dick. Julian kept his hands at his side while he chose a blade of grass in his mind. When he'd made his choice, he plucked it out of Tim's hand like a striking cobra.

Dave sighed with relief. His blade and Julian's were approximately the same length.

"Down to you and me, buddy." Tim offered his hands up to Cooper.

Cooper frowned down at Tim's tiny hands, then placed two giant fingers on either side of one of the two remaining grass blades.

Tim's gaze darted back and forth between Cooper's eyes and fingers. He swallowed hard. His relieved sigh when Cooper pulled the blade from his hand confirmed Julian's suspicion that Tim wasn't leaving this contest entirely up to chance.

Cooper's straw was half the length of Julian's and Dave's. Tim pulled the final blade, then wiped his hand on his pants. Julian watched half a grass blade flutter from Tim's hand to the ground. Though it was exactly what he'd expected to see, he told himself it didn't prove anything.

"Tough luck, Coop," said Dave. "Have fun probing the annis."

Cooper sighed. "It's a step up from your mom." He started back toward the tree. "Might as well get this over with."

Julian followed along behind, feeling a mixture of guilt and relief.

"Have you come to a decision?" asked Annie. Her two subordinate hags rubbed their fingernails together in anticipation. They sounded like tarnished silverware.

"It's your lucky day, lady," said Cooper. He pulled down his loincloth and stepped out of it. "So you wanna do this here? Or should we —"

"You can accompany me inside." Annie took Cooper by the arm and led him to the mound, not looking the least bit put off by the sight of his schlong, even though it looked like a Dali painting of a rotting ear of corn.

"I don't know who I feel worse for," said Julian.

Dave nodded grimly, but Tim had just up and disappeared.

The sneaky little jerk was walking out of the mound, sucking back stonepiss from his flask, as Annie and Cooper approached. As soon as he cleared the vines hanging over the entrance and saw Cooper's junk, he spit out what he'd been drinking.

"Jesus Christ, dude! You couldn't wait until you got inside?"

The next couple of minutes seemed like years. How is one supposed to pass the time while one's friend attempts to impregnate a giant blue hag a few yards away?

The other two annis didn't seem uncomfortable at all. They merely watched Dave, Tim, and Julian.

"Salut," said Tim. He took a small swig from his flask. One of the annis winked at him. He took a much larger swig.

Only about a minute of awkward silence followed before an ear-shattering scream sent birds flying out of trees all around the clearing. It was Annie.

"Ow!" said Cooper. "What the fuck is wrong with you, lady? No, don't — Ow, goddammit! Knock that shit off!" He ran out of the mound bleeding a pattern of diamonds from the chest. Four deep cuts from either shoulder, crisscrossing downward to his belly.

Annie came out after him, seething at the entrance, naked as the day she clawed her way out of her mother's wrinkly blue vag. Her breasts hung like a couple of moldy pomegranates in crusty tube socks. The carpet matched the drapes, right down to the bugs and worms.

"How dare you!" cried Annie. "We shall revel in your slow and agonizing deaths!"

"Hold on," said Julian. "Let's everyone just calm down, huh? Whatever happened, I'm sure we can come to some sort of agreement."

"You are in no position to negotiate, elf. You have nothing we want."

"But what about Option C? We could get you that omelet."

"Amulet," said Dave.

"Sorry. I'm just hungry. Amulet. What was it called? The —"

"The Amulet of Mighty Monkey Fisting!" said Cooper.

Annie's face briefly showed more confusion than anger.

Julian frowned. "I'm sure it wasn't that."

"The Amulet of Mighty Fists," said Tim. He glared at Cooper. "Worn by a monk. Not a monkey."

Annie didn't immediately reject the idea, but she was going to need some more convincing. Julian was trying to think of how best to exaggerate their qualifications for the job when the other two annis escorted Annie back into the mound.

"Think of the power!" said one of the other annis. "Think of Lord Wallace. How he disgraced us. The amulet will tip the balance of power. We can paint the walls of his keep with the blood of his sons."

"The amulet is gone," said Annie. "We searched the monk's body and could not find it. What makes you think those four fools will have any better fortune?"

"The elf is versed in the ways of magic. He can spot with ease what is hidden from our old eyes."

Annie re-emerged from the mound. Thankfully, she was once again dressed, and seemed to have calmed down a little.

"Very well, elf. You have one more chance. Fail me again and

all the sniveling in the world won't save your precious bird."

She wasn't bothering with niceties anymore. All they could do was find that amulet.

"Can we have our weapons back?" asked Dave.

"No."

Julian looked down at his feet, one booted, the other bare. He probably shouldn't push his luck, but one more good Diplomacy roll could make a hell of a difference strolling around in the woods.

"Can I at least have my boot?"

"GET OUT OF HERE!" screamed Annie. Even the bugs in her hair burrowed deeper in fear. Julian tried not to stare.

Julian backed away, and Cooper took a step toward his loincloth.

Annie hissed and brandished her fingernails, causing Cooper to stop dead in his tracks. She hobbled quickly to the loincloth, picked it up, tore it to pieces, and threw the pieces into the fire under the cauldron.

Cooper frowned. "That's just mean."

"Let's go," said Tim.

Julian looked up at Ravenus as they passed underneath him. "I'll be back for you."

"Very good, sir. Do try not to be too long."

Just before they exited the clearing, a haggard old voice called from behind them. "Wait."

One of the subordinate annis had followed them. She held up a blue gemstone hanging from a silver chain. "There is danger in the forest. Wear this." Strangely enough, she offered it specifically to Cooper.

"Okay, thanks." Cooper looped the chain over his head. The stone rested high on his chest. It was a gaudy piece of jewelry which looked especially out of place on his bleeding torso.

The annis twitched her fingernails. "Travel north until you reach a creek bed, full of stones and roots where once there ran water. Follow it eastward until you see the Great Elm. Beneath its mossy branches, you should find the remains of the deceased monk. I suggest you begin your search there."

"Awesome," said Tim. "Thanks for the tip." He clapped his hands together. "Well, daylight's a-wastin'." Not the most polite way to disengage conversation, but it got the job done. The hag retreated back to her mound, and Julian, Tim, Dave, and Cooper stepped into the forest.

Once they were a little ways out of the clearing, Tim turned around abruptly and glared up at Cooper. "Do you mind telling me just what the fuck happened back there?"

"I'm in a little bit of pain here," said Cooper. The entire front of his body was sticky with fresh blood, still running from his chest, coating his belly, and dripping from his dong. He pointed at Dave. "Dude, how about shooting me some fucking Hit Points?"

Dave touched Cooper's finger. "I heal thee."

Cooper farted ecstatically as his wounds closed up. "Oh that feels so much better."

"All right," said Tim. "Spill it. What did you do to piss her off like that?"

Cooper shrugged. "Fuck if I know. I stuck my finger up her ass, and she flipped the fuck out."

"What the... Why would you..." Tim was trembling with frustrated rage. "Do you even know how fucking babies are made?"

"I thought that was, like, their thing. You and Dave both told me to probe her anus."

"We said probe the... You know what? Never mind that. How would we even know if that was her thing?"

"Maybe it was in the Monster Manual. I thought it was weird, but you both insisted, so..."

"Have you ever seen anything like an anal fetish in any of the monster descriptions?"

"Hang on," said Dave. "Is that the finger I touched to heal you?"

"Um..."

"Goddammit, Cooper!"

"Shut up," said Julian. "Let's just go and find the amulet. She said to go north, right?"

"Maybe," said Dave. "She was so gross, I was having trouble paying attention."

Tim nodded. "I zoned in and out. North sounds good."

In the distance, some kind of beast let out a terrible howl.

"That came from the north, didn't it?" said Julian.

Dave sighed. "Of course it did."

They trudged along at the speed of Dave, which was just fine with Julian. His right foot was aching from all the rocks, twigs, and roots he was stepping on. Removing his other boot might have distributed the pain more evenly, or it might have just made his left foot as sore as his right one. He kept his one boot on for now.

Half an hour later, they came to a dry creek bed, which prompted a memory of the annis having mentioned one.

"Okay," said Julian. "This is a good place to take a rest." Before anyone could object, he sat down on a big rock and started rubbing his foot.

No one seemed remotely interested in objecting. Tim sat against a tree and had a drink. Dave picked bits of dried vomit out of his beard. Cooper scooped up a fistful of dirt and scrubbed the dried blood off his chest, belly, and junk.

As he massaged the soreness out of his foot, Julian looked down the creek bed to see if he could get some idea of the terrain. A deer nibbled on some leaves about fifty yards ahead. Just a deer. No wings or tentacles or extra legs or anything. Just a simple white-tailed deer. There was something reassuring in that. It put Julian's mind at ease.

"Guys," he whispered. "Take a look at that."

There was an air of peace and awe as everyone stared at the deer, soon broken as a blur of white crashed out of the branches above.

Julian, Tim, Cooper, and Dave ducked into the creek bed like they'd been sucked into it by a force more powerful than gravity.

"What the hell was that?" asked Julian.

"A girallon," said Dave.

Julian peeked over the bank.

The giant, four-armed, albino gorilla grabbed the deer by the antlers and savagely slammed its body against the trunk of the tree it had just been nibbling until the antlers snapped off. It paused for a second, staring first at the very dead deer on the ground, then at the antlers in its hands. Apparently not a fan of shoddy animal craftsmanship, the girallon screamed and pounced onto its prey, pounding the shit out of it with all four of its fists.

"Goddamn," whispered Cooper, who had joined Julian at the bank. He squeaked out a soft fart. "Sorry."

Julian couldn't blame him. He was relieved that he was able to remain in control of his own bodily functions while witnessing such a brutal attack on another living thing. And as Cooper's farts went, it was a pretty tame one.

The girallon bit into the side of the deer and tore away a massive amount of flesh and fur, which it spat on the ground so that it could continue tearing the rest of the corpse apart. After about ten more seconds of ripping apart the deer, the girallon froze. A second later, it turned around, vaguely facing Julian's direction. It twitched its nostrils, pivoting its head back and forth more and more narrowly, gradually homing in on Julian's exact location.

It took a step toward them, still sniffing the air. Julian and Cooper ducked down.

"It's coming this way," said Julian. "I think it picked up Cooper's fart."

Cooper stuck out his bottom lip. "I was nervous."

"I know. I was too. Maybe it'll just go away if we're really quiet and don't fart anymore."

Dave shook his head. "I don't think that's a good idea. We have to pass through its territory. Shouldn't we confront it while we know where it is instead of waiting for it to jump out of a tree and catch us off guard?"

"Confront it with what?" said Julian. "We don't have any weapons. Did you not see that thing?"

"What happened to 'That's so stupid. It's just a gorilla with two extra arms'?"

Julian couldn't believe Dave wanted to use what little time they had to gloat, but he felt he had to defend his statement. "Just because it's big and scary doesn't mean it's any less ridiculous a concept. Yeah, it could probably kill us all in under a minute, but that doesn't change the fact that it looks like a short guy waving his arms behind a tall guy."

"Brilliant," said Tim. He looked at Cooper, then at Dave.

Dave shook his head. "No fucking way."

Tim took a swig from his flask. "It's the only way, Dave." He offered the flask to Dave, who accepted it and gulped down most of what was left.

Cooper scratched under his armpit. "So... What's going on?"

A minute later, Dave was silently sobbing with the side of his face pressed into the small of Cooper's back.

"Stop crying, Dave," said Cooper. "This isn't any more fun for me than it is for you. And keep still. Your beard is tickling my ass."

Julian and Tim scrambled under some exposed tree roots so that they could watch without being seen.

Together, with tiny strides for Cooper and long strides for Dave, they walked out of the creek bed.

The girallon stopped sniffing the air when it spotted something not entirely unlike itself. It barked what Julian hoped was a friendly greeting. It didn't sound all that friendly. Dave waved his left hand.

They were all going to die.

Cooper barked back an impressive imitation of the girallon's initiating call.

The girallon approached warily on its legs and lower arms. Cooper and Dave stood their ground, probably because there was no way they'd be able to imitate the girallon's walk.

When it got within five feet of them, the girallon attempted to look over Cooper's left shoulder. Cooper turned left, and Dave sidestepped behind him. When it tried to look right, they repeated the move in the opposite direction.

"I think this is a good sign," said Julian. "It suspects something's amiss, but it's too dumb to know exactly what's wrong. It's not perfect, but under the circumstances..." He realized he was talking to himself. Tim was nowhere around.

The girallon leaned in to get a close look and a good sniff of Cooper's junk. A fart wheezed out like the last note of a dying trumpet player. Dave's fists balled up tight enough so that solid iron might ooze out from between his fingers if he'd been holding some.

The girallon stood on its legs alone, its head rising a good foot and a half above Cooper's. It roared what sounded to Julian like a challenge, and pounded its chest and abdomen with its fists. It sounded like it was carved out of wood.

"Raaaaahhhh!" said Cooper, thumping his own chest as Dave flailed his fists against the sides of his belly, which sounded more like someone slapping a waterbed.

A stream of urine spouted out from between the girallon's legs, forming a puddle at Cooper's feet. Perhaps the relative sizes of their members was another point of contention. Julian could hardly make out the tip of the girallon's penis poking out from its fur. It must have been as small as Tim's, which Julian had seen more times than he'd ever wanted to. But to the beast's credit, he put out some strong-smelling urine. Julian could smell it from way over by the creek bed, like spoiled meat marinated in vinegar.

Cooper was doing an admirable job of not pissing himself for once. He stood his ground while the girallon pissed gallons of urine in a stream that Julian thought would never end. It finally did end when the girallon lost its shit for what seemed like no reason at all.

It screamed and bared its fangs just before punching Cooper

in the side of the head, sending him a good five feet away from Dave.

The girallon stopped screaming and stared down at Dave, then at Cooper who was struggling back to his feet, and then at Dave again.

"Fuck," said Julian.

"Fuck," said Dave.

"FUCK YOU!" said Tim, from somewhere above everyone else.

The girallon looked up, and its face was met with a falling backpack. Judging by the impact, it was full of rocks.

Dave took advantage of the distraction, running between the girallon's legs and Super Mario punching it in the nuts.

There was no longer any point in hiding, so Julian grabbed a rock from the creek bed and ran over to join the fray.

While the girallon cradled his balls, Cooper jumped on its back and caught it around the neck in a choke hold.

The girallon backed up hard into a tree trunk.

"Ugh," said Cooper, squashed in between. But he kept his hold.

"Shit!" said Tim as he fell out of the tree. He caught one of the beast's flailing upper arms, wrapping his own arms and legs around it.

Dave did likewise, wrapping his arms and legs around one of the girallon's legs. The poor creature looked like it was working at a daycare for troubled youths.

By the time Julian reached the fight, it looked to be just about over. The girallon's formerly pink face was now a deep shade of purple, and the arm supporting Tim's weight hung limp at its side. Its free upper arm took some desperate swipes at Cooper, but didn't have the reach.

Finally, it just couldn't stand anymore. It fell forward to its preferred walking position on legs and lower arms, then the arms buckled and it collapsed onto its face.

"Hurry up!" Cooper said to Julian. "Bash its brains in with your rock."

Julian frowned down at his rock. "It's helpless. Can't we just leave it unconscious?"

"You can be such an idiot," said Dave, pushing himself up from between the creature's legs. "It was your stupid idea that almost got us killed. And now you want to leave it alive so it can wake up pissed off and have another go at us?"

"It was my idea," said Tim. "Julian only inspired it." He too had let go of the girallon, and was now staring down into its piss puddle. "And it worked. Cooper, punch it in the head a few times if you like, but stick to non-lethal damage. It doesn't deserve to die for defending its territory."

Dave stomped over toward Tim. "Have you all lost your minds? Since when do you give a shit about animal rights or whatever? And how can you possibly say that your stupid idea worked?"

Tim looked down at Dave's crotch, then at his legs where his armor was dripping. "You pissed yourself, didn't you?"

"And you, of all people, are going to judge me for that? Do you know how many times you've pissed yourself since we've been stuck in this game? It's like you think you're going to win a prize if you do it enough. I thought I was going to die with my face in Cooper's ass, so don't even —"

"I'm not judging you," said Tim. "I'm just saying that my idea was working until you blew it." He gestured down to the piss puddle.

"What are you talking about?"

Tim squatted down over the puddle. "See this big puddle here? That's where the girallon pissed. He was marking his territory. And that little puddle over there, that's where you pissed. And see this little stream running from that one to this one? When your urine mixed with his, you challenged his territorial claim. That's when he went apeshit, if you'll pardon the pun."

"Nice going, Dave," said Cooper, who had finished his business with the girallon and joined the rest of them. "Don't cross the streams, dude. Didn't you see Ghostbusters?"

Tim dumped the rocks out of his backpack. "Stay here for a minute. I'll be right back." He darted back toward the creek bed.

It was an awkward wait. Julian didn't want to start up anymore shit with Dave, but he couldn't very well make small talk either. Any idle chatter on his part would be interpreted as "I'm deliberately not talking about how you endangered all of our lives by pissing yourself, because I'm a better person than you." Fortunately, Tim didn't take too long. He returned wearing a refilled backpack, and holding his seemingly endless flask of stonepiss.

"Maybe we should tie this thing up," said Julian. "We could knock him out again and cut him loose on our way back." He looked at Tim. "You got any rope in there?"

"Nope." Tim necked back the last few drops from his flask. It had a finite supply of booze after all. Next, he did something that Julian felt safe in assuming that none of them were expecting. He knelt next to the puddle of girallon piss and submerged his empty flask, holding it there until the bubbles stopped.

"Dude," said Cooper. "Who the fuck are you? Chipmunk Grylls? I'm sure there's a stream or something nearby."

Tim smiled up at Cooper. "Better to have it and not need it than need it and not have it."

As Tim stoppered his flask, Julian tried to envision a scenario in which one might need a flask full of gorilla urine. None came to mind.

"Um... Okay," said Dave, clapping his hands together. "Now that that's done, shall we continue on our way?" He seemed in better spirits now that someone had taken the pee spotlight off of him.

Tim put the flask inside his backpack. "Not yet. Girallons track by scent. Before we leave this girallon's territory, we should mask our own scents as best we can."

"Should we all piss ourselves?" asked Cooper.

"No. That's like ringing a cowbell. In fact, you and Dave are going to have to work extra hard to mask your scents."

"With what?" asked Dave.

Tim plucked a five-pointed leaf from a vine wrapped around a nearby tree trunk. "Smell this." He passed it to Dave.

Dave sniffed. "Smells kind of minty. What is it?"

"How the fuck should I know?" said Tim. "But it's the most pungent thing around, it's native to the area, and there's a shit-ton of it growing all over the place. It's our best bet." He climbed up the tree trunk, using the vine for hand and foot holds, then crawled out onto a branch where a similar vine was hanging down almost to the ground. He slid down the vine like a fire pole, stripping leaves off all the way down. He packed some into his backpack, and stuffed the rest into his tunic and pants.

Fifteen minutes later, Dave, Julian, and Tim were all stuffed like fat scarecrows, and Cooper looked like Swamp Thing, wrapped up from head to toe in vines.

"That should do us," said Tim.

After thirty minutes of traveling up the creek bed, Tim stopped. He sniffed the air, looked north, then pulled his flask back out.

Dave cringed. "Please tell me you aren't going to drink that."

"Shh," whispered Tim. "Don't worry. It's empty."

"You drank all that gorilla piss already?" asked Cooper. "You should pace yourself, man."

"Just stay quiet and keep me covered." Tim silently crept out of the creek bed and tiptoed northward from tree to tree, keeping his eyes focused on the treetops.

When Tim was about sixty yards away, Cooper started to get fidgety.

Julian put his hand on Cooper's shoulder. "I'm sure he knows what he's doing, and has a good reason to —" His words lost their credibility when Tim knelt down and submerged his flask in another puddle.

"What the fuck?" said Cooper. "Do girallons piss scotch?"

When Tim was done refilling his flask, he hurried back to the creek bed. "Let's keep moving."

They repeated this bizarre ritual three more times before Julian finally spotted a tree worthy of being called the Great anything. He didn't really know his trees, but it was probably an

elm. Its roots were responsible for diverting the water that once flowed down the bed they'd been traveling. A younger, shallower creek ran from the tree to the northwest.

"I guess we're here," said Dave. "I'm going to go wash my finger." He waddled off toward the stream.

Julian looked up into the massive branches of the tree, hoping not to see a giant four-armed gorilla monster. "This is an elm?"

"Yeah." Tim picked up a stick and prodded a conspicuously writhing pile of worms and beetles, some of which scattered to reveal black decomposing flesh. "And this is an arm. I guess this is our dead monk." He unstoppered his flask and didn't flinch at all as he sucked down a couple of gulps of the liquid inside.

"Jesus, Tim," said Cooper. "There's a running stream right fucking there." He pointed at where Dave was squatting.

Out of instinct, Julian looked in the direction Cooper was pointing, but he saw something out of place in the leaves about halfway between where he stood and the stream. Something rectangular and brown, but a different shade of brown than any of the nearby fallen leaves.

"Hey guys, check this out." Julian led Cooper and Tim toward the conspicuous object.

Dave waddled toward them excitedly, as if he too had just made an unexpected discovery. He held up the soggy leafy part of a carrot. Only a sliver of orange dangled beneath it. "Look what I found!"

Julian and Tim frowned at Dave. They were all hungry, but Dave's excitement at about one cubic centimeter of carrot was a little sad.

Cooper's stomach rumbled. "You wanna split it?"

The enthusiasm faded from Dave's eyes and was replaced with annoyance. "Do you know what this means?"

Julian, Cooper, and Tim shook their heads.

"It's a domesticated plant. Look at the bottom. It's clearly been cut with a knife."

Cooper scratched his ass. "You want to avenge it?"

"Goddammit, no! This means that somewhere upstream from here there is a farm. Civilization. And they might be cooking."

"Excellent," said Julian. "That will be useful information to know after we rescue Ravenus."

Dave looked up at the gem hanging around Cooper's neck. "Of course."

"I found something too." Julian bent over and picked up the object he'd spotted before.

It was a book. Or rather, the cover of a book. The pages had all been ripped out. The cover was made from thin, flexible leather, and was smeared with blood, which covered a large portion of the letters on the front.

T_E J_UR__L OF
BR_____ _______STER

"What do you make of this?" Julian held out the journal for the others to see.

Dave stroked his beard. "Tejurlof? Sounds dwarven, but I don't recognize it. Maybe gnomish?"

"Focus, Dave," said Julian. "This could be a clue. Some of the letters are covered in blood. I'm guessing the first word is THE."

"Second word is JOURNAL," said Tim.

Julian looked closely, filling in the missing letters with his mind. "I think you're right. How did you figure that out so fast?"

"I'm Pat Sajak's bastard son."

Julian bit his lower lip. "THE JOURNAL OF who?"

Cooper frowned. "If it says CHESTER COPPERPOT, we're fucked."

Julian held the cover in front of Tim's face. "What can you make out of the rest of it?"

Tim shrugged. "I don't know. Brewster?"

"Too much empty space for that."

"Monky Brewster," said Cooper. "I like it."

Julian looked up from the book. "What is it with you and monkeys today?"

"That's not what I meant," said Cooper. "I was talking about... Never mind. It was before your time."

Dave's eyes lit up. "Brandon! The dog's name was Brandon. That starts with BR!"

"Why the fuck do you remember that?" asked Tim. "And what makes you think that this monk has any relationship to a shitty 80s sitcom?"

Dave looked at his feet. "I liked it."

Tim snatched the leather cover out of Julian's hands. "I'll tell you what it says." He ran his finger along the words as he read them. "THE JOURNAL OF A DEAD MONK TORN TO PIECES BY FUCKING GIRALLONS WHOSE NAME ISN'T GOING TO HELP US FIND ANY GODDAMN AMULETS."

Cooper frowned. "I know I'm illiterate and all, but I feel like that's a lot to fit in to that space."

"The amulet's got to be around here somewhere," said Tim. "Let's start poking around in the leaves and see if we can find this dead fucker's neck."

"Or I could use a Detect Magic spell," said Julian, failing to give credit to the annis for that idea.

Tim raised his flask. "Now you're thinking. Get on it." He proceeded to imbibe a healthy dose of girallon pee.

Julian cringed, then regained his composure. "Detect Magic!" His vision turned grey and hazy. He scanned left and right. The gem Cooper wore around his neck glowed bright blue, but everything else was grey as far as he could see in any direction... until he looked up.

A green aura radiated out from a clump of leafy branches high in the Great Elm.

Julian pointed and whispered, "Up there."

A blurry white stream spouted out from the magical aura, hitting Julian before he had a chance to react. It was wet, and smelled like —

"Get out of the way," said Tim. He shoved Julian away from

the stream, sucked down what was left in his flask, and held it under the stream.

"Goddamn," said Cooper. "I guess if that's what you're into, it doesn't get any fresher than this."

Julian's vision returned to normal, his concentration on maintaining his spell broken by Tim's sudden insatiable thirst for animal piss.

"What the hell are you —"

Tim shut him up with a severe look. "Keep your voice down or we're all going to die." His look and tone suggested that he had a far better idea of their situation than Julian did.

"What are you thinking?" Julian whispered.

Tim waved Dave and Cooper over into a close huddle before responding. "How tough would a monk have to be to go walking in these woods alone?"

Dave shrugged. "Pretty tough."

"Give it a number. Let's say the girallon we faced earlier today was a six."

"I don't know," said Dave. "He'd be a ten maybe?"

"With or without the Amulet of Mighty Fists?"

Dave sighed. "I have no idea."

"It's just for illustrative purposes. Make a guess."

"Fine. Ten without. Twelve with."

"Okay. Now let's say there's a bigger girallon around here. One that claimed the Great Elm as his territory. And let's say that it kicked this monk's ass, even while he wore the amulet. How tough would you say that girallon had to be?"

"Fourteen." Dave's tone was bored. He was just spouting numbers at this point to get Tim to his point.

"And if that same girallon were then to adorn itself with the Amulet of Mighty Fists?" Tim now had Dave's full attention.

Dave squinted up into the branches. "Fuck."

Tim nodded. "I'd say that's an accurate assessment of our current situation."

"I'm with you so far," said Julian. "So how do we get the amulet away from the girallon?"

"We don't," said Tim. "We're probably a collective four in this situation. The only reason that first girallon didn't rip us apart was because we surprised it."

"So what do we do?" asked Dave.

Tim shrugged. "We go with Plan B."

"Shit," said Cooper. "We have to go fuck the hags again?"

"That was Option B, in a different set of circumstances."

"So what's Plan B?" asked Julian.

"First, we retreat very slowly and quietly back to the creek bed."

They stepped as quietly as they could. Dave and Cooper made a little noise, but it was covered by the stream of girallon pee still flowing down out from the branches of the Great Elm.

"How many Level 1 spells do you have left?" Tim asked Julian once they were about thirty yards down the creek bed.

"Three."

"That'll do. We need three fast horses, and I need your boot."

Walking around on one boot was something Julian was more than ready to discontinue. He started to take off his boot, then hesitated.

"Come on, Julian," said Tim. "You can have it back when we're done."

"It's not that. I just wanted to make sure... I mean, you're not going to use the horses as bait, are you?"

"No more than I'm going to use the rest of us."

Julian frowned. "I guess that's fair." He removed his boot and handed it to Tim. "Three horses coming up."

"Wait," said Dave. He looked at Cooper, then turned away from him. "Cooper, you need to give that necklace to Julian."

"Fine with me. It hasn't done shit to protect me anyway."

"That's because it's got nothing to do with protection. Don't take it off just yet."

"What do you know, Dave?" asked Tim.

"It's a Hag Eye. I remember it from the Monster Manual.

They're using it to spy on us. I didn't say anything before because I didn't want any of you to act weird around it and let on that we know what it is. But if Tim's plan involves double crossing the annis, —"

"It does," said Tim.

"Then they might kill Ravenus long before we can get to them."

Tim gave Dave a thumbs up. "Well done. So what the fuck are we waiting for?"

"Cooper can't just hand it over to Julian for no reason. That will arouse suspicion. We need a credible reason to take such an action. Cooper, crouch down in front of me."

Cooper crouched down in front of Dave, not looking at all amused.

Dave put his finger over his lips, pointed away in a random direction, then did some kind of weird gorilla dance. Again, he put his finger over his lips, then pointed at Cooper. He made a show of flexing his muscles, roaring, and beating his chest. Then he pointed at Julian, after which he wrung his fists under his eyes in a crying gesture. Adding more than what Julian deemed necessary, he made twisting motions with his thumbs and index fingers over imaginary nipples on his breastplate. Finally, he pointed at the gem hanging from Cooper's neck, then at Julian.

"Are you done?" asked Cooper.

Dave nodded.

Cooper pulled the silver chain over his head and handed it to Dave. "What the fuck was any of that supposed to mean?"

"I was saying that you're big and strong, and that Julian's a little titty baby, and so he needs protection more than you do."

"I'm not sure you communicated anything of the sort," said Tim.

"Titty baby?" said Julian.

Dave offered the necklace to Julian. "Put this on, but casually slip the gem underneath your shirt."

That was the first thing Dave said that made any sense.

When Julian had donned the necklace, Tim cleared his throat. "Now can we summon some goddamn horses?"

"Horse. Horse. Horse," said Julian, pointing at three spots on the dry creek bed, and consequently summoning three horses in rapid succession. They whinnied nervously.

"Keep them quiet!" snapped Tim.

Julian stood in front of the horses, rubbing their noses, but keeping his eye on Tim.

Tim set his backpack on the ground and pulled out a flask.

Julian shook his head. No point in dying sober.

To Julian's surprise, Tim set the flask on the ground and pulled out another, then another, and still another. When he was done, he had seven flasks in all. He unstoppered the last two and sniffed each, cringing at the first one and drinking deeply from the second. He slipped the flask with his preferred vintage into his vest pocket and handed two flasks each to both Cooper and Dave, keeping the remaining two for himself.

Tim, Cooper, and Dave huddled around Julian's boot.

Tim licked his lips and looked into Dave's and Cooper's eyes. "When I say go, we pour."

Cooper frowned. "We're going to cross the streams?"

"Exactly. You guys ready?"

Dave and Cooper nodded.

"Come on, guys," said Julian. "I need to wear that."

"Pour."

Tim, Cooper, and Dave emptied their flasks into Julian's boot. Before the flasks were empty, a roar boomed out from the treetops like an angry god had just finished the series finale of Dexter.

"Time to move!" said Tim, no longer bothering to keep quiet. "Cooper, help Dave onto his horse. I'm riding with you." He dropped his empty piss flasks and picked up the boot.

As soon as they had Dave mounted, the ground shook beneath Julian's bare feet. He slipped one foot into the stirrup and pulled himself up.

"GO! GO! GO!" shouted Tim, mounted in front of Cooper and hugging his boot full of urine.

The horses didn't move.

"Julian!"

"Shit, that's right," said Julian. "GO! GO! GO!"

The horses went full-throttle into a gallop along the creek bed. Julian chanced a peek behind him.

"Holy fucking shit!"

It was the biggest, meanest-looking girallon Julian had ever seen. Sure, it was only the second one he'd ever seen, but this one could have been that first one's daddy fresh out of prison. It crashed through the trees and bounded after the horses in a curious six-limbed gallop, and it was catching up to them, slowly but steadily. Sure enough, Julian could see a green amulet around its meaty neck.

"We're not going to make it!" cried Julian.

"Just hang on a little longer!" said Tim.

Riding in front of Cooper, Tim obviously didn't have an appreciation for just how little longer they all had to live.

"Drop the boot!" said Julian. "We'll think of something else!"

Tim hugged the boot tight, trying to minimize the amount of piss sloshing out of it. "Just... a little... longer..."

"I'm telling you, man! It's right on top of —"

Something crashed out from the trees at Julian's five o'clock. Two angry girallon screams rang in his sensitive ears. He looked back, and found that they were re-gaining their lead as the huge girallon, and a second smaller, yet still very scary girallon, stumbled over one another, the creek bed being too small for the both of them.

"Ha!" cried Julian. "You crazy son of a bitch, you did it!"

Tim cocked an eyebrow and casually sipped from his flask.

The third and forth girallon slowed the whole pack even more.

The fifth girallon leapt out from a tree branch overhanging the creek bed. It's timing was off, and it landed hard behind them, just missing the ass end of Dave's horse.

"How many of these were there again?" asked Julian.

"One more," said Tim. "I think."

And there it was, the first girallon they'd faced, standing ahead of them in the creek bed. It looked even more pissed off than the others. Beyond urine-induced territorial instincts, it had personal reasons to want to tear them apart. It screamed and bounded toward them.

"Go left, into the woods," cried Julian, not waiting for any deliberation. Now that they'd reached this girallon's territory, it was pretty much time to start heading south anyway.

Any one of the girallons could have caught up to them with ease, but even in the open forest, they continued to bark and swipe at one another as they gave chase. More importantly, they continued to lose ground.

"Ravenus!" cried Julian when he thought they must be getting close. He realized that there were no landmarks which would lead them directly to the clearing, and he didn't want to waste a lot of time seeking it out.

Off in the distance, a raven let out a mighty caw.

"This way," said Julian, guiding his horse slightly to the right. He shouted ahead, "We're coming for you buddy!"

A couple of minutes later, they trotted into the clearing. Ravenus still hung from the tree branch. The annis were assembled in front of their mound. Greedily rubbing their blue hands together.

"Do you have it?" asked Annie excitedly. "Where is it? Let me see!"

"You heard her, Julian," said Dave. "Let her see."

Julian looked at Dave. "What?"

Dave whispered, "Give me the eye."

Julian pulled the silver chain over his head and handed the hanging gem to Dave.

Dave pointed his middle finger at the gem in his hand. "See this, bitches." He shoved the gem deep in his mouth.

"No!" screamed the annis who had given Cooper the eye.

Dave bit down hard. The gem crunched, eliciting ear-piercing screams from all three annis.

Annies eyes bulged until they popped and ran down the sides of her face.

"You fools!" cried Annie. "You think that will save you?" She grinned wickedly. "I won't need eyes to savor your screams. When I'm finished with you, you'll wish you'd never —"

Girallon howls and screams grew closer.

"What's that?" said one of the lesser annis.

Tim smiled. "We invited a couple of friends."

"Girallons?" said Annie. "How many?"

Tim guided his horse forward. "Hopefully enough." He threw the boot at Annie, hitting her in the tit and splashing girallon urine all over the three of them.

The first girallon crashed out from the trees and into the clearing, heading straight for the annis. Aside from punching Dave off his horse, it paid the rest of them no mind.

Tim guided his horse to the tree where Ravenus hung upside down. Cooper tossed him onto the branch, where he easily untied the knot.

All three annis had their claws buried deep in the attacking girallon. It barked and swiped at them, but was gushing gallons of blood from dozens of holes.

Julian, Tim, Cooper, and Dave stood out of the way as five more girallons came barreling into the clearing.

Cooper helped Dave back onto his horse. "Let's get our annises out of here."

When they made it back to the creek bed, and the sounds of screaming hags and girallons began to fade in the distance behind them, Julian looked at Dave. "You knew about the eye this whole time?"

"I suspected it was a Hag Eye when the annis handed it to Cooper. He's taller, which would give them a better field of vision, and he's the only one that wasn't wearing any clothes."

"Why didn't you crush it right then and there?"

Dave shrugged. "I might have been wrong. It wouldn't have

made a big enough difference anyway. They still would have probably killed us."

Julian pulled aside his serape, where Ravenus sat nestled against his chest. "You holding up okay?"

"No worse for the wear, sir. Just a bit peckish is all."

"You and me both, buddy." Julian really hoped Dave was right about there being a farm nearby, and that they were cooking something. They should at least be able to barter a meal from the silver chain which had held the Hag Eye. But Ravenus's culinary tastes and nutritional needs differed from theirs. "Fly on ahead until you see a big tree. There's some good monk up that way."

The End

ABOUT THE AUTHOR

Robert Bevan took his first steps in comedy with The Hitchhiker's Guide to the Galaxy, and his first steps in fantasy with Dungeons & Dragons. Over the years, these two loves mingled, festered, and congealed into the ever expanding Caverns & Creatures series of comedy/fantasy novels and short stories.

Robert is a writer, blogger, and a player on the Authors & Dragons podcast. He lives in Atlanta, Georgia, with his wife, two kids, and his dog, Speck.

Don't stop now! The adventure continues!

Discover the entire Caverns & Creatures collection at
www.caverns-and-creatures.com/books/

And please visit me on Facebook at
www.facebook.com/robertbevanbooks

Made in the USA
Columbia, SC
15 December 2017